Praise for
THE SALTY SWAN

"A gripping tale of love, mystery, and the supernatural, this novel takes readers on a thrilling journey through the unknown. With rich, unique characters and unexpected twists, it reminds us that sometimes the greatest adventures begin when we step into the unknown and embrace the magic around us."

—Jake Stehman, author of *A Battle for Fire*

"Mackrides's debut novel creates an enchanting world where legends come alive and love triumphs over darkness. With a spellbinding blend of romance and suspense set against the backdrop of untamed forests and natural wonders, this book is a captivating must-read that will leave you yearning to be part of Lily's extraordinary adventure."

—Erika Lewis, cofounder,
The Sage & Scribe Book Club

"*The Salty Swan* reminds readers to act in kindness over fear, trust and lead with your heart, question but respect what's lurking in the shadows, and lead with courage. A satisfying read that playfully bounces between fantasy and reality, love and fear."

—Miranda Faye Dillon, author of *The Unshatterables*

"Katrina's voice as an author is unique and refreshing. You can tell she spent a lot of time researching the local lore, and you really fall in love with the characters. It's a fun read from start to finish, and I can't wait for the story to continue."

—Lela Merriam, The Boozy Bookworms blog

"The Salty Swan story reminded me again that life is filled with choices. Expect to get lost in this romantic story."

—Rachel Williamson,
founder and chief strategic retail advisor,
Running Great Stores, LLC

"Katrina Mackrides has a way of transporting you with her vivid details and well-developed characters. With a unique storyline that is the perfect blend of fantasy and romance, be prepared to be left wanting more!"

—Wendy Clark Rahmouni, regional manager

"Brimming with excitement, tender new love, and twists of fate, this author's first novel is a page-turner. An amazing coming-of-age read with exciting psychic and spiritual layers that keeps the reader wanting more!"

—Angela Santrock, retail specialist

"A fantastical coming-of-age romance that'll make you question just how far you'd go for your own happy ending."

—Desirai Labrada, book influencer @LibriLabra.

"I was instantly captivated within the first several pages of *The Salty Swan*! Lily, Kai, Berly, and the rich cast of characters drew me in and took me on an enchanting ride; I could not turn the pages quickly enough! In the vast genre of literary works with mystical creatures, this author has created an inventive and unique world this avid reader has not yet encountered. How refreshing! *The Salty Swan* left me with an eagerness to be swept away more with this story. How thrilled I was to discover that I can look forward to further adventures in the second book of *The Salty Swan* saga! Bravo!"

—Elizabeth Baker, retail specialist

"*The Salty Swan* is a beautiful love story full of mystic enchantment. I enjoyed everything about this book and can't wait to read more."

—Kimberly Parker, reader

"*The Salty Swan* is an adventure story of first love that illustrates the power of acceptance and community unity."

—Penny Davis, SHRM-SCP, SPHR

"*The Salty Swan* will bring up memories of your first love. The characters are interesting, and the story is so full of twists and turns that it will keep you turning the pages."

—Laura Sliker, reader

"I absolutely loved this novel and can't wait for the next installment in the series! If you're a fan of well-developed characters, blossoming romances, and captivating mysteries intertwined with magic, crystals, and powerful curses, then this book's for you!"

—Natacha Belair, award-winning author, *A Stellar Purpose* trilogy

"Mackrides takes you on an enchanting ride in her debut novel. She has managed to seamlessly weave love and fantasy through Lily's story, leading readers on an adventure they won't want to put down."

—Michelle Wishner, author of *Ever the Same*

"Lily takes you on a thrilling and captivating adventure uncovering the secrets but also unleashing her inner strength. This page turning novel will have you wanting to know more about the fascinating unearthly creatures in this world leaving eager to know how everything works out in the end. There is something for everyone in this enthralling story, it's one I'm sure everyone will love."

—Sarah Alserhaid, author of *Etched in Stone*

The Salty Swan
by Katrina Mackrides

© Copyright 2024 Katrina Mackrides

ISBN 979-8-88824-472-2

All rights reserved. No part of this publication may be reproduced, stored in a retrieval system, or transmitted in any form or by any means—electronic, mechanical, photocopy, recording, or any other—except for brief quotations in printed reviews, without the prior written permission of the author.

This is a work of fiction. All the characters in this book are fictitious, and any resemblance to actual persons, living or dead, is purely coincidental. The names, incidents, dialogue, and opinions expressed are products of the author's imagination and are not to be construed as real.

Edited by Hannah Woodlan
Cover design by Catherine Herold

Published by

köehlerbooks™

3705 Shore Drive
Virginia Beach, VA 23455
800-435-4811
www.koehlerbooks.com

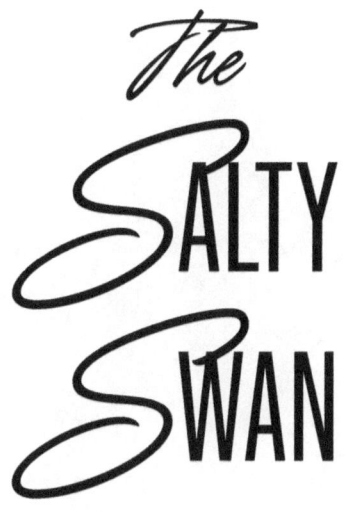

KATRINA MACKRIDES

VIRGINIA BEACH
CAPE CHARLES

To my husband, Steve.
Thank you for your unwavering love and support.

CHAPTER 1

THE MORNING SUN streamed between the curtains. I had woken up early to explore the jogging trails, despite a needling headache growing behind my ears. I couldn't shake the memory of that awful dream. My heart was still pounding as I railed at myself. *Why does that dream continue to haunt me? What does it mean?* I had hoped my nightmare would end once I was in college, that it had all been based on feeling trapped in high school, but that was clearly not the case.

When I emerged from the dorm, the air was crisp and energizing. My head cleared as I reached a comfortable pace down the smooth, wide trail. The sun warmed the dampness, but a half mile in, the forest thickened, blocking the sun and closing around the trail. My eagerness faded.

After another half mile, the trees began to thin, and each step added to the cloud of dust behind me. As I turned the corner, the forest vanished completely, revealing a stagnant marsh. The water was brackish and foul smelling. Besides a few dead trees surrounding the water, the spot was empty and looked abandoned, even haunted.

A small wooden bridge crossed the water. I slowed and stopped in the middle to take in the landscape. The silence was acute without the plodding of my feet. Even the birds had fallen silent.

Dark clouds drifted overhead, casting ghostly gray shadows across the water. The thick, pungent air gave me an uneasy feeling. I realized jogging alone was a dumb thing to do. Especially on trails I didn't know in an unfamiliar place. The last thing my mom told me before I got on the plane was "Use your street smarts." Yet here I was. *What if I can't find my way back or I run into a bear?*

I shook my head at my imagination. Fighting the instinct to turn back toward campus, I focused on making it to the trail's end.

Wind brushed my face, and my breath quickened. It was dead quiet except for my blood pulsing in my ears. The sound throbbed in unison with each stride on the dusty trail. A restless feeling grew—like I was being watched.

I noticed an old three-story house at the edge of my vision and stopped abruptly, frowning. It looked eerily like the house from my dream. For a moment, the connection flooded me with fear.

I struggled to shake off the lingering strangeness.

"It was only a dream. It is not real. Forget it."

Trying to think practically, I wondered how old the house was and why someone built it way out here in the marsh. But the longer I stood there, the more anxious I grew. Wanting to get far away, I resumed my pace. My lungs labored as I headed up the trail. A light breeze sent a shiver down my scalp.

I found myself glancing back over my shoulder every few minutes. The endless forest grew denser, and dark clouds added to the dreariness.

Slowing to read the sign at a fork on the narrow trail, I stumbled when a dark figure stepped from behind a tree. It moved slowly away from the trail and into the trees. I couldn't tell whether it had seen me.

And then suddenly I was darting into the forest in pursuit. Stomping bravely through the underbrush, I felt a force pulling me toward the figure. I followed it deeper into the forest, ducking overhanging limbs, scratching my shins on thick undergrowth.

No matter how close I got, the shadowy thing eluded me. Sometimes it glimmered, resembling polished stone. Finally, it halted unexpectedly, turned my direction, and disappeared with a loud pop.

A yelp escaped me as I awoke from my trance. *What am I doing?!*

I hurried back the way I'd come, the dry leaves crunching loudly under my feet. All at once, I started to sprint, ignoring the sting of spindly branches slapping my arms and legs. I had no idea if I was heading the right way.

Panic was beginning to take over when I glimpsed the white trail.

Surging out of the forest, I ran directly into another person. The full-body slam knocked the breath right out of me. He stood solid as a tree, gripping my shoulders so I wouldn't fall over.

Stunned and attempting to catch my breath, I stepped back to apologize—and to take in the full height of this towering man.

"Please pardon me. I didn't . . ." I lost my train of thought as I took in his wildly handsome face. Staring at my wide-eyed, gawking reflection in his sunglasses, I could barely form words. "I hope I didn't hurt you."

My knees felt weak when the man released me. His warmth lingered on my shoulders.

Standing tall in his uniform, he placed his hands formally behind his back. I wished I could see the eyes hidden behind those dark sunglasses.

"What were you doing in the forest?" he asked sternly. His deep voice sent a thrill through me.

"I was chasing a figure or something." Instantly, I felt foolish for telling the truth.

Leaning toward my face, so close that his long, silky black hair almost brushed my cheek, he ordered in a low but authoritative voice, "Stay out of the forest." I felt his breath on my forehead. "The forest is hazardous. You must always stay on the trails."

His tone implied that I should already know the dangers.

I stumbled for a logical response. "You don't understand. I don't know why I followed that thing. It was like a force pulled me toward it."

My cheeks warmed. *What kind of explanation is that? I sound insane.*

"Followed what, exactly?"

"A dark little creature that shimmered like polished stone. I don't know what it was." I screamed at myself to stop talking.

He regarded me condescendingly as if addressing a child. "Promise me you will never wander into the forest again. It's dangerous. Stay on the trails." His tone was lighter, but it still sounded like he was scolding me. His voice dropped to just above a whisper. "It is much more dangerous than you know." I caught a sense of sorrow in his tone.

"I promise," I sheepishly replied, involuntarily swaying toward him.

One side of his cheek lifted and quivered, almost like he was suppressing a smile. He turned and nodded over his shoulder before unceremoniously marching off.

Stunned to silence, I simply watched him stride out of sight.

I ran at a swift pace back to campus, full of nervous energy and unconcerned with saving my strength for soccer this afternoon. I was running away from the forest, the creepy house, and the stagnant marsh. And from the forest ranger's rebuke.

I was such a coward. *So why did I follow that creepy shadow?* I never did anything remotely like that.

By the time I made it back to campus, I was heaving for air. I bent over with my hands on my knees for a good five minutes. Once I'd calmed my breathing, I headed into the dining hall to find my new roommate, Berly. My cheeks were hot from more than exertion when I plopped down beside her.

"How was your jog on the trails?"

I shook my head. "Honestly, it was scary. I should not have gone alone. There wasn't much jogging. It was more like a full-out sprint. This creepy feeling that I was being watched washed over me. The whole marsh looks like death, and it smells like rotten eggs."

My embarrassment inspired me to withhold the details about chasing the strange creature and being yelled at by a handsome forest ranger.

"'Marsh.' Even the word sounds scary," she commiserated.

I showed her the trail map on my phone, and we reviewed other possible routes. Secretly, though, I wondered if I would run into that ranger again.

"Maybe I'll try the Wood and Waters or the Black Pond Trail tomorrow. They're both far from the marsh."

Berly smiled over the rim of her coffee cup. "Hey, maybe we should ask the guys to picnic on one of the trails. After all, it will be our last day of fun before we get swamped with homework."

"Great idea. I hope they'll be up for it."

Someone behind me cleared their throat. "Excuse me."

I turned to find a stunning man standing there—muscular, with a square jawline and black hair styled precisely. He had dark eyes and the longest eyelashes I had ever seen.

I placed my hand on my chest in a "Who, me?" gesture and replied, "Can I help you?"

"Good morning, beautiful. Please allow me to introduce myself. I am Benton Weston the Third."

"Lily," I replied, confused.

"I noticed you from across the room. I couldn't help but overhear your conversation about hiking the trails. I assume you might need a strong companion like me—to stroll with, perhaps hold hands with—while walking on the trails?"

My eyebrow shot up so hard that my forehead cramped. *Now, that was forward.* I huffed out a large breath of air. He reminded me of so many jerks from high school. "No thanks. I'm good." I held my hand up to signal him to back off and turned away. Berly's face twitched.

"I'll be around if you change your mind. I'm sure you can find me," Benton said, his self-importance unwavering.

I waved my fingers bye-bye behind my head.

"What the heck was that?" Berly exclaimed.

She looked impressed—whether with the man or my reaction, I wasn't sure.

Imitating his introduction, she simpered, "Pardon me, I'm Sir Benton the Third. Please melt into my arms."

We could not suppress our laughter.

"A strong companion, really? What a moron. Who talks like that? Stroll and hold hands. This day is getting weirder by the minute," I said, shaking my head.

"He got a look at those long legs and blond hair down to your waist and said, 'I need to hit that.'"

I stuck my finger in my mouth and made a gagging noise.

Despite my name, Liliana Swan Makris, I'd never felt like a swan. My grandmother had always told me I would be a beauty, saying to be patient, give it time. For most of my youth, kids made fun of me for being tall and thin. I was taller than most of the boys in my grade throughout the years. But I "blossomed" during the summer before my senior year in high school—filled out in all the right places, I guess you could say.

I supposed I finally resembled the swan I was born to be.

CHAPTER 2

IT FELT LIKE Berly and I had known each other for years. It was hard to believe that I had been in Florida only yesterday, rushing around my room and trying to pack everything I owned into two suitcases.

After loading my luggage into the car, I glanced back at the house, and the realization hit me like a dodgeball to the face. I was moving 1,500 miles away.

What am I doing? I don't even own a winter coat!

I paced beside the car, berating myself for constantly worrying. There was no way I was going to pass up this amazing scholarship to Paul Smith's College. This was my ticket out of my hometown, a new beginning. I had been a fool to think my teammates would be happy for me, and their jealous reactions to my good fortune confirmed it was time to get as far away as possible. I needed a new start, with new friends. Real friends.

I took a deep breath, proud of my college decision. Suddenly, I was smiling with newfound bravery—unaware of what the spirits had planned for me.

Mom was a nonstop chatterbox on the way to the airport, reminding me of all the arrangements once I made it to New York.

I was half listening and half thinking about my recurring dream. *Maybe it's not about being trapped in high school. Maybe my future is chasing me, and I'm afraid to make the wrong decision.*

"Are you listening to me?" she asked.

"Of course I am. Don't worry. I'm going to be just fine," I said, trying to convince myself it was the truth.

Mom wrung her hands as she checked my luggage tags for the third time.

"I can't believe my baby is going so far away. You are going to freeze to death."

I hugged her tightly. "I'll be home for the holidays. And I'll text you when I land and again after I get settled in my dorm room. You'll barely miss me. I love you."

Hustling away before my eyes teared up, I wondered if she believed I could handle the change.

"I love you," she called. "Be careful, and use your street smarts."

I waved. "I will."

***

Waiting for my bags to appear in the baggage claim after the flight landed, I spotted the bus driver with the Paul Smith's College sign. I sighed in relief. Everything was going as planned.

The volume of the chattering students on the crowded bus increased with every mile. As the shuttle rounded a hairpin curve at the top of the mountain, I got my first view of the college nestled at the bottom of the valley. Large wooden buildings with forest-green roofs reflected in the lake. Tall trees cushioned the campus. An intense blue sky spread overhead, and the sun cast a luminescent glow over the colorful mountainside. It looked like an oil painting.

Although the view was captivating, a terrible sinking feeling came over me as I eyed that dense forest. Leaning forward to peer closer at the tall pines and gloomy shadows dancing around the dark trunks, I bit my nails.

"Beautiful, isn't it?" someone suddenly asked beside me.

I jumped, and the girl leaned away, but her expression showed concern.

"Are you okay?"

I shook my head, amused and ashamed. "Oh, I'm sorry. I spooked myself. I was remembering a scary dream I had last night."

The petite girl's smile revealed dimples, and I relaxed enough to ask, "Have you seen these mountains before?"

"As a matter of fact, I have. My dad and stepmom purchased a house a few miles away from here so we could ski in the winter. After our first visit here, I fell in love with the place. I knew this was where I wanted to go to college." She spoke with an easy confidence. I liked her immediately.

I held out my hand. "I'm Lily."

"Nice to meet you. I'm Berly."

"That's a great name."

"It's short for Kimberly. I am not a 'Kim' type of girl," she replied with air quotes.

"Mine is short for Liliana. Berly suits you."

When the bus stopped, incautious students scrambled off with their gear. It was a madhouse, with everyone milling about like a flock of sheep waiting to be herded in the right direction.

I made my way through registration. The registrar handed me my schedule, my room assignment, a map of the campus, and a map of all the hiking and cross-country ski trails. At least twenty different trails surrounded the campus.

All the campus buildings were constructed from huge natural logs, including the dorms. I navigated to my assigned room with my nostrils flared to welcome in the scent of the wood. The pictures from the website didn't begin to capture the campus's grandeur.

The furniture in my room was also crafted from natural wood. A bit rustic but workable. I swung my suitcases onto a bed and started unpacking. The door flew open, and Berly stepped in.

"I guess we were destined to be friends," I said with a grin.

"The spirits are in our favor," she declared.

We unpacked our gear, and I hung a large dream catcher on the wall. Berly tacked up a few bohemian wall hangings she had made with wood and beads. The beads matched the wooden furniture and really pulled the room together. She also strung remote-controlled lights across the ceiling.

We stepped back to admire our work.

"It looks good," I said.

Berly placed her hands on her hips. "Better than good. We are artists."

I smiled, and my stomach rumbled. "What time is dinner? I'm starving."

Berly looked at the time and yelled, "Now! We're late!"

We scrambled to get our IDs and keys and ran full speed to the dining hall, laughing the entire way.

The crowd was blaring like a flock of geese as we pushed the doors open. My stomach growled. Waiting in the long line, I was prepared to eat anything they offered. The smell alone was intoxicating.

After selecting several delicious-looking foods, we clutched our trays and scanned the room for a table. Berly tilted her head and signaled with her eyes. I followed her gesture toward a few open spots, and we strode briskly to the seats and asked if they were available. Receiving an affirmative, I nodded gratefully to our table partners and sat.

Everyone was so consumed with eating that nobody made eye contact or bothered with introductions. After a while, I sank back in my chair and sighed.

"This is so good. I don't think I even chewed. I inhaled it."

The guy across from me chuckled. When Berly and I turned our attention his way, he held out his hand across the table.

"Good day. I'm Martin, and this is Max, my flatmate." Martin had a pronounced British accent.

I sat up and shook his hand. "Pleased to meet you. I'm Lily." I waved toward Berly. "This is my flatmate, Berly."

Berly burst out laughing. "'Flatmate'? 'Pleased to meet you'? Ta-ta!"

Laughter erupted across the table.

"A tallyho to you too!" Martin said.

"You sounded so proper. I was trying to be polite," I defended myself.

My words were swamped by their laughter. Martin snorted, sending us into another uproar. Berly's face was bright red, and Martin held his sides.

Once the hysteria subsided, Max said, "I think this is going to be a bloody good year."

"Where are you from?" I asked.

"Bournemouth, about a hundred miles from London," Max answered.

"How did you decide to come here for college?" The place was a gem, but I was curious how the college's reputation had reached across the Atlantic.

I learned they were friends from back home who had transferred here as juniors in the biology program, and they loved skiing.

As the crowds in the cafeteria dwindled, I stood up.

"Do you guys want to check out the campus while it's still light out?" I asked the table.

The boys were amenable. We grabbed our maps and headed out to explore.

"Where should we go first?" Martin asked.

"I would like to find all the academic buildings so I know where my classes are on Monday. And I need to find the Saunders Sports Complex for soccer practice," I said.

"So, you play football, do ya?" Martin asked.

Heat rose in my cheeks as it always did when the focus was on me. "I'm here on a soccer scholarship."

"We'll have to give it a go sometime," he said with a smirk.

"That would be great! I need to stretch my legs and get ready for the season. What about tomorrow?" I asked eagerly, looking at the three of them. "We could play on the Great Lawn. Maybe around eleven before the sun gets too hot?"

"Bangin' idea, mate! I'm in. I could use a good run," Max said. Martin nodded in agreement.

Berly bit her bottom lip. "I'm in, but I'll be the handicap player."

"Soccer tomorrow. It's a date." I pointed to the campus map. "If we follow this path, it will lead us past the academic buildings and out to the complex."

"Lead the way, mate," Martin said.

❦ ❦ ❦

We exited the sports complex through the side, with me at the rear of the group. The hard metal door slammed behind me. Before us loomed the forest, alive with animal and insect activity.

Being this close to the forest gave me an ominous feeling, like a dark cloud promising a storm. A branch snapped, and I whipped my gaze in that direction. A shadow moved between two trees. I narrowed my eyes. The shadow moved again. A chill washed over my skin, and I sprinted to catch up with my new schoolmates, hoping they wouldn't notice the fright on my face. They might think I was crazy.

The first day had been exciting yet exhausting. Berly and I made it back to the dorm late, and after a hot shower, I sat on my bed, drying my hair with a towel.

Berly fell back on her pillow and stared at the ceiling.

"Those two were quite interesting. I think they're going to be fun to hang out with. Do you think they're cute?"

I considered the question.

"Martin's cute, and his eyes are nice. Max is cute in a cheeky sort of way. Still, he seems like a player. I'm not sure about him, but they're both hilarious. What do you think?"

"I think Martin is adorable and Max is a riot. I think you're right, though. And I'm not loving all the tattoos. I wonder how many he has."

"I'm sure he has a story for each one of them," I said.

Berly chuckled, then yawned. "It was a great first day. I'm exhausted," she added with a satisfied look.

"Me too," I said, though my mind was still racing, stuck on the uncanniness of the shadow in the forest and the vestiges of my scary dream. I wondered what lived in that forest. Rolling over, I tried to shift my thoughts to the coming days. I was galvanized about this chapter of my life. I was ready for college and to continue pursuing my passion for soccer.

CHAPTER 3

EVEN AFTER MY adventurous morning jog, Berly and I arrived at the Great Lawn before the boys the following day. I sat on a bench to retie my shoes, laughing at myself because it was my second day on campus, and I was already playing soccer. A chipmunk sprang on the bench beside me and sat up, revealing his little white belly.

"Hey, little guy. Sorry, I have nothing to give you."

"It looks like you're making friends all over the place. Be careful. He might want to go for a stroll," Berly said with a grin.

I gave her a snarky glance, making us both giggle.

"What's so funny?" Martin asked as he and Max wandered up.

I told them about my interaction with Benton this morning.

"Sounds like a real cretin," Max scoffed.

Berly raised her eyebrows. "A what?"

"Cretin. You know, a right pompous bloke."

"An idiot," Berly clarified.

"Oh, now I get it. Benton is certainly a cretin," I said.

We started kicking the ball around. Martin and Max were good, as I expected. They said I was not bad for a girl, which made me roll my eyes. Berly, on the other hand, was way out of her league and didn't care a bit. She had fun anyway.

The sun fried our backs, and I reveled in the feel of sweat building on my brow. We played until we were all starving—but then, I was always starving.

During lunch, Berly shared our idea for a Sunday hike and picnic. The guys were keen to go.

When we finished eating, I excused myself to buy the books I would need for the semester.

Berly spent the afternoon at the recreation center with the guys. The caretaker for her parents' winter cabin had brought her a jeep to use for the semester, so they also headed to the local market to get supplies for our hike.

I met Berly back at our dorm room, where she greeted me with hectic arm flailing.

"Quick, shower and get dressed! We have to get to dinner early because the guys entered a lumberjack competition tonight."

"What on earth is a lumberjack competition?"

"I don't know for sure. It's all woodsman stuff, but apparently we can't miss it."

* * *

A crowd had already gathered by the time we made it to the arena, and boisterous laughter filled the air. We scanned for the guys but had no luck and decided securing a good seat was more important. Fresh-cut logs had been arranged in a half circle up the hillside, to be used as bleachers.

I turned to Berly. "This is seriously a cool place. Look, they even have zip-lining over there. We should try that out soon."

"Yes!"

The announcer, one of the professors, introduced the four teams. First up were the Woodchucks. Martin and Max had named themselves the Oxford M & Ms, the next team was called the Axe Men, and the last team was Jacked Up.

Berly and I exchanged looks, and I slapped my hand to my mouth to suppress a laugh. Benton was on team Jacked Up. He arrogantly marched by us, slowing to wink directly at me before continuing onto the field for the competition.

I cringed. "Ew, did you see that?"

"How could I miss it? Giiirl, he has his eyes on you." She smirked. "But sorry to tell you, he is in love with himself."

The first event was the two-handed saw. Each group was greeted by the cheering crowd.

Martin caught our attention and pointed at Benton, mouthing, "Is that the bloke?" We nodded in unison. Martin ran his index finger across his throat, and I gave him a thumbs-up.

The next event was the log split. The Woodchucks split the log with three strikes. The Axe Men and Jacked Up both split a log in two strikes. Max and Martin were whispering to each other before their turn came.

When the Oxford M & Ms were called, I whistled, and Berly yelled, "Break a log!"

Martin hefted the axe, and Max grabbed a sledgehammer. Martin placed the axe on top of the log, and Max swung the sledgehammer back and around, hitting the axe-head squarely. Their log split with one hit. Cheers erupted when Max bowed low to the stands as if greeting royalty.

The third event was the tree climb. The competitors had to climb sixty feet using only a rope and a harness. Benton, with his puffed-up chest, had changed into silver-spiked cleats specially made for tree climbing.

So far, everyone had been evenly paced. The announcer called for Max. He waved to the crowd and signaled us to turn up the volume, then hopped up the tree like a frog in a few easy bounds, wearing a devilish grin. He had the fastest time of the night. When he reached the top, he saluted the crowd and yelled, "Cheerio!" before dropping like a rock to the padding below.

Everyone surged to their feet, cheering, and the sound was deafening.

Jacked Up ended up last despite their groovy spiked shoes.

The final event was axe throwing. The Oxford M & Ms went first, scoring 120 points. Team Jacked Up was next. Benton pointed at Max as he walked past and said, "Nice try. Let me show you how it is done."

Benton's face contorted with rage when Max waved cheerfully and said, "Thanks for the tip, mate."

When Jacked Up scored ten points fewer than the M & Ms, Benton spun on his heels and stomped away.

The last team to be called were the Axe Men.

The first guy hit a bullseye, and his second axe almost split the first. The crowd went wild. Bullseyes were fifty points each, which was almost enough to win the event. I enthusiastically cheered them on. The second guy scored ninety points. The audience screamed.

The Axe Men handily won the whole competition.

People swarmed to congratulate them on the win. We learned that the Axe Men, Troy and Nate, were from Idaho and had done lumberjack competitions as kids.

Martin pulled a massive cooler out from behind one of the logs.

"Bloody hell, that was smashing. On to the lake." He waved others to follow.

The crowd was jazzed and talking about the contest as they trailed behind him. Martin set the cooler down by the shore and opened it to reveal that it was full of beer.

"Cheers," he said, handing them out.

Max sauntered over, looking smug. "Quite a match, eh?"

I noticed four girls watching his every move. He had become quite a fan favorite.

"You have a few admirers," I said, tilting my head their way.

"Excellent, I will have to go chat with them!" He scooted off to meet his fans. I took the reprieve to scan for my other friends. A few students were building a fire in the dedicated firepit near the arena, and Martin and Berly stood nearby.

Martin's arms were flying with animation as he spoke. He spotted me and made a beckoning motion.

"Where's Mr. Prissy Pantaloons? He might want to take a stroll and hold hands after his loss."

"I think he ran home to cry about his defeat. That competition was banging. How did you learn about it?" I asked.

"Someone told us at breakfast, so we thought we would give it a go."

"Without any practice?"

Berly tapped one finger on Martin's chest. "You are crazy. Did you know that?" She flashed both dimples. "Although I'm glad you entered. What a fun night. I can't believe how you split that log so fast. It was brilliant."

Martin beamed.

Slowly backing out of the conversation, I meandered toward the lake and ran into the set of twins Berly and I shared a suite with, Aspen and Brooklyn. They were also on the soccer team, and I learned they had run the same trail I had followed that morning. I daydreamed about having running partners on the spooky trails. I also wondered if they had seen the handsome forest ranger. I invited them on our Sunday hike to Black Pond.

It soon grew very dark by the lake. Huge floodlights had been directed at the arena for the competition, but at some point, they had been shut off. I searched for Berly. A shadow shifted behind the trees. I shivered with the awareness of how close we were to the forest. This was the time of night animals came out—and who knew what else.

I glanced at my watch. It was 11:11 p.m., the perfect time. No other time involved four of the same number. You could get three of the same, like 4:44 or 5:55, and 10:10 was cool, but nothing was better than 11:11 in my book.

Gazing one last time at the lake, I watched the moon's reflection cast silver swirls across the water. It was so beautiful and peaceful until I heard a twig snap, making me jolt. The ranger's voice echoed in my head: *"Stay out of the forest. You must always stay on the trails."* I jogged back to the arena with no intention of seeing any more shadows.

I found Berly by the fire. "Are you ready to go?"

"Yeah." She turned to remind Martin and Max to meet us at the dining hall around ten, and then we headed down the path back to the dorms.

The twins ran to catch up.

"Can we walk with you?" Aspen asked. She wore her hair down and looked less sporty than her sister, but I wasn't sure I would be able to tell them apart if they both wore their hair the same.

"Of course. Safety in numbers," Berly said warmly.

"It's kind of spooky out here," Brooklyn remarked.

"The forest is so dark and foreboding," I couldn't help adding. "Who knows what kinds of animals live out there? I keep seeing dark shadows moving between the trees."

I was embarrassed yet relieved to admit what I had seen.

"My dad said this campus is full of wildlife. He told me to always carry bear spray with me," Berly said, a hint of sarcasm in her voice.

Aspen replied too quickly, "It's true. Moose walk right through the campus, looking for food. I heard they can get a bit ornery."

"I hope we never have to find out!" I exclaimed, and we picked up our pace.

CHAPTER 4

THE NEXT MORNING, Berly and I packed our gear for the day.

"Do you think we should wear swimsuits under our clothes?" I asked.

"Heck yeah. You know we're gonna end up jumping into a pond at some point," she replied. I sent Aspen and Brooklyn a text suggesting they do the same.

The four of us met up to walk to the dining hall together. The PSC campus had a kitchen where students could prepare meals or practice culinary skills. We assembled some lunches and went to the cafeteria to wait outside for the guys.

Berly tapped my arm. "Watch out. Casanova is coming your way."

I glanced up to see Benton and his lackeys approaching.

Benton stopped directly in front of me. He ignored my friends and drawled, "Hello there, Lily." He ran one hand through his hair. "How did you like the competition last night?"

I replied in my perkiest voice, "It was great! The Axe Men were amazing. I couldn't believe how good they were."

He frowned. "Did you cheer for me at all?"

I shrugged. "I cheered for all the winners."

Benton let out a grunt but seemed to shake off the disappointment. "I came over to see what you're doing today. My friends and I are taking out the canoes. Would you and your friends like to join us?" He dragged out the word "my" as if his companions were the most important people in the world.

"Thank you, but we already have plans," I said politely.

The timing was perfect: Martin and Max burst through the doors.

Benton leaned on the pole beside me and muttered, "Here comes the Obnoxious M & Ms."

"It's Oxford," I corrected snippily, crossing my arms.

Max strode up and planted a kiss on each girl's cheeks. "G'day, mate. Are you lovely ladies ready to roll?"

"What are you, Australian?" Benton scoffed.

Martin likewise gave us the double-cheek-kiss greeting, ignoring the interloper.

"Hiya. I'm one lucky bloke to hang with this lush group of birds."

Benton rolled his eyes. "See what I mean? Obnoxious M & Ms."

I looked directly at him, placing my hands on my hips. "It's better than being one of the Jack-Offs!"

Berly let out a howl.

I wiggled my fingers, saying, "Ta-ta" as I stepped past him.

Max scrambled to catch up with me, wearing a curious grin. "Are you two having a lovers' spat?"

I rolled my eyes. "I was just dealing with a— What did you call it? Oh yeah, a cretin."

The guys had grabbed a few breakfast sandwiches and downed a coffee in the cafeteria. I asked if they needed to fill their water bottles. Max placed his hand on Martin's shoulder, and they exchanged a secret look of amusement.

All six of us circled up to review the trail map.

"If we go around the pond clockwise, we should make it to the dam in a few hours. That would be a good place to stop for lunch," I proposed. "From that spot, it's only two miles back to campus."

The others cheerfully agreed with my plan.

The first mile was pleasurable. The path was clear and the ground relatively flat. We passed the first lake, its calm surface dappled with water lilies. The flowers attracted insects, and those attracted birds.

We ambled through a symphony of chirps, tweets, and chatter.

Martin prattled on about the competition and how he planned to train for the next one. Max ambled between Aspen and Brooklyn with his arms around their shoulders.

"Not one but two beautiful lasses. I'm one lucky bloke. Martin, get a snap of this. I need to send it back home to the fam."

Martin and Berly paused in front of a lean-to built near the intersection with the next trail, looking back at me for directions. I checked my watch and called ahead to them, "Turn left." The time was 11:11.

I lagged behind, enjoying the sunshine. Before I made the turn, I glanced right and caught my breath. He was there. The ranger stood less than thirty feet away, looking magnificent in his uniform. I stood frozen for an endless moment before he abruptly walked away with long, quick strides. The sight of him unnerved me. I ran to catch up with my new friends.

Black Pond was much darker than the other ponds in the area due to the dark river rock. The water itself was clear, and I spied multiple fish swimming gracefully past me. But as the water darkened, so did my mood. *He couldn't get away fast enough*.

The sun grew hotter and hotter as it crept toward its noontime position. Max whined about how bloody hot he was and kept pleading for volunteers to carry him back. Finally, I heard splashing up ahead.

"We're here. Chill out," I said as we reached a break in the trees and beheld the dam.

Max cheered. "Break time!" He ran over to a big rock on the bank and dropped his backpack. Stripping off his shirt, shoes, and shorts, he leaped in the pond wearing only his blue-striped boxer briefs.

We shed our packs and scrambled to get undressed. I noticed a rope hanging from the tree and grabbed a long stick to untangle it from another branch. Tugging on the rope to ensure it was sturdy enough to hold me, I took off running and swung far out into the water.

"That's bangin'. Let's give it a go," Martin yelled.

After a good ten minutes of splashing about, Max climbed out of the water and opened his backpack.

"Bottoms up!" He handed out beers.

Brooklyn wrinkled her nose. "Won't they be warm? You've been carrying them for over an hour."

He raised a condescending eyebrow. "That is the way ale should be drunk."

So that was what we did. The lukewarm beer wasn't too bad after the hike, but no wonder Max was complaining. He was probably carrying thirty extra pounds of weight. Martin's backpack was also full of beer.

We spent the next hour drinking and swinging from the rope, trying to perfect our leaps. The more we drank, the funnier our landings got. I could not stop myself from scanning the trails every so often, keeping an eye out for the ranger.

"I'm so glad we came. You guys are nuts," Aspen said.

We ended up stretching out on the big rock, enjoying the sunny summer day.

"Does anyone want something to eat?" I asked.

"Don't harsh me buzz," Max barked. I marveled at this uncharacteristic refusal of food.

Around 1:30, we ran out of beer. Max raised his hand like a kid in school.

"Who's going to make the beer run?"

"We are SOL," Berly said.

Martin looked perplexed. "Eh?"

"Shit out of luck," she explained.

He laughed. "Good one, mate."

Brooklyn handed out the sandwiches and snacks. I sat cross-legged, enjoying my food with the heat massaging my shoulders. Casually scanning the shore, I glimpsed a dark shape in the bushes. This figure was more defined than the shadow I'd seen in the forest; it looked like it was wearing a theatrical mask. I shook my head, and the figure vanished. *I must be hallucinating.* Maybe it was the combination of alcohol and heat.

We collected the empty cans and stuffed them into the guys' packs. I could only imagine what the ranger would say if we left anything more than footprints.

Our hike back was swift and easy. The empty beer cans jiggling in the guy's backpacks made for an unmusical soundtrack. Other hikers we passed regarded us with puzzled expressions. We just waved and kept walking.

Martin grinned wickedly. "How about a beer run? When we get back, we can play pool at the rec hall."

"Why stop now?" Berly agreed. "It's our last day of freedom!"

🦢 🦢 🦢

We ran into the Axe Men, Nate and Troy, on the Great Lawn. Martin shared our plan to get more beer and head to the hall and invited them to join us.

The rec hall comprised a little kitchen area with a fridge, lots of sitting areas, a big-screen TV, tables for pool, ping-pong, and air hockey, arcade basketball, and two dartboards.

Silently reflecting as the twins and I waited for the guys and Berly to return, I wondered what I had been so afraid of. This was only my third day, and I had made so many friends. It seemed like we had been here and known each other for months.

That thought jogged my memory. I needed to call my parents and check in.

I retreated to the lounge area for privacy to call home. Mom picked up straightaway, only briefly scolding me for not calling sooner. I filled her in on my first few days, minus the beer. Just as I hung up, Berly, Nate, and Martin entered with more beer.

The tall, sandy-blond Axe Man approached me.

"Want to play a game of pool?"

"Sure, sounds fun."

In high school, I quickly learned to be suspicious of good-looking guys, but I was hopeful that the guys I met in college would be different, more mature. I was sick of fake people. Thankfully, Nate seemed honest and a bit shy. He was certainly easy to get along with. I was outmatched, but he patiently gave me tips on how to line up different shots.

Aspen watched our game with interest. When the round was over, she leaned on the table, and Nate's eyes darted to her cleavage.

"Can I play too?"

Nate waved Troy over so we could play doubles.

When deciding on teams, Nate chose me to be his partner. Aspen's forehead wrinkled, and she pouted. Her expression reminded me of some girls I had known back home. Aware of her displeasure, I was careful about how I interacted with the guys. I did not want to spark any jealousy.

Max was relishing his new celebrity status. The more he drank, the louder he became. He told everyone the new moniker I had given Benton's team. Frankly, I was a bit embarrassed but also impressed with myself for coming up with the name. It was funnier when Max told the story in his British accent.

I gazed around, happy, knowing I had made the right choice for college.

CHAPTER 5

THE FIRST WEEK of school rushed by in the blink of an eye. Luckily, my classes were all on Mondays, Wednesdays, and Fridays, except for a two-hour lab on Tuesday afternoons. I had soccer practice every day except Saturdays and Sundays. I was starting to get into a groove by the third week, but I still hadn't figured out how to fit doing laundry into the mix.

Dedicated to jogging even with soccer practice every day, I ran on the trails at least three times a week, looking for my mysterious ranger. I didn't know his name, but a surge of energy accompanied the few times I saw him. Unfortunately, in each instance, he swiftly disappeared as if fleeing from danger. He was never close enough to talk to.

Maybe he was avoiding me, embarrassed by how he had barked at me. No, he probably thought I was mental for following some glittering shadow into the forest.

I had the opposite problem with Nate. Everywhere I went on campus, he seemed to find me. I was relieved that he was too bashful to ask me out. However, one morning he asked, "Would it be okay if I join you on one of your morning jogs?"

I kept my face very still, searching for a polite way to answer.

"Well, um . . . my morning jogs are a way to clear my head, my alone time. I'm afraid I wouldn't be much company. You understand, don't you?" It was a lame excuse at best, but I couldn't imagine running into the ranger with another guy by my side.

He looked away. "I understand completely. When I want to clear my head, I go to the woodsman arena."

I felt terrible hearing his sheepish response but couldn't think of anything else to say.

"Sorry, Nate, I have to get to class."

"See you later."

***

My favorite class so far was Ecological Restoration, which had the two-hour lab. The first week, we were assigned a group project to design and implement river and stream restoration projects. With access to data from previous years, we could compare and note environmental changes. This campus was a dream with its 14,000 acres of forest to use for the research.

Our professor had been teaching this class for fifteen years and knew the area well. During lab one day, I asked him, "What's up with that abandoned house in the marsh?"

He rested his hands flat on the table and adopted a mysterious expression as if preparing to tell a ghost story.

"That house was built long ago. For years, mystical travelers lived there from time to time. They never stayed long before moving to another area. When one group left, another moved in."

His voice deepened.

"It is said that they practiced witchcraft, made potions, and could manipulate the weather. Although some of the travelers were helpful, others were not. They practiced darker magic. Long ago, the locals tried to get them to leave. According to legend, the travelers conjured up a swarm of locusts that destroyed crops in the area. Many people died that winter. These mystical travelers stopped using that house long ago but still come to town from time to time. Locals have learned to stay away from them or suffer their wrath."

Shocked by his answer, I stood speechless. The whole class had fallen silent.

The professor let out a short, lighthearted laugh and patted me on the back. "Don't worry. They keep to themselves."

Nevertheless, his story gave me chills.

My lab ran long, so I went directly to the dining hall afterward. I was the last in our group to arrive. A few unfamiliar girls were plastered to Max. He loved the attention.

Berly patted the chair beside her. "I saved you a seat."

"Thanks, I'm starving. I love pasta night."

"Hey, does anyone want to go shopping downtown next weekend?" Brooklyn asked. "We have four days off for Columbus Day."

"Absolutely," I said. "I need to purchase a proper winter coat. We couldn't find any coats in Florida, and I am going to die without one."

"I'm in! We can shop till we drop!" Berly chimed in.

"We'll be at the pub," Martin said, clearly disinterested in shopping.

"Since we have the whole weekend, why don't we stay at my parents' house? We would be closer to downtown," Berly offered.

"That sounds great. Do you think they would mind?" I asked.

She flashed her dimples. "Not at all. That's why they purchased the house—so we could use it. My parents only use it in the winter months. The house is free to use anytime we want." She glanced at Martin. "You two blokes are invited too. We have plenty of room."

"Maybe we'll pop over on Saturday or Sunday, if you have enough ale," Martin answered playfully.

"We'll have plenty of beer, kayaks, a firepit, a hot tub, and a game room."

Her description of the house thoroughly won them over.

"Bloody hell, we're in." Martin pounded his fist on the table.

After dinner, Berly and I walked back to the dorm. "How big is this house?"

"It's five bedrooms with four and a half baths and a loft."

"It sounds huge."

"I love it. It's three stories with loads of balconies. A crystal-clear river runs across the back of the lot and down the side of the mountain. My stepbrother and I spent hours playing in the river and building forts."

"How many houses do your parents own?"

"Only four," she replied nonchalantly.

I shook my head in amazement. "What does your father do for a living?"

"He's a neurosurgeon."

"Wow, that's impressive." What was most impressive was how down-to-earth Berly was despite it all.

***

The following week, I found it hard to concentrate on schoolwork. Amid a grueling soccer season, I looked forward to the long weekend off, but time passed at a turtle's pace.

My lab partners and I were working on an Ecological Restoration assignment. Using the float method, we tested the flow of the water in the rivers and designed ways to save them from erosion and pollution and restore them if needed.

My lab partners returned to campus to log our results while I ran back to the river to collect water samples. Kneeling on the bank, I filled and labeled the vials, then carefully placed them back into the carrier. When I stood to leave, I heard voices. The deep voice sounded familiar.

I padded away from the river and back onto the trail. The ranger was less than ten feet away, giving hikers directions. The glass vials clinked against each other as the carrier dangled from my shaking hands. Silently, I stared at his profile.

When the hikers left, his head snapped in my direction. His whole body stiffened, and his mouth opened slightly. He even took a step back.

Heat flushed over me. *Why does this man dislike me?* We stood in silence, staring at each other. I closed my eyes and took a breath, uncertain whether I should get angry or burst out crying.

For once, I decided on anger. He didn't deserve my attention. I marched right past him without looking at him or saying a word. The knot in my stomach loosened after I passed. Proud of myself, I ran the rest of the way back to campus, leaving him and my frustration behind me.

That night, full of angst, I stared blindly at the ceiling. My mind raced with the possibilities ahead of me, but I couldn't help returning to the question of why the ranger loathed me. Like a chicken on a rotisserie, I tossed and turned, silently watching the hours tick past.

Eventually sleep took me, and my old nightmare returned.

❦ ❦ ❦

I grabbed the window, pulled and tugged, but it was nailed shut. I ran to the other window. It wouldn't budge.

Sunlight stabbed through slits between the planks nailed over the windows, casting dusty beams on the floor. My chest tightened when fog swirled in, bringing a musty smell as it twisted and squirmed and sent ghostly shadows dancing across the walls.

A clock on the wall ticked in time with the pulse in my temples. My throat constricted. I rushed to the door and snatched the handle. It opened freely. Behind the door, to my despair, was a brick wall. Someone had intentionally blocked the way out.

Heedlessly pounding my hands on the bricks, I tried to scream, but no sound came out. I swallowed and tried to scream again, but I was voiceless. The wooden floors creaked with the thud of forceful footsteps approaching behind me. I reluctantly glanced back as a dark shadow elongated across the wall.

I had to get away. I flung myself up the stairs, opening the first door on the left. This room also had no windows, no way out.

My heart pounded louder as the footsteps closed in. The door directly across from the top of the stairs was barred shut. I spun around and scuttled down the hall like a rat being chased by a cat.

The door on the right opened. I ran to the window, but it wasn't real. It was just a painting.

I fled again. The shadow inexorably advanced down the hall in my direction. Insensible with fear, I took two large steps to the last door. It opened, and behind it was another staircase. I slammed the door behind me and leaped up the stairs two at a time.

The staircase led to nothing. I pushed on the walls, banged on the roof. Everything remained impenetrable. I dropped my head and struggled to hold back tears.

Hearing a click, I cut my eyes back to the bottom of the stairs. The doorknob began to turn. Trapped like a bird in a cage, I had nowhere to go. Over the thunder of my pulse, I heard the squeak of the door opening.

Then I heard something outside the house; it sounded like a horn used on a foxhunt. A small glimmer of hope crept over me. Was someone here to save me? The horn sounded a second time, this time closer. The horn blasted for the third time, even louder.

✻ ✻ ✻

Groggy and confused, I reached over to turn off my alarm clock.

CHAPTER 6

Packed comfortably in Berly's jeep, the four of us girls headed off-campus. We were more than ready for a break.

The view from the winding road was spectacular. Fall had splashed fiery colors across the mountainside. As Berly pulled up the steep driveway, she said, "We'll drop off our gear and head out shopping."

The house was built high atop multiple acres. Multitiered decks of rich cedar wrapped around the house like a fancy ribbon on a gift. The front stairs led up to the second level. The moment we stepped out of the jeep, we were bathed in soothing sounds from the river flowing along the backside of the property.

"This house is amazing!" I cooed. The twins remained speechless.

We entered on the main floor. The interior boasted a modern rustic Adirondack style, with natural wood features. The pleasant smell of timber filled the house. The great room boasted a substantial wood-burning fireplace and stone hearth. Logs braced the massive ceilings, and floor-to-ceiling picture windows offered a breathtaking view of the mountainside.

We left the bedroom on the bottom floor for Max and Martin. It had a bunk bed and two single beds and was attached to the game room.

Berly wagged her finger. "You know what? You shouldn't purchase a winter coat. We have plenty of them." She walked me to the bottom floor and into the mudroom. "My stepmother has at least six coats in this closet. Here, pick one and save some money. She won't wear them again; she only wears the latest fashion. We like to keep a few in case a visitor needs a warmer coat."

I blinked. "Are you sure?"

"I'm sure. I should probably grab one too. It'll be getting cold soon. Go ahead. Try one on," she encouraged.

I reached for an olive-green one and discovered it was a perfect fit.

"Check the pockets. She always gets matching gloves."

Berly was right. There was also a scarf.

"This is too much!"

"Welcome to my world."

I hugged her. "Thank you so much. We just can't forget to grab them before we head back to campus."

"If we forget, we can always have the caretaker drop them off." Berly craned her neck and called up to the twins, "Are you two ready to go shopping?"

"Coming."

Berly stopped in the kitchen and grabbed a set of keys. "Let's take the Land Rover."

"Why, of course. After all, we are going shopping," I said in my best snooty voice. Berly snickered.

Main Street was less than three miles from her house and had an eclectic mix of shops. We took our time trying to browse them all. Berly introduced me to fleece-lined leggings, which were the biggest score of the day. I had no idea such things existed.

Berly pointed to one of the first pubs on the strip.

"Should we see if the guys are in here?"

"It can't hurt to look," Brooklyn replied.

We walked in and looked around.

"This place would be a lot louder if the two of them were here," I concluded.

Berly flashed a single dimple. "You are so right. Let's keep shopping."

After lunch, we hit the jackpot as far as the others were concerned:

a boutique showcasing fantastic style.

"I want to go in here," the twins announced simultaneously.

Berly was all in. "Let's do it! This is a great store."

I, however, was immediately intrigued by a shop across the street called the Salty Swan.

"What's that place?" I asked Berly.

"They sell jewelry, gems, crystals, and gift stuff. Go on and check it out! We'll be in here for a while."

"I think I will. I'll meet you back here."

Apropos of my middle name, my great-grandmother once told me, "Lily, you are a swan. Swans are beautiful creatures, but they can be salty when they need to. They will fiercely defend their loved ones. People can be deceived by the swan's beauty and never expect they are fierce. Be proud to be a swan." And I was.

I pushed open the door, activating a harmonious sound of chimes. Incense swirled around me as calming music played softly in the background.

I perused the jewelry section, immediately drawn to a lovely necklace with a swan pendant. Shown in profile, the animal's eye was crafted from pink crystal, and the tail had four larger crystals of the same color. Unbidden, I thought about the ranger for the first time that day. I couldn't believe I had the nerve to stomp right past him. Maybe I had a little salty swan in me after all.

I turned over the tag and frowned: $85. I set the necklace down.

"The red-tag jewelry is sixty percent off today," the clerk said over my shoulder.

I smiled and faced her.

"What kind of crystal is this?"

"Pink tourmaline, the rarest and prettiest of the tourmaline stones."

She showed them to me in raw-crystal form and as polished stones. When I held them in my hand, I swore I felt a gush of positive energy.

I purchased the necklace, a small natural crystal, and a polished one shaped like a heart. When I turned to leave, the clerk said in a dreamy voice, "It's already working for you. You are the swan, the protector who connects heart with head."

I had no clue what she meant. "Thank you, bye," I blurted and scampered across the street.

Berly had deposited a pile of clothes on the counter. Aspen held a large bag in her hand as she poked through displays near the door, and Brooklyn was still sorting through racks; she carried a bunch of items in her hands.

Berly waved me over. "You still have time to look around."

I wandered the store and found a dark-green long-sleeve shirt with a tan lace design on the bottom of the sleeve. I held it up.

"Do you guys like this?"

It was a unanimous yes. Before long, I had purchased the top, a few sweaters, and two pairs of pants. The place wasn't as pricey as it looked.

"Did you find anything in the Salty Swan?" Berly asked as we left the store.

"A few things. I'll show you when we get back."

We continued down the street. At the next intersection, we heard loud voices and laughing from a pub. We exchanged looks.

"I think we've found them," Berly said, flashing both dimples.

The four of us charged in.

"Look who's crashed the pub just when we're getting merry," Max yelled. Martin moved a stool next to him, motioning to Berly.

I leaned toward Berly's ear. "I will be the designated driver. Enjoy."

"Thanks," she mouthed back to me.

It was the least I could do. After all, she had just saved me at least $100 on a coat. The one she gave me was probably ten times better than any I could have purchased. Plus, she was hosting us in her incredible house.

The school had arranged for cheap hourly bus rides to and from the school to the Olympic Village at Lake Placid and Main Street. The guys had been here since noon. Quite a few other students had shown up, and it seemed like Max knew every one of them.

Max and Martin got louder and funnier the more they drank. Half the time, we had no idea what they were saying in their British slang, but they cracked us up with their animated delivery. Thankfully, the bartender—or as the boys called him, the barman—also thought they were hilarious and kept pouring them free ale.

After a few hours, Berly met my eyes and signaled. "Are you ready to head out?"

"Fine with me."

After making our farewells, we left the boys behind and started the long walk back to the car.

"Now, this is when it gets dangerous. A nice buzz makes you buy stupid stuff. Ladies, keep your head down and eyes on the sidewalk, or you will spend more than you intended," Berly slurred. I laughed, and she handed me the keys.

"Should we stop for some dinner and breakfast supplies?" I asked as we all climbed in. Berly slid into the front passenger seat.

"No, I've got it covered. I called the caretaker, and he stocked the house for us. He'll send the bill to Daddy."

"Wow, you are spoiling us."

"That's how I roll."

Aspen stuck her head between us from the back seat.

"Berls, I think Martin has taken a shine to you. Did you notice the way he always saves you a seat and whispers in your ear?"

Brooklyn squeezed forward beside her twin. "What do you think of him? Would you date him?"

Berly shrugged, but her dimple betrayed her. "Who knows? Only time will tell."

🦢 🦢 🦢

When we arrived back at the house, I scanned the kitchen for food.

But first things first.

"I could use a glass of wine."

"Coming right up." Berly opened a cabinet to reveal it was filled floor to ceiling with wine. "Red or white?"

"You choose."

She handed me a glass of white wine. I took a sip.

"Oh my, this is good."

Berly winked. "Vivi, my stepmom, only buys the best."

I found some mushroom ravioli in the refrigerator and heated it up because it was quick and easy.

"I don't know whether it's the beer buzz or this just tastes amazing," Brooklyn said after taking a bite.

"I think it's good, and I'm not even drunk," I said.

"I'm drunk, and I love it," Berly declared.

"Maybe we should call it drunk pasta," I suggested.

Berly raised one fist. "Drunk pasta it is!"

After dinner I took the bottle of wine outside on the front balcony. The evening air was cool, and the moon cast a charming glow on everything it touched.

The others went upstairs to shower. Brooklyn was the first to join me outside. She was carrying a handful of cookies. "Do you want one?"

"No thanks. I'm just enjoying my wine and this view." The night air was bracing. "I feel like we're in a dream. This house is amazing."

"I know. Berly is so matter-of-fact about it all, it's cute. She is so sweet."

"How lucky was I to get assigned as her roommate?"

Brooklyn leaned toward me. "It was meant to be."

"I'm starting to think so. It feels like I've known her for years," I said. "She is so easygoing. It's refreshing how comfortable she is with herself. I think that's why Martin likes her. She just does what she wants without any worries."

Brooklyn finished her cookie. "I'm going to bed. Good night."

"Night."

I meandered the deck to check out the views. The river flowed past the front balcony. The firepit and hammocks were on one side of the property, while the other side revealed forest as far as the eye could see. The back led to the steep driveway.

Leaning on the railing out front, listening to the water gurgle past, I saw a dark shape move in the trees. It was probably an animal, but it still gave me a chill. The bright moon illuminated the immediate environs, but the forest remained dark and mysterious.

I thought about what the professor had told the lab students. Maybe evil spirits roamed these woods and the mystical travelers created them.

I peeked at my watch, and a gust of wind lifted my hair. It was 11:11.

I flinched when the door opened, but it was just Berly joining me outside.

"It is such a nice night. Thanks for driving." Berly hooked her arm in mine. "Those two are crazy. How did we make such a connection with them on our first day?"

I repeated what Brooklyn had said: "It was meant to be. Thank you again for letting us stay here."

She waved her hand like she was shooing a fly. "I love it when the house gets used."

"Today was so much fun. What a great start to a long weekend." I gazed up at the moon.

Berly nodded with an expression of satisfaction. Her eyes brightened. "Hey, you never showed me what you purchased in that store."

"Hold on, I'll go get it." I popped into the house and returned with my purchases. "The clerk said something strange to me. Let me think. Oh yeah! 'It's already working for you. You are the swan, the protector who connects heart with head.' What do you think that means?"

"Maybe it's because you bought the swan necklace?"

I told Berly about my middle name and the things my grandmother had told me.

"That's why I got the swan necklace—and because it was so pretty."

She took the necklace and inspected it closely. "It's beautiful, so dainty. What kind of stone is this again?"

"Pink tourmaline. I was instantly drawn to it when I walked into the store."

"Crystals are used by psychics, healers, gypsies—all kinds of people that believe they have different types of powerful energy."

With the story about the creepy house fresh in my mind, I did not want to think about such things.

She handed the necklace back to me. "What do you want to do tomorrow?"

"What are our options?"

She ticked them off on her fingers. "We could take out the kayaks, go to the Olympic Village, go horseback riding, zip-lining, fishing, do the Skyride."

"I would be up for anything at the Olympic Village. I heard it was fun."

"I'm in, but nothing too early. I need to sleep this off."

"We can play it by ear."

We headed back inside.

"Good night." She waved from the doorway of her bedroom and closed the door.

CHAPTER 7

THE NEXT MORNING, wanting to give the girls time to rest, I quietly padded to the kitchen for a cup of coffee and left a note on the counter so they would know where I was. I grabbed a croissant, my cell phone, and a jacket and headed out for a walk. Realizing I was still carrying the notepad, I stuffed it into the jacket pocket.

The weather was perfect, the crisp air and clear sky energizing. I chose the path following the stream down the mountain but didn't bother turning my outing into a jog. I had done enough running for soccer this week; I just wanted to get a closer look at the river and enjoy myself.

The walk made me recall Benton's line about strolling and holding hands. The memory made me chuckle.

The river was pristine. *It must be spring fed.* I thought of my project. *This would be a great river to study.* Not too wide or deep, the water flowed at a steady pace.

I looked around for something to float down the river. I tried using a small piece of wood, but it sank. Remembering the notepad, I settled down on a log to try to fold a boat that would float. The water was moving swiftly enough to splash against the rocks, and my first boat was too skinny to handle the force and tipped over. I folded three pieces together and tried again.

This paper boat was much better. When I let it go, it took off swiftly. I raced to keep up with it; I couldn't litter, or the ranger might yell at me. Using a broken branch, I stopped it and pulled it out. I marked lines in the sand to measure how fast it was going. Setting the timer on my phone, I placed the boat back in the water.

A terrible cry erupted downriver. I jumped up from my crouch, straining to see what it was, my hand pressed to my pounding heart. My little boat sailed along.

Walking briskly to discern where the noise came from, I scanned the trees. I heard a different sound—a snort and a shrill cry. I picked up my pace and soon found the source of the sound.

A deer lay on the opposite bank, struggling to free itself from something tangled in his antlers. He shook his head vigorously to get loose. My heart grew heavy as he continued to snort and cry. *He might break his neck or even die.* Behind him, a few deer watched anxiously.

My adrenaline took over, and I stepped into the river and sloshed across.

"It's okay, boy. It's okay. I'm going to help you."

I glanced down the river when I reached the other side and glimpsed a flash of white slipping behind a tree. My boat was gone. I pushed it from my mind. Sweat beaded at my temples as I knelt beside the deer to assess the situation.

I spoke to him in a low, calm voice. Miraculously, he seemed to settle down, so I slowly removed my jacket, hoping that if I covered his eyes, I could keep him still. Moving with caution, I stroked his back. He looked at me with gentle eyes that begged for help.

"Everything is going to be all right," I said quietly.

I tugged the line that he was tangled in. It was hard and thick, some kind of wire. I tried to pull it off, but it cut into my fingers. I was only able to free two of the loops before the deer started shaking his head again and snorting.

Slipping my jacket over his eyes, I kept patting his back until he quieted down. I had to straddle him to get a better grip. The wire was too strong to break, and the blood on my fingers made them slippery. I managed to get one more loop off, but he was still stuck.

I started pulling on the wire and kicking at the tree it was snagged on to see if I could find what it was attached to.

"Come on, just break free, stupid wire. Break free! I can't let him die," I yelled at the wire like a fool.

My jacket fell from the deer's head as he grew agitated, and I grasped the antlers, afraid he was going to gore me. My hair fell across my face and stuck to my cheeks. Only then did I realize I was crying.

I heard a splash in the river. Peeking through my hair, I saw only a pair of hands.

"Please help me. I can't get him untangled from this wire." My voice cracked.

"You hold his antlers still. Let me try to get the wire free."

The poor deer was exhausted. His snorts slowed to soft bursts. The guy grabbed the wire in one hand, pulled out a multitool with his other, and pulled out the pliers. My arms ached, but I held on as he snipped and unraveled the wire.

His voice was stern but hushed. "Be very careful. I am going to hold his antlers while you step off his back. Grab your jacket and move away before I let him go."

He held the antlers steady. I vaulted off, grabbed my coat, and hopped backward. He looked into the deer's eyes. "Luck is with you. Go, you are free," he said in a familiar deep voice. He released the deer. The buck scrambled to his feet, snorting a few times.

"Go, my friend. Go back to your herd."

The deer swung his head from side to side. He was either confused or out of breath. Finally, he turned and ran off.

Swiping at my eyes with the back of my hand, I gasped, "Oh my God, that was crazy. Thank you so much for helping me. I just couldn't get him free." I tried to push the hair from my face. "You were my angel today."

"No, I believe you were his angel today."

"I guess we were both his angels," I conceded.

My pants were wet and covered in dirt. I tried to wipe it away.

"Look at me, I'm a mess."

"I am looking at you. I think you look perfect. Those are just clothes; it is your heart that counts."

I raised my head. My heart seemed to stumble in my chest. "It's you."

The ranger flashed his pearly white teeth.

"Hi, I'm Lily," I said in a quavering voice.

"Nice to meet you. I'm Kai." His voice was almost perky as he reached for my hand. "Come, let me help you back across."

When I placed my hand in his, a tingle zipped to my toes. He helped me to my feet and supported me as we crossed the river.

He was perfect. His skin glowed a beautiful bronze as he moved gracefully through the water. He was not wearing those annoying sunglasses, so I could see his high cheekbones and mesmerizing, emerald-green eyes flecked with gold.

He was staring at me as intently as I was staring at him. Once we made it out of the river, still looking at each other, we mindlessly started downhill in the same direction I was headed before.

"Why are you here?" he asked.

"I'm staying the weekend with my friends at a house near the top of this trail. I grew up in Florida, so this winter will be a big change for me." *Where did that non sequitur come from?* I chided myself, but he seemed genuinely interested in me, asking all kinds of questions.

"Why did you decide to come here for college?"

"I was awarded a soccer scholarship. I chose this school because I wanted to get far away, and I liked the environmental science program."

I was immediately worried I had overshared.

"What did you want to get away from?" he asked directly.

"I was sick of malicious gossip from jealous people I thought were friends," I muttered darkly, surprised I had told the truth.

A smile flashed across his face. "I can see why they were jealous of you."

I couldn't focus on anything except his perfect lips and didn't know how to interpret his words.

"Enough about me," I said quickly. "What about you? Are you from around here?"

I tried to sound attentive so he wouldn't turn the focus back on me.

"I've been here my entire life. I live down at the bottom of the mountain."

I relaxed as his voice grew lively.

"When I was a kid, my friends and I would come to this river to float down on homemade rafts. They were never very good, but occasionally, we made one that worked. We would spend entire summers trying to perfect our rafts. It was so much fun, like our own personal waterslide." He was beaming.

I was relieved that it was my turn to ask a barrage of questions about his life in the Adirondacks.

Eventually changing the subject, I asked, "What made you walk up the river path this morning? Did you hear me screaming?"

"This." He pulled the paper boat from his pocket. "I'm a forest ranger. Part of my job is to make sure no one is doing any harm to the forest."

"Oh, that was me. I was trying to measure the flow of the water." I dropped my gaze to my feet, bracing myself for a scolding. "Sorry, I didn't mean to litter, but the deer distracted me. Are you going to give me a fine?"

He laughed. "Yes, the fine is that I get to keep this paper boat."

"Deal." I was dazed. *Why is he acting so nice?* Before, it had seemed like I had the plague.

He looked away. "I'm sorry for the way I talked to you the day we met on the trails."

I didn't know what came over me, but I told the truth again.

"You scared the crap out of me, and I was already scared to death. I've been angry with you ever since." Just mentioning it made some of that resentment return.

"I wasn't kidding about the forest. It is a dangerous place." He enunciated each word slowly.

"You spoke to me like I was a child," I muttered.

"Please forgive me, but I intended to scare you. To protect you."

"Protect me from what?"

His voice softened. "What exactly did you follow into the forest?"

I cleared my throat self-consciously. "Well, a dark shadow about three feet tall was gliding between the trees. I couldn't take my eyes off it and felt a strange impulse to follow it. So, I did. That was weird for me because I'm usually a coward. The shadow started to seem solid, like stone. It disappeared with a loud pop. That's when I panicked and ran out of the forest, smashing into you."

"Have you seen it any other times?"

"Yes, actually. In the forest by Black Pond and last night, from the balcony up at the cabin." The hair on my arms was standing up. "Do you know what it is?"

"I have heard folklore about creatures of the forest. Some people believe they're otherworldly. They were never described as stonelike, as far as I remember. I would have to ask my grandmother to be certain."

My mouth was dry. "Are they dangerous?"

"Extremely," he answered without hesitation.

A loud caw above our heads made me jerk.

"Okay, enough about that."

I could tell he was intentionally changing the subject, like he knew more but didn't want to tell me.

He brightened. "Hey, I can show you how the elders measure the flow of the water."

"Please do," I answered a bit too eagerly.

He let go of my hand and grabbed four long, thin branches. I felt dizzy. I had not even realized we were still holding hands all this time. Heat rose in my cheeks, and I laughed internally at the irony. *I just strolled the hiking trail hand in hand with a guy I just met. That's how it's done, Benton, you jerk!*

Kai waded in and stood all four branches upright in a straight line across the river, equidistant from one another.

"Now observe them for a few minutes, and tell me what you see."

We both knelt to watch the branches. His leg against mine made it difficult to concentrate on anything else. But I forced myself to study the water flow because Kai was watching my face. I felt his breath light on my cheek. My heart throbbed in my ears.

"Do you notice anything in the flow as they pass each branch?" Kai asked.

"They all create a good wake around them as the water flows. The one on the far right has a bigger wake than the others."

"Correct, and a good observation. What do you think that means?"

"More water is flowing from the right, or it's flowing faster on the right side," I replied uncertainly.

"You can tell it's flowing faster if the water makes white bubbles passing the stick. You can also add more sticks farther down the river to test whether the flow is the same. The watermark on each stick lets you know if the flow is increasing or decreasing."

He continued with confidence. "Now we need to fix the issue you noticed of the water flowing faster and stronger on the right side; otherwise, you'll get erosion in this bank. My grandfather would look for a solid log or big piece of bark and bury it at an angle on the right side where the water is picking up speed." He found a rotting log a few feet from the bank and demonstrated. "You can adjust the angle of the log according to the speed of the flow like this. Pack some mud around it, and your erosion problem has been diverted."

"That's amazing. No math or crazy calculations. I could listen to you all day."

"I wish I had all day."

My heart sank when he looked at his watch.

"Why don't I walk you back to your house before I go to work?"

"Sure, if you have the time."

His grin gave me my answer.

We stood, brushed the dirt from our pants, and started back up the path. We discussed all the rivers I was studying. He knew everything about them, and there was barely a pause in conversation. When I finally looked up, I discovered we were all the way back to the house and were holding hands again. *When did that happen?*

I looked up into his face. When our eyes locked, everything around us seemed to melt away. His emerald eyes sparkled, and I felt my heartbeat in my throat.

Trying to sound nonchalant, I said, "Feel free to stop by to see me whenever you're working near campus."

Kai raised an eyebrow. "How long are you staying in this house?"

"Until Monday," I answered.

"Would you mind if I come by tonight after work? It's going to be a full moon," he said with that same twinkle in his eye. "Is ten okay with you?"

Heat rose in my veins as if I had stepped into a sauna. I could not contain my smile.

"That sounds great. See you soon."

He touched my cheek, gazing into my eyes for a long, intense moment. Slowly he leaned in and kissed my forehead. He moved his lips to my ear.

"You have a beautiful heart."

He turned and jogged back down the path, his silky black hair swaying. Dusted with sunlight, the black sheen took on a hue of navy-blue marbling. I could not take my eyes off this breathtaking mystery man.

When I finally managed to take a breath, I looked up to the balcony and found all three girls standing at the railing, their mouths open with mock surprise. I waved cheerfully and dashed around to the door.

They were squealing and hopping a little with suppressed excitement when I walked in.

"Who was that?" Berly demanded. "What are you, some kind of hot-guy magnet?"

My smile was so broad that it hurt.

Aspen placed her hands on her hips. "Spill it."

Holding up my hand, signaling for them to wait, I hurried down to the mudroom, took off my wet, muddy shoes, and placed them in a cubby. I shucked off my dirty pants and tossed them in the washer. Back upstairs, all three of them goggled at me.

"Give me a minute to grab some leggings. I'll be right back."

Then we went into the great room, and I told them the whole story.

"Oh my God, what a morning. Do you think you'll see him again?" Berly asked.

"I hope so." I found it hard to contain my exhilaration. "Enough about me. What have you guys been doing? Any ideas about what you want to do today?"

Berly crossed her arms and tapped her foot. "Don't try to change the subject. You were holding hands with a hot guy, and he kissed you before he left."

"I know! I could not stop thinking about Benton Cretin's pickup line and how I was strolling down a trail with a hot a guy I had just met. It's funny when you think about it. Kai just swept me away while Benton made me want to puke."

"I had forgotten that classic pickup line."

The twins looked puzzled, so we filled them in on our first encounter with Benton.

"I don't think I'll ever be able to look at him again without thinking of that line," Aspen giggled.

Brooklyn shook her head. "He really thought that would work?"

"Maybe he's had luck before, but I found it creepy."

"So, let me get this straight. You saved a deer, walked hand in hand by the river, and he kissed you, right?" Berly asked.

"I know it sounds crazy, but that is what happened. But it's not entirely random. I have seen him before while running the trails near school. He's a forest ranger." I withheld the details of our first encounter. "He said he was going to stop by after work tonight."

Aspen's eyes bugged out with delight. "That's all I know. Now, really, what are we doing today?"

CHAPTER 8

I WAS SO ABSORBED in my thoughts of Kai that I was hardly aware of the wait in the bobsled line at the Olympic Sports Complex. Kai seemed to be hiding something about the forest. He'd used the words "folklore" and "otherworldly." *Could whatever he was warning me away from be connected to mystical travelers?* I wondered. *And why was I so honest with him?* Most importantly: *Is he thinking about me as much as I'm thinking about him?*

"You're up," the attendant said, jolting me out of my private conversation with myself. I had not paid any attention to his directions.

He strapped me in, saying, "Hang on tight and have fun," and launched my cart. I was flying down the track before I even took a breath. It went so fast I feared it would jump the track on the turns. The pure adrenaline had me screaming and laughing at the same time. Finally, the track leveled off, and the cart slowed. Another attendant helped me out. I wiped my shaky, sweaty palms on my jeans and stepped off the platform.

"What did you think?" Berly's dimple told me she'd loved it.

"That was exhilarating! How fast do you think that thing goes?"

"It can go up to sixty miles per hour."

"It felt like a hundred to me. I was worried I was going to flip off the track."

"Me too," Berly admitted.

We turned to see Aspen and Brooklyn climb out of their carts.

They were both laughing. We waved them over, and I asked, "Should we go again?"

"I'm in."

After our third ride, we grabbed lunch, went to the museum, and ended up stumbling upon an outside festival. Aspen pointed to the stage. "Hey look, it's the Axe Men."

Nate and Troy were showcasing their skills with axe throwing. When they finished up, Nate waved us over to the stage.

"How did you like the show?" he asked me.

"It was great. We only saw the end, but the crowd seemed to love it."

Aspen had a firm look of displeasure on her face. I turned to her. "What did you think, Aspen?"

She livened up, answering Nate directly. "You were amazing! I didn't know you could split an apple." Her level tone was sweet and polite.

Berly wore a devilish grin. "I dig the lumberjack flannel."

Nate winked. "A man's got to play the part."

"I like the shirts," Aspen defended him.

Berly invited Nate and Troy to the house for dinner, drinks, and fun. They seemed more willing to join us when she told them Max and Martin were coming.

On the drive back to the cabin, Aspen asked, "Do you guys think Nate is cute? He is so tall and rugged. No, not cute. He is handsome and humble."

Brooklyn rolled her eyes. "Aspen likes a lumberjack, but I think he has eyes for Lily."

The scowl returned to Aspen's face. I kept my mouth shut and looked out the window.

***

My stomach did flips thinking about Kai and what I should wear and if he would even show up. *Why didn't he ask for my number? What if he has a girlfriend? What if he's married?* I began to spiral and drive myself crazy.

I tried to blank my mind as I pulled on my new green top from the boutique, dried my hair, and put on a little makeup and the swan necklace.

Berly was setting up the kitchen. "Wow, you look great in green."

"Is that the sweater you bought? It's adorable," I said. "We might have to go to the boutique again."

Nate and Troy were the first to arrive. Berly asked them to set the wood up so we could use the firepit. It was a perfect task for the lumberjacks, and Nate in particular was eager to help.

Troy gazed around. "This is a beautiful place."

Berly replied, "Thanks, my dad likes his toys."

"This is quite the toy."

Martin and Max set up the cornhole game as soon as they arrived. Then Martin promptly got into the hammock tied between two trees and started asking for beer deliveries because he could not get back out.

Nate and Troy dominated cornhole. Nate asked if I wanted to play, and Aspen grimaced. Not wanting to hurt his feelings, and to keep Aspen happy, I did my best to divert his attention.

"I think Aspen wanted to play. Why don't you ask her?"

Her cheeks reddened, and she stepped forward. Nate, being the gentleman he was, asked her to join him. She accepted with a smile.

Tired of pacing, I went inside to straighten the already clean kitchen. I folded my laundry, brushed my teeth and hair, cleaned the bathroom mirrors, and wiped down the tables. It was only 9:30. Time was dragging.

Back downstairs, the party had moved to the game room. Aspen and Nate were playing table tennis, and she was markedly cheerful. Nate's smile widened when I entered the room.

"There you are. Do you want to play?"

Aspen glared at me.

I sighed and thought quickly, trying to keep my voice lively.

"Sure! Troy, do you want to play doubles? I need a partner."

Aspen seemed pleased with that. She had to know I was not the enemy.

Troy set the arcade basketball down. "Sure."

Much like Nate, Troy was friendly and considerate. They were both very likable.

"Do you think we should start the fire in the firepit?" Nate asked the room after we had gone a few rounds.

"That sounds like a good idea," Aspen answered in a jovial voice. "Do we have enough wood?"

Her question made him laugh. "I can always chop some more."

She giggled, and the two of them headed out to get the fire started.

I ran upstairs to put a tray together with supplies for s'mores. Enjoying the quiet of the empty kitchen, I checked the time every five minutes. It dawned on me that my first real conversation with Kai had occurred only around twelve hours ago.

After I brought out the tray, I realized I had forgotten the skewers and ran back upstairs to get them.

Walking back onto the deck, I spotted Kai coming up the path by the creek. I set the skewers down gently and descended the stairs. My heart thudded. I drifted toward him as if pulled, never breaking eye contact. A big smile grew on his face as he approached.

"Good evening," I murmured. "I'm so glad you came."

I felt eyes burning into the back of my head as Kai took my hands in his. "Nothing could keep me away." He kissed my hands.

Heat flushed my body.

"Come with me. I'd like you to meet my friends."

We went to the firepit, and I introduced him to Aspen and Nate. The disapproval on Nate's face was unmistakable. Aspen, on the other hand, was beaming.

Inside, I introduced Kai to the others. Looking up at his perfect face, I felt my mind go blank. I stood staring like a fool.

Martin came to the rescue, handing Kai a beer. "Brewski, mate?"

Kai took the beer and popped it open. "Thank you."

"Cheers. Eh, it's good to be a bit merry."

I composed myself. "Do you want a tour of the house?" I asked.

"Sure. I've always wondered what this house looked like inside. It's beautiful, and it smells so nice."

"It's the natural wood. Berly told us the builder used the trees cleared from the property to build the house."

He nodded in approval.

The tour was brief. I didn't know much about the house and ended up gazing at Kai as we wandered from floor to floor.

Back down on the main floor, I asked, "Do you want to go out to the firepit?"

"I will go anywhere with you."

An alarm sounded in my head. Maybe he was a player, but he sounded sincere. He took my hand in his, and we returned to the fire.

Martin, who had never had s'mores before, gushed about how good they were.

"These are brilliant. I bloody love them."

We sat on one of the oversized chairs and made some of our own. When I took my first bite, I had to agree. "He's right. They are brilliant."

Max stood and thumped his chest with his fists like a gorilla. "Max is chuffed. Time for another beer. Who wants to get in the hot tub?"

Everyone except Kai and I went inside to change, leaving us alone by the fire.

My swan necklace fell forward as I reached over to grab a blanket from the back of a chair. Kai took hold of the pendant, inspecting it as I leaned toward him.

"A swan? That is interesting. And beautiful. What made you choose a swan?" he asked, draping the blanket around our shoulders and placing his arm behind my back. I felt so warm and safe beside him.

"My middle name is Swan: Liliana Swan Makris. Swan was my grandmother's maiden name. Both my sister and I have Swan for our middle name, and so do our cousins. My great-grandmother used to tell me to be proud of being a swan and that swans were fierce in protecting their loved ones." I smiled and admitted, "I'm still wondering if I can be fierce. I bought this yesterday in a downtown store called the Salty Swan."

"That reminds me of a story the elders used to tell. Would you like to hear it?"

I turned to him. "Absolutely I would."

"Let me see if I can remember how it goes." He licked his perfect lips and started the story in a hushed voice.

※ ※ ※

Swans are powerful creatures of infinite grace and almost heavenly in appearance. They are sacred to our people, and witnessing their beauty is considered an honor. They are also symbolic of angels and are said to bring us life lessons from spiritual planes.

Long ago, there was a beautiful swan princess whom the animals adored. They would bring her gifts just to gaze upon her. Wherever she went, everyone praised her. They wrote songs and poems about her beauty.

Her parents, the king and queen of the land, were very pleased with her. But the princess was so used to everyone giving her everything she wanted because of her beauty that she expected it. She was not very kind to others. In fact, she was conceited and rude.

For her sixteenth birthday, the beautiful princess demanded an elaborate party. Everyone from the village worked tirelessly to prepare. She wanted it to be the grandest celebration anyone had ever seen. Nothing was ever good enough, and she continued to demand more extravagance.

The village residents began to resent her and no longer liked her for her beauty. They recognized that she was ugly on the inside.

During the party, someone toasted the princess and her health. The queen exclaimed that the swan princess was the most beautiful creature on the planet and in the heavens above.

This angered the Great Spirit. In a puff of smoke, he materialized in the middle of the party. His thunderous voice brought silence to the crowd.

"The swan princess may be beautiful in the physical world, but her spirit is far from pretty. In eleven days, little princess, you must make a choice. You can save the animals of your village by giving up your beauty, or you can keep your beauty, and they will all suffer. I will return for your answer."

He disappeared in a swirling mist.

The animals gasped. They pleaded with the princess, but she was far too selfish and did not want to live without her beauty.

The residents of the village stopped attending to the princess. They started to ignore her altogether. She heard them say things like "Why is she so selfish?" "She is not beautiful on the inside." "I think she is quite ugly."

She did not know what to do. She had no one to talk to.

So she walked down to the river to think. While sitting on the bank, she met a vulture. He was not a good-looking creature. He had a red, scaly, featherless head, a long, hooked beak, and dull brownish-black feathers. She wondered if she would look like him if she agreed to give up her beauty. No one would ever bring her gifts or attend to her if she looked like that.

"What is troubling you, pretty one?" the vulture asked her.

"No one will love me if I am not beautiful."

"Look at me. I am not beautiful, but I am one of the most powerful, adaptable creatures with a strong survival instinct. I live in a solid community that loves and protects each other. Vultures are messengers between life and death, the physical world and the spirit world."

He looked directly into the swan princess's eyes. "What good is beauty if you have no one to love, no one to be with? I consider myself fortunate to be a vulture. I am loved by so many."

The princess swan thought about what the vulture told her but could not imagine life without her beauty.

For the next few days, no one spoke to her as she wandered the village. Sometimes she was angry at her mother for putting her in this situation. At other times, she was embarrassed about the way she treated everyone.

No one even looked at her anymore, which really drove her crazy because she craved the attention. They were all busy preparing for disaster. Many were packing up their families to leave the village.

The swan princess was sad and very lonely. She asked her mother what she should do.

Her mother's head hung low, her voice barely over a whisper. "I am ashamed of what I said that angered the Great Spirit, and I hope you can forgive me. But this decision must be made by you and you alone. You must choose what is right."

On the eleventh day, the Great Spirit returned to the village square to ask the swan princess for her answer. Everyone gathered to learn their fate.

The swan princess walked slowly, dragging her feet toward the town square. Then a little duckling stopped the princess. With a sweet smile, the creature handed her a small pink stone.

"Hold this. It will give you strength and clarity."

The swan princess gently took the stone from the little duckling, nodding in thanks.

This was the first kind gesture she had experienced in days. Warmth spread through her. This little duckling was genuinely trying to help her.

The princess started thinking about her interactions with the animals of the village. Did they only do things for her because she ordered them to? Did anyone even like her? Would she have to find a new home if she chose her beauty? Would she have to live with the vultures?

When she made it to the center square, she knew what she wanted to do.

The Great Spirit asked for her answer. "Do you choose to keep your beauty or to rescue the animals of the village?"

The swan princess held the stone tight, closing her eyes. "I choose the animals!"

Everyone cheered loudly and hugged one another.

"Then let it be done." The Great Spirit waved his hand, and dust gathered around the beautiful swan princess. When the dust cleared, she looked down. Her beautiful angelic features were gone, and her white feathers had turned jet black. The Great Spirit vanished, and the swan princess cried and cried.

The animals comforted the princess and thanked her for the sacrifice. And they loved the princess more than ever. They showered her with flowers, songs, poems, even erected a statue of her in the middle of the village. Animals everywhere heard about the princess and her sacrifice. They came from all over to meet her, to become friends with her.

She learned to be humble, caring, and kind to others. She was more greatly loved by the animals than anyone had ever been loved before. She was so fulfilled by all the love and support that her beauty returned to her, except the color of her feathers. They remained black as a reminder. To this day, we see an occasional black swan, reminding us to be kind to others and open our hearts to understand the miraculous power of love.

Kai's voice was strong and soothing, and I was utterly engrossed by the story.

"What a beautiful tale. I felt sorry for her, but I wanted her to choose the animals."

"Not everyone would make that kind of sacrifice."

"I'm sure most would. Think of how many lives she would ruin if she didn't."

"I knew you had a good heart."

Embarrassed, I rolled my eyes, feeling the heat spread across my face.

"Do you know any other stories?"

"I know plenty of them."

A burst of laughter came from the back of the house.

"Maybe we should see what's going on." I sighed.

Martin, Max, Berly, and Brooklyn were still in the hot tub. Max was singing way out of tune and getting all the words wrong, which made it even funnier. The others gasped with laughter.

Brooklyn regained her composure. "Are you guys going inside?"

"Yep."

"Can you grab me one of the towels from the stand?"

"Of course." I grabbed towels for all of them, returning to hand her one and placing the other three on the hot tub platform.

Kai and I entered the game room on the bottom floor, where we found Nate, Troy, and Aspen. Nate was playing arcade basketball while Aspen watched and Troy tried his hand at darts.

"Max is quite the character, isn't he?" Kai said to me—more a statement than a question.

"We never know what he's going to do or say next. He certainly keeps it interesting."

Kai and I played a round of darts with Troy. Nate glared at us as he threw the ball over and over with force. I heard him curse a few times, which was a first, as he was usually very calm. His cheeks were red when he stomped over.

"I'd like to challenge you to a game of pool," he said curtly to Kai.

Kai looked at me.

"Sounds like fun; go ahead," I encouraged Kai, though I loathed the tense feeling in the room.

Dried and dressed, Brooklyn came down the stairs.

"Hey, what's going on down here?" she asked, immediately lightening the mood.

Troy answered obliviously, "Nate challenged Kai to a game of pool."

She plopped on a stool next to me. The sound of a solid crack started the game. Nate rested his stern face on his pool cue as he lined up his next shot.

Brooklyn leaned down to whisper, "What's up with him?"

"I don't think he's happy I invited Kai to the party." I tried to keep my voice low.

She raised her eyebrows and peered across the room at her sister. Aspen was leaning against the wall with her arms crossed, expressionless. "I don't think Aspen is so happy either."

I sighed. "I just wish we would all get along. I hate when people are angry or jealous."

"Don't worry about it. You can't control the way people act. How's it going with your mystery man?"

"Great. He is so pleasant, easy to like, and his voice is mesmerizing. I can't fathom why he came to see me. Look at him. He is impossibly handsome."

Brooklyn scoffed. "Don't you have any idea how beautiful you are?"

Her comment reminded me of my senior year. I remembered the eyes glaring at me, the jealous girls with their heads together, hands covering their mouths to hide what they were saying, speculating that I had plastic surgery. Even my closest friends became catty, telling me I looked great in one breath and asking what I had gotten done in the next. It was beyond annoying.

Then Brooklyn crushed my spirit. "I hope there's not a bad side, like he has a girlfriend. What if he's married, or worse, a player?"

My ears grew hot.

Nate won the first round, and his mood seemed to lift. Meanwhile, Aspen relaxed and sat with me and her sister. Kai won the second game. As the guys competed for the tiebreaker, the room quieted. All eyes were on each shot.

They were evenly matched, and I was biting my nails. I didn't watch the game as much as I watched Kai—his muscular arms, hard, flat stomach, and the way his long black hair swept the table when he shot.

Kai sank the winning shot. Cheering, I unthinkingly jumped up and leaped into his arms. His hold tightened around my waist. I loosened my grip, wondering if my reaction seemed too forward. But I didn't let go.

With my arms still around his neck, Kai said to Nate, "Good game" and flashed a radiant smile, exposing his perfectly white teeth. Kai reached out to shake Nate's hand.

Nate took the defeat with class. "Thanks. Great game." Kindness had returned to his voice.

"I just got lucky. You totally earned my respect," Kai said, patting Nate's shoulder.

Relieved that things had settled down, I poured a glass of wine and handed another beer to Kai. "Cheers."

The conversation in the room shifted to the festival. Nate and Troy were performing again tomorrow, and Berly, the twins, and I promised to go again. Berly tried to persuade Martin and Max to join us.

Kai turned to me. "I don't have to work tomorrow. I was hoping you would spend the day with me." He regarded me with probing eyes.

I paused because my thoughts were unmanageable. I didn't want to make the girls angry for ditching them. I didn't want to lead Nate on by going. But I feverishly wanted to be with Kai, so I decided on a compromise. "What if I go with the girls to the first show at eleven? You can meet me there. After that, we can spend the rest of the day together."

"That sounds perfect."

Troy racked the balls for the next game. Kai moved away to give the players room and pulled me with him until my back was pressed against his chest. He encircled his long, firm arms around me, and his hands landed on my waist. My skin thrummed where his fingers rested.

We stayed this way for I didn't know how long, until he bent down and whispered in my ear, "Do you want to get some fresh air?"

I nodded. We walked hand in hand upstairs to the great room and onto the balcony.

The moon was bright and full.

"Isn't it magical?" he said, looking up.

"The moon?"

"Yes, the moon." He turned to face me, taking my other hand in his. "We have a saying about the moon. The glow of a full moon can place you in a trance with its beauty." He added, "Like your beauty has placed a trance on me."

Is this guy for real? Again, it sounded like he meant it.

Gazing up at the luminous moon, I replied, "You certainly have plenty of great sayings, but I think you're right about this one. It is magical."

Kai leaned down and pressed his lips to mine for the first time. *He is magical*, I couldn't help thinking. He pulled back, smiling, and leaned in for another kiss. This time it was harder, passionate. I felt like I was dreaming. Nothing had ever felt so right.

Breathless, we looked back at the powerful moon. I shivered.

"Is it too cold out here for you?"

"Yes, sorry I'm such a wimp. Why don't we go back inside to the loft? That way we can still see the full moon and stay warm."

The loft provided a glorious view of the night sky. We lay back on the oversized daybed and looked into each other's eyes. The moonlight in his hair gave it that blue sheen. He wrapped his arms around me, and I placed mine at his neck. I could not resist running my fingers through his silky hair.

"I feel like I've known you forever," I admitted.

His eyes brightened. "I feel the same about you. I could hardly wait for tonight."

"I was worried you weren't going to show up," I confessed, then blurted without thinking, "You run like a frightened deer every time I see you on the trails."

"To tell you the truth, after the first day I met you, I couldn't get you out of my mind. I switched shifts with other rangers just to try to see you again. But when I found you, I had no idea what to say, so I fled. If it weren't for that deer, I don't know if I would have ever approached you."

"I assumed you thought I was a lunatic, and I was positive you were trying to ignore me." I was stunned by his honesty and surprised by my own candor.

"Ignore you?"

"I jogged out on the trails more often than I want to admit, hoping to run into you. I'm so glad you came tonight."

"I could not stay away if I tried," he whispered. A tingle traveled up my spine.

We talked for hours about everything and anything. We made plans for the next day and kissed some more. His scent was intoxicating, his face perfect, and his eyes sparkled. I loved watching the grace of his hands moving while he talked. I was attracted to everything about him. I wondered if this was some type of spiritual connection.

It took quite some time to recognize that the activity in the house had quieted down. I looked at my watch; it was almost five in the morning. I moaned.

"Oh my God, does time stop when I'm with you? It feels like you just got here."

"It's the energy coming from the full moon," he said decidedly. I could not look away from his piercing stare. "And not only the energy from the full moon. It's also the energy I have had since I met you."

We kissed again. My heart pounded so loudly that I was sure he could hear it.

He whispered, "I'd better go so you can get some rest."

I wished he didn't have to.

"Will you be okay getting home in the dark?"

He chuckled. "The moon is lighting the way. I'll be fine. I will meet you tomorrow, before noon at the festival. We should exchange cell numbers so we can find each other."

I pulled out my phone and handed it to him. He did the same. We entered our numbers into each other's phones and pressed SAVE.

We kissed one last time before he loped down the trail, just as he had that morning. I watched the moonlight dance off his hair.

Then I readied for bed, thinking maybe I could get four or five hours of sleep. Kai's smell lingered on my skin. My mind could not stop reliving his tender touch.

My phone buzzed with an incoming text: "GOOD NIGHT, MY BEAUTIFUL SWAN."

I replied, "SWEET DREAMS."

My heart skipped a beat when I noticed the last four digits of his phone number: 1111. My brain swirled in a thousand different directions. This was more than a coincidence.

"Thank you, spirits," I whispered.

CHAPTER 9

IN THE MORNING, everyone moved at a slow pace. The drinking had finally caught up to the others. Aspen slumped on a stool, cradling her coffee mug. Brooklyn stared out the window as she munched on toast, and Berly rubbed at her temple with one hand and poured a cup of coffee with the other.

Berly heard me walk in. "Good morning, sunshine. How was your night?"

"Perfect—better than perfect. Kai is amazing and says the most romantic things. We talked until 5 a.m. We're going to spend the afternoon together."

She looked intrigued. "Good for you."

"I still think he's a player. No one is that perfect," Brooklyn noted.

I scowled at her comment.

Aspen protested, "Brooklyn! That was a mean thing to say. I think they're great together."

She sounded like she was defending me, but I thought I knew better. She only wanted to keep me away from Nate. I tried to push away those thoughts, hoping that our friendship wouldn't devolve into the same cattiness I'd escaped in Florida.

* * *

At the festival, the stands quickly filled with a spirited crowd. Nate waved me over to the side of the stage. "Do you want to help me do a trick?"

"Um, well, I . . . I don't think I can," I stammered.

His face seemed to shutter. "Oh, he's coming, isn't he?"

"Yes, he is," I answered dryly, wishing I hadn't come.

I returned to my seat, my stomach flipping with the anticipation. Berly noticed my fidgeting and said, "Chill out. He'll be here soon."

I was obsessively scanning the crowd when my phone pinged.

"Seeing you makes my heart open to all possibilities."

My heart leaped when I spotted him leaning on a pole, watching me. He made it to me in a few long strides, placed a hand on the back of my head, and leaned in for a kiss.

He pulled back and pressed his forehead to mine. "How is my beautiful swan?"

"I'm glad you're here."

Taking the seat next to me, he curled an arm around my waist, pulling me closer to him. We kissed again, deeper this time, like no one was watching. Our lips parted, and we stared into each other's eyes.

A shrill voice behind us declared, "Looks like someone isn't a cold fish after all."

An uproar of laughter came from Benton and his friends. My eyes never left Kai's. Clearly Benton wanted to annoy me, so I ignored him. After a few minutes and some more passive-aggressive insults, the rowdy group walked away.

Kai looked confused. "What's that all about?"

I filled him in on the Benton story. How he continued to ask me out and how I continued to refuse him. "He doesn't take rejection well. Now he's getting ornery."

"Well, at least he has good taste."

The first demonstration began, and Nate hit the bullseye five times in a row. The crowd cheered with each throw. Troy threw an axe while blindfolded, splitting an apple. Nate asked for a volunteer to be strapped on a spinning target. The audience went quiet. No one was willing to stand in front of a man throwing an axe at them. I was glad I'd had an excuse not to volunteer.

Of course, Aspen jumped up. "I'll do it!" The crowd moaned in disbelief when she bounded onto the stage.

Troy strapped her to the target and spun it. Nate reared back and hurled the axe. I think I closed my eyes as I dug my fingernails into Kai's arm. The crowd shrieked, and Troy stopped the target to reveal the axe had landed directly above her head. Noise exploded all around us.

Troy unstrapped Aspen and walked her to the front of the stage to take a bow with Nate, hand in hand. She cheerfully waved to the audience. I wasn't sure if she was beaming from the rush of the trick or the thrill of holding Nate's hand. Aspen skipped back to her seat.

A red-faced Brooklyn screamed, "Are you crazy!"

Aspen leaned in and whispered, "It's just a trick. Be cool."

"You have some crazy friends." Kai chuckled.

I nodded in agreement, pleased with myself for making so many new ones.

Kai and I left swiftly after the show ended. I personally did not want to run into Nate again. We walked out to the parking lot, glancing often at each other.

"I would love to show you a few special places around the mountains if you don't mind." Kai stopped in front of a motorcycle and handed me a helmet. "Are you ready for an adventure?"

I swallowed hard but said, "I have never been surer of anything."

The road wound north, unveiling a breathtaking view of four waterfalls cascading over rocks. My mind went directly to the insane volume of water plunging over the cliff. I certainly had no clue how to determine the speed or velocity of that beast.

Kai knew the area and took hidden trails up the backside of the mountain. We traveled along the path for a bit until he parked the bike on the side and placed our helmets on the seat. "We'll have to walk from here so we don't disturb them."

"What are we going to disturb?"

Kai placed one finger to his lips. Each footstep sounded like a clink from a jack-in-the-box waiting to explode as we traveled up the path in quiet anticipation.

Suddenly we were bathed in sunlight as we came to a grassy clearing that ended in a ledge.

Kai took my hand. "This way."

I leaned over the precipice and was stunned by what I saw.

Rich green pastures tumbled over the rolling hills. If I closed my eyes, I could smell the grass. The lush meadow directly below us was picturesque, covered with assorted wild grasses and wildflowers.

The best part was the herd of wild horses, their tails flying like silken banners flapping in the wind at a joust.

"Wild horses are powerful, almost majestic, like swans," Kai said admiringly. "It's the most beautiful thing to see them living free out here. Every time I see them, I feel a pulse of energy from their pure, unbridled spirit. Look at the combinations of colors. My favorite one is the big white stallion to the right. Do you see him?" he asked.

"Yes, I do. He is magnificent. The swan of the horses," I replied.

Kai's eyes flickered with excitement. "The first time I ran across the wild herd, something awoke inside me." He propped his chin on his hands. "My best friend, Ben, and I would roam the forest almost every day during our summer breaks. We set traps, checked existing traps, fished, camped, or built forts. We were always busy doing something.

"One summer afternoon, we were lying in the meadow, eating our lunch, and enjoying a beautiful sun. Suddenly the earth shook. Rocks on the ground were trembling. We looked at each other for answers. I assumed it was an earthquake.

"The sound intensified, like a bass drum, a sound you can feel in your chest. A herd of wild horses thundered past. It happened so fast that it was hard to comprehend what I was seeing. Dozens flew by in a blur, snorting, bucking, and kicking up dust with their hooves.

Colorful manes and tales whipped in the wind.

"They disappeared as quickly as they had arrived, leaving only a trail of dust. That was the moment I decided to protect this land and its wildlife."

Hearing the wonder in his voice, I was overcome with admiration. This rare, unexpected story and his honesty only intensified my attraction to him. If this man was a player, he had me hook, line, and sinker.

"They are breathtaking. I see how they captivated you. I'm glad you chose to protect them."

We stayed on the ridge for at least half an hour, observing the herd in silence.

Kai slowly relaxed back into the thick grass, crossing his arms behind his head. His voice was low and serious. "I don't think I can stay away from you."

"Why would you want to stay away?" I blurted, stung by his comment.

"We live very different lives; it could get difficult."

I wasn't sure what he was getting at. His tone teetered on the edge of unease.

My stomach twisted. "I believe we'll figure it out as we go along," I said, enunciating each word.

"Do you?"

I sighed, hopelessly enamored by this man, and my irritation melted away. "I know our schedules will be difficult to navigate. People do it all the time. I mean, things have a way of working out. I hope we can work it out. Don't you?"

"I hope the same."

Finding unseen courage, I said, "I don't want to stay away from you. I have no doubts we can work it out."

"Then it's settled." After a short pause he continued, "When I'm with you, I feel alive. I have hope. I am overjoyed that we met."

He left me speechless. I couldn't control the conflicting emotions within me. Then Kai leaned over and kissed me softly, squeezing all the doubt out of my head. All I knew was that I adored him and wanted him by my side.

"I feel like I knew you before I met you. You electrified my heart," he said, dazzling me again with his words.

"I feel the same way. Maybe we have old souls that knew each other in a different life."

He kissed the backs of my hands.

It had been such a beautiful afternoon. My cheeks hurt from smiling. Holding his hand as we rambled back down the trail, I asked, "By the way, I'm amazed you got 1111 as the last four digits of your phone number."

He flashed his white teeth. "I asked for the number, and they gave it to me because it was available. No other time gives you four of the same number. I consider it pure."

I halted abruptly. "I cannot believe you just said that. I've always believed 11:11 is the perfect time too. I used to drive my parents crazy with numbers. If I had to get up at 6, I would set my alarm for 5:55 and wouldn't go to sleep until it was 11:11. You're the first person I've met who shares my obsession."

He grinned and kissed my temple. "You are too cute."

The sun sank toward the horizon as we rode back down the mountain. Kai pulled into a parking lot at the bottom and grabbed my hand with bright eyes.

"Quickly, I want to show you Mirror Lake."

With a springy step, we moseyed out onto a viewing deck.

"This looks like a dream," I said in awe.

The fiery image of the sun was doubled by its reflection on the lake. The bright orange, red, and yellow saturating the sky and water dazzled and stunned me.

"Mirror Lake," I murmured.

"It's the perfect name, don't you think? I can spend hours here."

"Mother Nature does amazing work. Thank you for showing me

these treasures. I understand why you love living here. It's incredible."

"I feel like I need to share everything with you. I feel safe when I'm with you."

"I'm so glad that you do. I love spending time with you," I replied, though I thought his word choice odd. *Safe?*

We waited until the sun dipped below the trees and the full moon brightened before leaving the dock. Arm in arm, we walked slowly. I did not want our time together to end. The sound of our steps echoed off the wooden walkway. My heart beat in unison with the rhythm of our steps, reminding me of his description of the pounding hooves of the horses.

A long black town car with blacked-out windows pulled into the parking lot. Kai stopped suddenly, his body stiff as he stared at the vehicle. Tightening his arm around my back, he pressed me forward, ducking left and away from the car. Our pace quickened with unmistakable tension.

I looked back to see who was getting out of the car. Three tall men dressed in navy-blue uniforms emerged first. One opened the back door, offering his hand to help a woman step out. She was not tall but moved with self-assurance and was dressed exceptionally well. She looked mysterious in oversized sunglasses that were unnecessary at dusk.

"Who is that? Why are you hurrying to get away from her?"

"Don't worry about it. Let's just say she's someone I don't care to see." He sounded bitter. "She is repulsive." His voice was so low I wondered whether he was talking to me or himself.

My face had always been an open book, making it easy for Kai to detect my unease. He placed his hands on my cheeks. "She has a great deal of influence around here and has harmed many people I know. Please trust me: we do not want to run into her."

His eyes were intense. I believed him and resisted asking more questions as I slipped on the helmet.

Clinching my arms around Kai's chest, I breathed deeply and

enjoyed his alluring scent. But as we sped down the mountain, my mind whirled. I had so much to process. *Who was that woman, and who did she harm? What did he mean by "safe"?*

I didn't want to get off the motorcycle when we arrived at the cabin.

"I can't thank you enough for such a wonderful day."

"My pleasure," he drawled with an enticing wink. "What time are you heading back to campus?"

"I think around noon. Why?"

"If you don't mind, I would like to see you off. It may be a while before our schedules align again."

"That sounds perfect. What time?" I was doing a horrible job of hiding my enthusiasm.

He cut his eyes toward me with a devilish grin. "How about 11:11?" He paused. "Really, does nine sound good so I can get to work on time?" I nodded yes. "Thank you for sharing your day with me."

"Thank you for showing me part of your world."

"I will only think of your face when I look at the moon tonight."

I wondered how he came up with all these corny lines and hated to admit they were working on me. We kissed one more time before I went inside.

The girls were already home and accosted me with questions. Reluctantly, I gave them as few details as possible, but my face probably told a different story. I omitted the part about the strange lady.

"Holy cow, it sounds like you hit the jackpot," Brooklyn said.

Images of our day ran through my head. *Who knew rescuing a deer would lead to all this?*

Getting into bed that night, I glanced at the time. It was 11:11 p.m., and my phone chimed.

"Goodnight, swan. You shine brighter than the moon."

"Tonight, I will dream of you," I texted, hoping I didn't sound cheesy.

CHAPTER 10

IN THE MORNING, reality hit me. Kai was right. We were going to have a hard time getting together with school, my crazy soccer schedule, and his full-time job. Our action-packed weekend already felt like a dream.

After I dragged my things to the car, I trudged down to the trail, kicking the dirt with the tip of my shoe. A gust of wind scattered leaves and dust along the path, and an eerie feeling swept over me. *This forest is full of eyes.*

I checked the time. Kai would be here soon, which excited and saddened me at the same time. We did not know when we would be able to see each other again. But I knew deep down that nothing was ever going to be the same.

My heart thumped when Kai strode up the path. Without thinking, I ran to him. He picked me up and swung me around in a big circle. He smelled fresh.

"So, did you have good dreams last night?"

"They were perfect because of you," I said, not caring how I sounded.

A slight breeze lifted my hair. Kai ran his fingers through it and tucked it behind my ears, cradling my head between his hands. Then he bent to fit his mouth to mine. Heat coursed through my body. I loved the way he smelled, the way he held me and kissed me, but I was also slightly afraid to trust him completely.

We ambled back up the path and climbed into the hammock. Snuggled together, gently rocking, I asked, "How did you get your name?"

"It comes from a Mohican word, Ktuh. It means heart. Over the years it somehow evolved into Kai."

"Heart? No wonder you stole mine."

"I did?" His voice, soft in my ear, sounded surprised.

"You did, a few days ago."

"You have captured mine too."

I reveled in his deep voice, praying he wasn't lying.

With a heavy heart, we said our goodbyes. Kai touched my chin softly.

"My swan."

Heat rose through my body. "My heart."

The girls spilled out onto the deck, interrupting our moment. He kissed me anyway.

"I will see you soon," I said, fighting tears.

"I look forward to it."

I couldn't concentrate on the chatter on the ride back to campus. I leaned my head against the window, oblivious to the stunning canvas of color rolling past. All I saw was Kai's face.

CHAPTER 11

IT WAS AMAZING how everyone adjusted back to the fast pace of school after our four-day escape, but we had no choice. Midway through the semester, the workload only grew harder and heavier.

I showed my lab partners the technique Kai taught me for measuring water flow, and we started collecting data in record time. The results were much more accurate and took only a third of the time to calculate. We reviewed the new method with our professor, and he was pleased with the ingenuity. Kai found the circumstances comical, considering this "new" measuring technique had existed for centuries.

Our professor asked my lab team to measure the flow of a small stream north of the Heron Marsh. I was not crazy about this assignment. The stream was near the spot where I had followed the dark figure into the forest.

The sky was dark and dreary, and the temperature had dropped. My mood dropped with it. We hurried over the bridge and past the foul-smelling marsh and slowed in front of the old, weathered house. This was the first time some in my group had seen it, and the professor's story had made it an item of interest.

The chipped paint might have been white once, but now it was greenish gray, dingy, and faded. Traces of ornate detailing on the front porch reminded me of spiderwebs. The tall, narrow windows cast weird shadows on what looked like a tower, and the front door looked like an angry mouth—like the house wanted to eat me alive. Hair lifted on the back of my neck as we gawked at the structure.

"Does anyone else think that is the creepiest house you've ever seen?" I finally asked the group.

The guy closest to me shivered. "It must be haunted. After all, the professor said people used to do witchcraft there."

"It gives me goose bumps." I pulled up my sleeve to show them, relieved I wasn't the only one feeling this way.

"I say we get past it quickly. It gives me the creeps," said another girl.

Our path looped us back toward the marsh. We hastened across a long wooden walkway that went directly over it, with most of us holding our breath and plugging our noses because the water smelled like rotten eggs.

Our footsteps thumped along the wooden planks. Past the walkway, we had to leave the trail to get to the stream. Fully aware I was breaking my promise to Kai, I stepped into the forest. We set up the equipment and worked quickly to escape the stench.

I heard a loud crack behind me and whipped around. "Did you hear that?"

"Hear what?" our group leader asked, sounding annoyed.

"It sounded like branches breaking."

"You're imagining things. Get back to work so we can get out of here."

I glared at him over the data grid and hastily logged the data. Maybe I was being paranoid, but I knew I heard something. I steadied my stare, peering deep into the forest. It was there. A dark figure, staring back at me—with a little raccoon on its shoulder.

"Look over there. Do you see that shadowy bit?" I pointed into the forest. No one could see anything. They said I was imagining things and stared at me like I was deranged. I bit my lip and stayed quiet.

It started to sprinkle on the way back to campus, making our walk back even more unnerving. I shivered from the cold and the sensation of being watched. When we jogged past the old house, I refused to look at it.

✤ ✤ ✤

When I stopped by the dorm to change into dry clothes, Berly was sitting on her bed.

"A few of us are going to Anthony's for pizza tonight if you want to come."

"Sounds great. What time?"

"Seven. Meet me in the parking lot?"

"Okay, see you soon. I'm heading to soccer practice and then to the library to work on a paper for Environmental History."

The library was extremely busy. I found a table on the upper level and powered up my laptop to brainstorm topics. But my mind kept wandering to Kai—his masculine smell, his silky black hair, those mesmerizing emerald-green eyes. The intense experience of clasping his strong chest while riding on the back of his motorcycle. I wondered if he thought of me as often as I thought of him.

My wandering thoughts led me to research Mohicans. Their name meant "The people of the waters that are never still." They were a powerful, highly organized tribe. Tribes could pack up their entire village in a few days and move to a different location to prevent ecological overshoot.

Like most Native American tribes, they had been devastated by foreign invaders and forced to leave their homelands. It was heartbreaking to read about the destruction of such an amazing people.

I found an article about creatures that existed in Mohican myths. The first one listed was the Wauntht Mennitow or "the Great Spirit." I remembered the story of the swan princess Kai had shared. Another creature, the pukwudgie, apparently had magical powers that included the ability to turn invisible, thereby luring people to their deaths. It was only two to three feet tall. Their name literally meant "person of the wilderness," and they were considered forest spirits.

Is that what I keep seeing? I felt queasy thinking about it and wanted to ask Kai what he knew about them.

Stopping myself from going way off topic, I returned to the original article. I planned to write my paper on how the Native Americans adapted to the environment. After setting a general outline of what I wanted to cover, I headed back to the dorms.

The weather was growing chillier every day, so I searched for something warm to wear. I came across the green shirt I had worn my first night with Kai. The memory of him grabbing my hands and saying, "Nothing could keep me away" flashed across my mind.

I jumped when my phone rang. My heart skipped when I saw the caller ID.

"Hello, I was just thinking of you."

"I'm always thinking of you," he replied, sounding smooth as molasses.

How does he do that?

With my crazy soccer schedule and his busy work schedule, we had not seen each other in two weeks. "Would you like to spend time together Saturday morning before I go to work?"

Utterly elated, I answered, "Of course! I have so many things I want to share with you."

"I wish we could spend more time together, but I'm imprisoned by work. Any time with you is better than none." The way he said "imprisoned" made me wonder if work was the only thing getting in our way.

"Saturday morning sounds great. I have a soccer game in the late afternoon."

"It's a date. See you at ten on Saturday, my swan."

"I'll be counting the hours. See you soon."

When I approached Berly's jeep in the parking lot, I was grinning.

"I know who you're thinking about," Berly said. She was perceptive but respected my privacy. I got the feeling she was genuinely happy for me.

"Guilty as charged. Who else is coming to Anthony's?"

"Martin and Brooklyn are riding with us. Nate, Aspen, and Troy are meeting us there."

I wondered how Aspen managed that arrangement.

"What about Max?"

"He's staying on campus to have dinner with his 'flavor' of the week," she said with air quotes.

I enjoyed my night out with my friends, but the hours until I could see Kai again dragged on like a baseball game with extra innings. My phone pinged at 11:11 p.m.

"I will be with you in less than twelve hours."

"I can't wait," I sent back.

My nightmare returned that night. This time, a few things had changed.

※ ※ ※

I peeked over my shoulder as dense fog rolled through the trees, casting ghostly shadows. A squat creature rose from the mist and drifted silently toward me.

My heart pumped like a bass drum, and I turned to run. I couldn't let this creature near me. My breath froze in puffs before me, and I realized I was running and running but gaining little ground. My legs felt like lead. I plodded slowly into the stagnant marsh, my feet sinking in the mud. I let out a cry. The marsh grew thicker and deeper, like freshly poured cement just starting to dry. I had to press on, so I started crawling, the rancid slime squeezing between my fingers.

My legs were stiff like ice when I finally broke free—directly in front of the haunted house. I grasped frantically for the railing to pull myself out of the bog. As soon as the tips of my fingers touched the wood, the doors and windows of the house flew open with a bang.

More of those little creatures poured out of the house. Fog flicked around them like snake tongues. They were heading straight for me.

I squeezed my eyes shut, feeling cold hands grab feverishly for my arms and a clammy grip on my leg. I screamed, punched, and crawled with my eyes closed until I made it inside the house. As I kicked the door closed with both feet, it disappeared into the wall. I scrambled upright, trapped in the old house again.

The pungent, musty smell hit me square in the face. The doors and windows were boarded up, blocked off. I had no way out. A dark shadow stretched across the wall above the swirling fog. Déjà vu hit me as I rushed up the stairs. *Who is after me? Why don't I ever stop to find out?*

¤ ¤ ¤

I woke in a sweat with the memory of those evil little creatures pawing at me.

Irritated with my overactive mind, I dragged myself out of bed and took a long, hot shower. It didn't wash away my frustration and embarrassment.

CHAPTER 12

THE NEXT MORNING, I walked down by the lake to kill time. I was still brooding about my dream returning. My mood lightened when a pair of swans swam past, gliding on the water with beauty and grace.

Is this a sign? I wondered. *A sign to be fierce as my great-grandmother insisted I could be?* This dream would never go away if I didn't confront things head-on. I reminded myself that college was my fresh start; I had promised myself I would be strong.

I passed through the dining hall on my way to the parking lot. Berly and Martin waved me over. I raised an eyebrow at Berly, and she smirked. It seemed she liked Martin more than she had let on.

"What are you up to?" Berly asked.

"Kai is coming over before work for a few hours. What about you two?"

"We're going to brave the Sky Flyer Zipline at the Olympic complex."

"That sounds like a blast. I bet the view will be amazing."

"The view may not be so brilliant if I retch," Martin moaned.

"That is why I'm going first, so the breeze doesn't shower me with your spew," Berly sniffed.

"It would be an honor to wear my spew, innit, Lily?"

"I'll take your word for it. I personally don't want to experience it. I have to get going. Have fun flying high above the ground at incredible speeds."

"I think she might bloody well be trying to get rid of me," Martin whined.

"Really? You wouldn't want to be called a squawker, would you?" Berly retorted. I was still giggling when I walked away.

I perched on the stone wall near the entrance of the south parking lot.

A few minutes later, a rumble reached me before I spotted the motorcycle. I felt profound joy when Kai rounded the corner. He pulled up beside me, lifting his visor.

"Howdy, ma'am. It looks like you're in need of a ride."

"That depends on where you're heading."

"It's a secret." One side of his mouth lifted.

"Count me in," I said eagerly.

He dismounted the bike and pulled off his helmet in one swift motion, then lifted me from the wall. "I was hoping you would say that."

His soft lips met mine, sending heat coursing through my veins.

"Sorry for the short window, but I couldn't bear another day without seeing you." He set me down, pressing my hand to his lips. "You are hard to resist."

"Then don't resist," I replied coyly.

He handed me a helmet and helped me fasten it. I climbed on behind him, wrapping my arms around his muscular chest, and breathed in his familiar scent.

He drove to the south side of the lake to the Treetop Cafe, a restaurant in an actual treehouse. I scanned the structure in awe before we entered.

"That is a big tree. How did they build this so high up?"

"The construction was insane. It took them over a year to complete it using cranes and pulleys. I think it was worth the wait. This was one of my mom's favorite places."

I gulped as we found a table and sat. "Was? Is she no longer around?"

"Sorry, I did not mean to make it sound that way. She does not go out much anymore." His disheartened look told me to drop it.

"I'm sorry to hear that."

The waitress interrupted, and Kai ordered cappuccinos and a bag of donuts.

"I cannot wait for you to try these donuts. They're out of this world. I must limit myself because I will not stop eating them once I start."

I smiled. "I feel like I have so much to tell you, and I can't remember any of it now that we're together."

"First of all, how was your week?"

I shared what had happened on lab day and my encounter with the creature near the creepy house.

"I know exactly what house you're talking about. It must be over a hundred years old. It's hard to believe it's still standing. People say the house was used by itinerate mystics who practiced spiritual rituals."

"The marsh and that house give me the creeps. Last night I had a nightmare about them both." I told him the details.

"Nightmares about being attacked or chased mean you might be sensing danger. You try to evade the monster in the dream, but deep down you know it's something you must face."

"That's quite deep. How do you know so much about scary dreams?"

He looked down. "I have had similar nightmares for the past few years. Usually, I am running from a dark figure, and my legs stop working. Sometimes I'm riding my motorcycle, trying to get away from whatever is chasing me, and I keep passing the same landmarks over and over like I'm driving in a little circle, never getting away."

He stared blankly at the wall, then continued, "I know the feeling when you wake up exhausted and terrified. I started researching the meanings of dreams to find out what they mean."

"Do you think it's peculiar that our dreams sound so similar?"

The server arrived before he could answer and set down an

oil-stained paper bag and a tray of dipping sauces. "Be careful," she warned. "They're really hot."

Kai's eyes sparkled, and a childlike expression crossed his face. "I always burn the roof of my mouth on the first one because I can't wait." Steam plumed from the bag when he opened it, carrying the scent of sugar and cinnamon.

He placed a donut on my plate and one on his. "If you cut them into bite-sized pieces, they're easier to dip."

"Which one should I try first?"

"They are all so good. You just have to try each one."

I tried the red sauce, a raspberry jam, first. It was indeed scalding but also incredibly delicious.

Kai smiled smugly. "See? These things are dangerous!"

"Yum, it just melts in your mouth."

After we were sated, Kai stood. "I want to show you one more thing."

On the front side of the dining deck, a set of spiral stairs led up to another deck built on the highest part of the tree. He placed a steadying hand on the small of my back as we climbed.

"Be careful. This level is called the crow's nest."

I rounded the last curve and beheld a panoramic view of the lake, the college, the mountains, and the winding roads up the mountainside. I took in a deep breath, turning slowly to see everything. "This is truly amazing. I cannot believe how far you can see from up here."

Kai hugged me from behind and rested his chin on my shoulder. "This view is almost as breathtaking as you," he said quietly into my ear.

I leaned back and kissed his cheek. "Thank you for showing me all your secret places. You amaze me."

"I'm trying to amaze you so you won't forget me."

I turned to look him in the eye. "Impossible! All I ever do is think of you."

His lips pressed to my ear as he replied in his velvety voice,

"I'm glad."

I hooked my arms around his neck, and our bodies pressed together. Feeling his strong heartbeat against my chest, I surrendered to his warm embrace. We kissed for a while, becoming familiar with each other's touch. With his arms around me, I felt secure, like he would always protect me. But it felt so right it terrified me. I was waiting for someone to burst my bubble.

Standing arm in arm with Kai at the railing, I noticed two swans. Perhaps they were the same two I had seen earlier.

"Look over there. Can you see the swans on the lake?"

"Wow, I haven't seen swans in years. They honor us with their pure spirit to remind us that we should appreciate the beauty all around us."

"My family believes a pair of swans can represent being on the right path," I said, unconsciously rubbing my swan necklace between my fingers.

"What does it mean if you see three swans?"

"It must mean you're lucky," I replied zestfully.

"I am." We kissed for what seemed like an eternity. My heart raced. Yet I couldn't help thinking, *Why don't we have more time?*

Kai was very elusive about his schedule and days off. We could only manage a few hours on Saturday or Sunday mornings and only if I had home games. Kai rarely got weekends off, and our campus didn't allow visitors after 10 p.m., so we were limited. Doubt about his intentions lingered in my mind like a cobweb.

"Would you like to meet again tomorrow at ten?" Kai asked after he parked back near the dorms. "I'm working the same shift."

Inside, I jumped for joy. "That sounds great. Next weekend I have away games on Saturday and Sunday, so tomorrow is perfect."

His smile widened.

"I know I wanted to tell you something else, and I can't think of it," I mused after a moment of silence.

"Maybe you'll remember it tomorrow."

"Until tomorrow." I stood on my toes for one last kiss.

"I find it hard to wait."

On my way to the dorm, Brooklyn and Aspen met me on the sidewalk.

"Where are you headed?" Brooklyn asked.

"Nowhere in particular. I just had breakfast with Kai. My afternoon is free until the game."

"We're heading to the Forestry Club to ride the zip line. Why don't you come with us?" Brooklyn asked cheerfully. Aspen's eyes narrowed.

"Why not? I just need to drop my bag in my room. Go ahead. I'll catch up."

Walking away, I overheard Aspen say, "Why did you invite her?"

My temper flared. I wanted to lash out, which surprised me because I was usually such a mouse.

I purposely took my time getting to the Forestry Club. Aspen was already strapped in the harness when I arrived. In a gesture of goodwill, I took out my phone to capture a video of her ride. She was hysterical. She screamed the entire way and kept her eyes closed. My video of her ride was shaky from laughing so hard.

Nate waved me up the ladder to the platform. After strapping Brooklyn into the harness, he said, "One, two, three, go!"

She screamed as she flew overhead.

My knees wobbled when I reached the top.

"I did not realize how high this platform was," I squeaked. I closed my eyes for a minute, trying to ignore the trembling.

Nate was all business while he strapped me in. He double-checked to see that I was secure and placed his hand on my shoulder.

"Relax. I wouldn't let anything happen to you."

He really was a great guy, so genuine and kind.

"I trust you. I'm just a little scared," I said, trying to keep my voice even so it wouldn't sound like I was flirting. Nate showed me where to place my hands, how to use the brake, and some other safety things that passed through my brain without registering.

"Are you ready?" His tone was pleasant. I nodded yes. Before I knew it, I was flying high over the trees. The wind whipped my hair from side to side. The trees blurred, and the blue lake sparkled from the sun. My mind drifted back to kissing Kai in the crow's nest. He said I was hard to resist. I could not shed the lingering elation.

I heard yelling below me and jerked back to reality when it registered what they were screaming: "Brake! Brake! Brake!"

I reached back, flailing for the handle dangling behind my head. My fingertips brushed it. Adrenaline pumped through me, and I reached again, catching hold of it and yanking with all my strength. Simultaneously, Troy appeared beside me, grabbing my harness. The brakes caught, and I screeched to a halt right before the last tree. My heart was lodged in my throat.

"What the heck, Lily. I didn't think you would brake in time. I was ready to tackle you," Troy said between breaths.

"I forgot about the brake," I apologized, feeling like an idiot. "Thanks for watching out for me."

"Do you want to go again?" Brooklyn asked.

"Heck yeah!"

"I think I'm good with my first run," Aspen murmured, clearly disappointed with herself.

Brooklyn and I ran back up the hill to get in line again. Paying more attention when I climbed the ladder this time, I saw another dark mask in the trees below and felt my pulse rocket. At the top, I used the 360-degree view to scan the forest again. From this high up, four dark figures were clearly visible. I tried to push down the surge of terror.

My mind drifted. *Why do I keep seeing those dark figures? Are they watching me?* I sensed the swan rise up within me. *Maybe it's time to confront them.*

"Lily, you're up."

I jolted a little, realizing my anxiety was not solely about the ride.

"I've got you," he said. I picked up a slight undertone. "Do you know where the brake is?" His voice was gentle, not mocking.

"Thanks. I've got it this time." I felt Aspen's stare boring into us and decided this would be my last run of the day.

After that ride, I showed Aspen the video I took to lighten her mood. Nate surprised us when he walked up with a playful grin. I hadn't seen him leave the platform.

"Who wants to try axe throwing?"

"I do," Aspen replied eagerly. Brooklyn agreed.

I was hoping to make a polite exit, to give Aspen room, but Nate placed his arm in mine. "Come on, give it a try. I bet you're a natural."

I hid my exasperation. Aspen was giving me a full-on death stare.

Trying to be crafty, juggling to keep them both happy, I said, "Excuse me, I need to use the restroom. Nate, why don't you show Aspen how to throw first?" I slipped my arm from his and pressed her forward. "I'll be back in a few."

Nate didn't seem happy, but Aspen did. I skipped away.

When I returned, Nate was attentively reviewing techniques with Aspen. She looked pleased. He did not see me return, so I chose a target on the other end. Troy handed me the axes and went through the rules and proper form. I hit my target with the first axe.

"Stand up straighter and square your shoulders."

I hit it again, this time closer to the center. Once I got the feel for the axe and relaxed, it was exhilarating.

Nate walked by my target. "Not bad. We may have to get you in one of our tournaments."

"Yeah right. I do not see that happening anytime soon."

"Did you have fun with Kai this morning?" Aspen asked. Nate's smile fell away.

"Yes, I did," I answered curtly. The audacity of her question brought a wave of disgust. Jealousy was becoming my biggest pet peeve.

"I'm so happy for you two."

She wasn't happy for me. She was happy for herself.

Collecting my axes, I glanced out at the forest, and my scalp prickled as I discerned two dark faces barely visible through the thick leaves. I flinched at a tap on my shoulder.

"Oh, you scared me," I gasped, facing Brooklyn.

"Why so jumpy? Did you see a ghost?"

I nodded toward the forest. "Do you see anything right over there?"

She squinted. "Nothing except trees."

"See the shadow behind that big tree?" I pointed to the spot.

She studied harder. "Sorry, I don't see anything."

"I must be imagining it."

"We should probably head to the field. Our game starts in an hour. These guys are going to the recreation hall later. Do you want to come?"

Not wanting to irritate Aspen or Nate, I lied. "I have some homework to do after the game. Maybe I'll join you later."

After everyone left, I headed back to the Forestry Club, wanting to see if I could get a closer look at those dark figures and possibly confront them once and for all. Hoping to catch it by surprise, I dashed into the forest and yelled, "Where are you? What do you want?"

A cloud passed in front of the sun, and darkness cloaked the forest. A strange pull grew in my stomach. Changing my mind about the confrontation, I hurried out of the trees like a rabbit running from a hawk. I didn't stop running until I made it to the dorms, fully aware I had chosen flight over fight again.

I threw my keys on the desk, angry with myself, both for going into the forest after promising not to and for wasting the risk I had taken. I changed into my uniform and headed to the soccer field.

* * *

Energized by winning the game, Aspen, Brooklyn, and I dragged Berly to the recreation hall to celebrate that afternoon.

I veered past Martin to ask, "Did you spew on the Skyride?"

"No spewing, mate," he said with a grin.

"Do you still think she's trying to get rid of you?"

"She'll have to try harder than that to give me the bum's rush."

The doors slammed open as a big group of students strode in. Benton was right up front with a blond girl hanging on his arm. She had an innocent look about her.

"Looks like someone finally fell for one of his lines," Berly said, flashing her dimples.

"Poor thing."

Benton and his crew headed for a pool table. Benton racked the balls, and his girlfriend blatantly pretended not to know how to shoot. In an overbearing tone, he barked orders while standing behind her. It looked fairly demeaning to me. But she seemed to think it was cute, and Benton was clearly enjoying it.

Brooklyn tugged my arm. "Lily, do you want to play air hockey? The table is free."

I jumped at the chance to get far away from Benton. He was being loud, seemingly determined to catch my attention, and I only assumed that because he kept glancing over.

After our game, I joined Berly on the bar stools. Benton finally sauntered over.

He cocked his head. "Where is your lover boy?"

Baffled by his stupid question, I placed my hand over my heart. "He's right here."

I waved bye to him and turned back to Berly. She was holding her nose and suppressing a chuckle.

Benton's girlfriend came over and stood by his side. Wearing a forced smile, she wrapped her arm in his, staking her claim.

She extended her hand. "Hi, I'm Brie. How do you know Benton?"

I replied in a sardonic tone but accepted her hand. "Hi, Brie. I don't really know Benton at all. He just likes to ask me dumb questions. What about you?"

Berly let out a snort.

Brie gazed up at him dreamily. "We met in class. He asked me to go canoeing, and we've been going out ever since. Right, honey?" Her voice was squeaky.

"You two make a great couple. Did he ask you to stroll hand in hand on the trails?"

Confused, she looked at Benton for an answer.

"Come on, let's go," he grumbled. Brie toddled after him like a lost puppy.

Berly, now overcome with laughter, had tears running from her eyes.

"What is it with that dude?" I asked. She was approaching hysteria and unable to answer. I couldn't help joining in as I wondered aloud, "And why do I always wave goodbye to him?"

Our uproar sparked Martin's curiosity. He came over to learn what brilliant nugget Benton had blessed us with this time. It took a few minutes to compose ourselves and tell him.

"That bloke has a burr up his bum," he said, sending us into another round of laughter.

CHAPTER 13

WHEN KAI ARRIVED Sunday morning, he again greeted me by lifting me off the rock wall. He spun me around, burying his face in my neck. "You light up my day every time I see you."

"There is no place I would rather be than with you," I replied. We kissed long and deeply.

"I have excellent plans for us this morning. I hope you are ready for another adventure."

"Every minute with you is an adventure."

We headed down to the waterfront and launched a kayak from the floating dock. Paddling across the lake, we beached the boat and hiked to the waterfall.

"You were not kidding about an adventurous morning."

"I wanted to make sure we made good use of the little time we have together."

We perched on the edge of a rock overlooking the lake, and Kai gestured across the water. "Look, it's the swans."

"Shouldn't they be migrating south?"

"I have never seen them this late in the year," he agreed. "Maybe you're attracting them, oh queen of the swans."

I smiled at his silly comment.

"I remembered what I . . ." Glancing at the falls, a glimmer in the trees on the other side of the cascade caught my eye. I squinted and made out a shape lurking in the shadows.

Kai leaned forward. "What is it?"

"Do you see anything in the bushes to the right of the water?" Pointing, I said, "In the trees near the bottom of the falls."

"To the right? How far down?"

"About three feet from the bottom, directly beside the largest tree."

The stone face faded into the brush.

Kai looked intently. "It certainly did look like something moved."

I was excited that someone else had finally seen something.

"That's what I followed into the forest the day we first met."

Kai kept squinting, searching the trees.

"Have you ever noticed any stonelike creatures? You're in the forest all the time," I pressed.

"It could be wind, an animal, or shadows. I can see how it could make you feel like you're being watched."

It sounded like he was trying to come up with a logical explanation. I held my breath to stem the frustration bubbling inside me. *He doesn't believe me.*

"Do you know anything about a mythical creature called a pukwudgie?" I demanded, watching for his reaction. I might have been saltier than I realized.

His face hardened. "I have heard stories about them, or should I say warnings."

I was sure my question had surprised him, but he continued in a deep, calm voice. "My grandmother used to tell us that if we saw a short, gray-faced creature with large ears in the forest, we had to get away from it. Never look it directly in the eyes. Never trust it. Stay far away." His tone lightened. "It's just folklore. How did you learn about them?"

"After meeting you, I was researching topics for an Environmental History paper and got curious. I researched Mohicans and stumbled on information about mythological creatures. I read about the Great Spirit, like in your swan princess story, and pukwudgies, who seem awfully scary." Pausing to watch him, I asked, "Do you think they exist?"

Kai inhaled deeply. He flexed the muscles in his jaw when he was thinking. "I don't think so, but it's hard to decide what is real or not when it comes to myths."

Things weren't adding up. *Why was he so stern about the forest being dangerous the first day we met?*

"I think they're real," I stated with conviction. "After I researched them, they crept into my nightmares. They are out there, and I can feel them."

"How frequently do you see them? Have you told anyone else?"

"Almost every day. I try to point them out to others, but they never see them. It's like the creatures only show themselves to me. When I see them clearly, it feels like a magnetic force pulls me toward them. I told you about it the day we met."

Kai placed his hands on my cheeks. "My love, this is not good. They are dangerous. Please stay out of the forest. I will talk to Grandmother Kateri." I was pleased that he was finally taking me seriously—and beyond thrilled that he called me "my love."

"Do you think they want to hurt me?"

"I won't let anything hurt you." Kai kissed me warmly, and his lips moved to my neck. I ran my fingers through his hair.

"Excuse me." A husky voice interrupted our moment.

Kai jumped up in an instant, pulling me with him. It was another forest ranger. He looked irritated, standing with his hands on his hips. He had a strapping build, thick like his voice, with black, short-cropped hair and dark eyes. His round face seemed like it could be friendly when it wasn't wearing a scowl.

"Hey, Ben." Kai cleared his throat. "Lily, this is Ben, my roommate. Ben, this is Lily." Kai's voice cracked. Ben looked at us hard enough to burn a hole through me.

Kai leaned in. "Can you give us a minute?"

He stalked over to Ben, grabbed his elbow, and whisked him away.

"What are you doing?" I heard Ben ask sharply.

I struggled to hear Kai's response. I only heard a few mumbling words, but it was crystal clear that Ben was mad. The only other thing I made out during this heated exchange was Kai saying, "This is not your concern."

Kai's face was flushed when he returned. He laced his fingers in mine. "Time to go."

It sounded like an order.

Kai's anger faded as we paddled back. "I'm so sorry about that. Ben can be a drama queen sometimes. He needs to learn to mind his own business."

"I take it your roommate doesn't approve of us dating."

"Something like that," Kai answered vaguely.

There was an awkward silence between us. Each stroke sent ripples across the calm water as we glided to the dock.

After we climbed out of the kayak, I blurted out, "Do you have a girlfriend? Are you married? Is it that lady in the black town car?" My voice shook, and I felt crazy.

"It's not like that. Nothing like that at all. Please believe me. It's . . . complicated." His voice was just above a whisper. "I have never felt like this before. All I ever think about is you. I don't want to stay away. I can't stay away."

"Then don't. I've never felt like this before either," I admitted in a faint voice. "It's kind of scary."

CHAPTER 14

I DID NOT SEE Kai again for weeks because of our schedules, but I received a text from him every night at 11:11, making my heart flutter every time.

After soccer season ended, I continued to run in the mornings to stay in shape, always shooting Kai a text in case he was assigned that area. One Tuesday morning, the twins and I ran the trail to Black Pond. Cold gusts reminded me that winter was near. Halfway through the run, we took a break on Lookout Point, one of the docks.

Aspen, Brooklyn, and I slowed when we spotted a small package in pink wrapping paper on the middle bench.

Aspen's breath froze in the air as she read the tag aloud: "Lily, my swan."

My eyes widened, and Aspen handed me the package.

"Open it!" Brooklyn cried.

My hands trembled when I untied the ribbon. Inside the pink box was a silver bracelet carved in the shape of a swan and inlaid with pink tourmaline. It matched my necklace perfectly. I brought my quivering hand to my mouth.

The note inside read: MY SWAN, I'M THANKFUL FOR THE DEER WHO BROUGHT US TOGETHER. NOTHING TRULY MADE SENSE UNTIL YOU CAME INTO MY LIFE. LOVE, KAI.

"How sweet," Aspen said, but it sounded like she was thinking how sweet it would be to tell Nate.

"He's making the rest of the guys look bad," Brooklyn said.

I wondered how Kai had deposited the present here so early. *How could he be sure I would find it?* I couldn't stop smiling.

I tried to think of how to let him know I was delighted with his gift. Pacing, I typed, "THE DAY I MET YOU WILL FOREVER BE ONE OF THE MOST AMAZING DAYS OF MY LIFE." No, too cheesy. Delete. "THANKS FOR MAKING ME FEEL SO SPECIAL." That sounded better—short and sweet. I pressed send. Kai sent back a heart emoji.

On the jog back to campus, I daydreamed about Kai. He was so handsome, so thoughtful; he was perfect. I floated along the trail, feeling like my feet never touched the ground.

CHAPTER 15

MY PARENTS WERE in Texas over Thanksgiving break to help my grandparents with some medical issues, so Berly skillfully convinced me to stay with her at the cabin. "Come on, we have plenty of room, and it will be fun. Besides, you can't say no. The dorms will be closed."

"Are you sure your parents don't mind?"

"Mind? They will be thrilled; they love a big party. Martin will be stopping by too. My dad will go overboard with the food and make you eat until you gain about five pounds. My stepmom will keep pouring the wine." She waggled a finger. "Consider yourself warned."

"Thank you so much. You are truly the best," I said, grateful for Berly's kindness and thankful I had such a loyal friend.

When I told Kai I was staying in town for the week, we started planning our visits together like two kids plotting playdates.

Berly and I got to the cabin early Friday afternoon. It was such a beautiful day that we ended up going downtown to shop. We perused the windows on the strip, having little luck until we reached our favorite boutique.

When we skipped out of the store, thrilled with our purchases, our gazes fell on the Salty Swan directly across the street.

Berly said, "Come on, I didn't go in last time. I want to see what they have."

As we passed through the ornate door, chimes alerted the clerk of our presence. Her head tilted up.

"Welcome back."

I was surprised she remembered me. It had been over a month since I last visited.

Berly went directly to the candles, and I headed for the pink tourmaline, selecting a few of the polished stones. I still carried the heart-shaped one in my pocket and found myself rubbing it when I was nervous or deep in thought.

I came across a pink tourmaline night-light that I could not resist. After searching a few more displays, I selected a leather men's bracelet with the image of a swan stamped into the material. Four pink tourmaline stones decorated the tail. The design matched my necklace and bracelet.

The clerk approached. "I ordered that one for you after your last visit."

A shiver passed through me. I barely recognized my own faint voice when I asked, "How did you know I would want something like this?"

She swirled her finger in the air. "The spirits are active, the swan is the key, you know in your heart what you cannot see."

I had no clue how to respond to her little poem. "Okay, thanks. How much for this bracelet?"

She let out a soft chuckle and pointed to the tag. "It is sixty percent off."

With unflinching determination, I purchased the bracelet, night-light, and six more polished stones. After Berly made her own purchase, I waved to the clerk.

"Thank you so much . . ." I paused because I did not know her name.

She looked directly at me and in a serious tone said, "Wanda. My name is Wanda. It's an honor to meet you."

I nodded, perplexed by her comment. "Thank you, Wanda."

Once we exited the store, I asked Berly if she'd heard what the clerk said to me.

"Yes, I did. It was kind of cool but odd at the same time."

"What do you think it meant?"

"I have no idea. Only time will tell."

"She told me she ordered this bracelet after my last visit. That was over a month ago. How did she know I would come back?"

Berly looked confused. "Weird, real weird."

"Maybe she's clairvoyant or something, because this bracelet is exactly what I was hoping to find. I love it. I hope Kai likes it."

Later that evening, as Berly and Martin set up the firepit, I stayed in to clean up the kitchen, then went upstairs to the third-floor balcony to bide my time until Kai arrived. The cool night air stung my face. I was going to need a heavier coat tonight. I turned to go back inside, then detected a small figure standing on the trail next to the river.

The firepit gave off enough light to see it clearly. A second later, another figure stepped out of the forest. This one carried a small raccoon on its shoulder. A second tiny raccoon huddled on the trail. The figures looked in my direction. I heard a pop, and they all disappeared.

I stood frozen, trying to comprehend what I had just seen. Either I was going crazy, or those creatures were real. Returning to the kitchen, I poured a glass of wine to calm my nerves.

I couldn't contain my enthusiasm at the sound of Kai's motorcycle approaching. I grabbed my coat and ran outside.

"Good evening, my swan."

We kissed.

"I'm so glad you're here. Come inside and get warm."

He handed me a bouquet of flowers and a wine bottle. "These are for you."

"Thank you. They are lovely." I set them on the table and took his hand. "Come upstairs. I want to show you something." My face grew hot at the implication, and I quickly explained, "I just saw two figures from up here. They vanished, but I know they're still out there."

Opening the door quietly, I placed one finger over my lips. We crept carefully to the railing, his body pressed against my side. We stared in silence, watching, waiting. A shadow brushed along my periphery. I tapped Kai's shoulder and pointed.

We silently stared as a figure toddled out of the forest and down to the trail by the river. A small raccoon trailed behind. I pulled Kai backward off the balcony before speaking.

"Did you see it? Do you believe me now?"

He stood silent. His jaw muscles were flexing, and his face looked white.

Fearing he was going in shock, I asked, "Are you all right?"

He blinked, placing both hands to his face and shaking his head. "Wow, Lily. It's . . . wow. This erases any doubt." He was quiet for a moment. I didn't speak, allowing him to process. "They are real. They're *real*. I always wanted to believe it. Stories about the magical creatures of the forest have been told for generations. I thought it would be incredible if they were true."

I hugged him. "I'm so glad you saw it. I thought I was losing my mind."

"They're dangerous. We must be careful." Kai sounded grave. "Why do they look like stone? We should talk to Grandmother Kateri."

"I think that is a great idea. I would love to hear her advice—and to meet her. Do you think we should tell Berly and Martin?"

"No, I wouldn't want to worry them, especially with her family coming. And they're only showing themselves to you. Let's wait until we can talk to Grandmother Kateri. She will know what to do."

"Okay, we won't let this ruin our night. I'm just thrilled I can finally share what I've been seeing for months." I paused, then added, "With someone I care for."

"I'm surprised how easily I could see it. I can't wait to tell Grandmother." We reached the bottom of the stairs. "Can I get you a glass of wine?" Warmth returned to his voice.

"That sounds good."

We settled by the fireplace with our wine and planned a visit to his grandmother's in the morning.

"How was work today?"

"Jon and I had to save two sets of hikers on Jenkins Mountain. They defy the rules, leave the trails, and wander into hazardous conditions. They call us in a panic. It takes hours to find them and escort them off the mountain." Kai shook his head with a sigh. "Enough about me. I want to hear about your day."

"Berly and I went shopping downtown." Looking over the top of my wineglass, I said, "I bought something for you," and handed him the bag. He opened it slowly. I held my breath, watching his expression. The corners of his mouth turned up.

He inspected the bracelet with an expression of approval.

"Where did you find this? It is just like your necklace." He immediately put it on, and my pulse quickened with pride.

He kissed me. "This means the world to me."

"I am so glad you like it. I wasn't sure if you would want to wear it or not."

"Are you kidding? I will never take it off. You will always be with me."

I told him about the clerk and what she had said to me.

"What do you think it means?"

He rubbed his chin while staring into the fire. "It's like she knows you're a swan, but what could the other part mean? Remind me what she said to you the first time you visited the store?"

"Something like, 'It is working for you. The swan is a protector who connects heart with head.'"

"She definitely picked up the swan connection." His cheeks went taut as he pondered. "You are a protector who connects heart with head. You know in your heart what you cannot see."

My stomach churned. "It reminded me of what you said about dreams. I might be trying to evade something I know in my heart. I will eventually have to face it."

He hugged me. "I will face it with you. When I went to that shop to purchase your bracelet, the clerk said, 'I was wondering when you were going to come in.' She walked me right over to the bracelets. I did not think much about it. I just purchased it and left."

"I think she's clairvoyant." That felt easier to say now that the existence of the pukwudgies had been verified.

"Probably. Many people who own shops like that are quite spiritual."

Just before midnight, I walked Kai outside. The air was biting, much colder than a few hours ago. "Are you going to freeze to death on your bike?"

"I will be fine, my love." We shared a passionate kiss. "Thank you for the gift."

"Thank you for believing me, about the pukwudgies."

"It worries me. What are they after?"

"Are they the danger you were warning me about the first day we met?"

"There are other dangers in the forest." He paused. "And I felt an overwhelming urge to protect you."

I pointed to his bracelet, saying, "Now you have a swan to protect you."

He kissed the tip of my nose and then my lips. A small current fired through my veins.

"Now get inside before you freeze to death," he growled.

I blew him a kiss and ran inside.

CHAPTER 16

THE NEXT MORNING, I sprang to my feet and ran upstairs to brush my teeth when I heard a motorcycle approaching. A shaft of sunlight through the window cast a prism across the bathroom counter. I knew it was going to be a beautiful day.

Rushing down the stairs, past the kitchen, I called out, "I'll see you in a few hours."

Berly flashed me a thumbs-up.

Kai was already heading up the path to meet me. I bounded out the door, plunged into his arms, and smooched him on the cheek. "Good morning."

His face lit up. "Yes, it is."

"It looks like it's going to be a perfect day." The weather was crisp and sunny.

"Are you ready? I can't wait for you to meet Grandmother Kateri." Kai's eyes sparkled.

"I'm looking forward to it."

He glanced at me with a half grin and kissed me quickly. Walking backward toward his bike, he swept his arms open and announced, "Your chariot awaits, milady." He handed me a helmet, bowing low. His giddiness offered a rare glimpse into what he might have been like as a kid.

I held on tight and let my eyes sweep our surroundings on the drive down the winding road. I wanted to absorb all the details of the area where Kai grew up. Many trees were already losing their leaves, but the view was still stunningly colorful. Farther down the mountain, the image began to change. A beautiful rock wall lined either side of the road. We passed picturesque farmhouses encircled by acres of green pastures where animals lazily grazed.

A quaint little town emerged ahead. Each building was constructed of thick logs painted vibrant colors that matched the fall foliage on the mountainside. From far away, the place blended right into the forest.

The walkways throughout town were all made from stone. In the center was a large fountain, also built from natural stone. On the right, a charming old stone church perched atop a hillside.

We traveled to the edge of town and up a narrow dirt road that ended at a charming log cabin surrounded by hills and a lake. Like the town, the house also had stone walls and walkways around the property.

"This looks like a fairy tale," I said after we parked and climbed off the bike.

He took hold of my hand. "Are you ready?"

"Of course."

He dragged me eagerly up the path and onto a wide front porch.

Kai called out, "Grandmother Kateri, we're here."

The door opened slowly to reveal a fragile-looking but radiant woman who was stooped from age. Kai's smile widened, and he hugged and kissed his grandmother on each cheek.

"My guiding star."

She touched his cheek with her hand. "My heart."

She turned to me, and Kai introduced us.

"Grandmother, this is Liliana Swan Makris." I was surprised he used my formal name—surprised he even remembered it. "Lily, this is Grandmother Kateri."

She had the same long features and piercing green eyes as Kai. The heavy wrinkles around her eyes revealed much resilience and wisdom. She stared at me with an intensity that gradually broke into a healthy smile. Her face became friendly and inviting. I hugged her lightly.

She placed my hand on her arm and patted it as she motioned me forward. "Please come in. I am so glad to meet you."

"I'm pleased to meet you too. You have a beautiful home."

"The land is fertile, and the spirits provide." Pride was evident in her voice.

We landed in a large living room. My first impression was of warmth but also strength.

One entire wall housed a beautiful stone fireplace. Our footsteps echoed on the rich cherrywood floors. Directly in the center of the room, the ceiling was elevated in the shape of an octagon. It was surrounded by stained glass windows that sent multicolored lights dancing around the room.

She motioned for us to have a seat. "Would you like some tea?"

"That sounds lovely."

Kai and I sat by a large window overlooking the lake. He took my hand and kissed the back of it, his eyes gleaming. It felt like he was letting me know everything would be all right.

Grandmother Kateri returned with a tray of tea and cookies. We each took a plate and a few cookies while she poured the tea.

Sitting next to me on the couch, she turned toward me. "Let me have a look at you."

She sandwiched my hands between hers, her grip soft and warm yet firm. I got the feeling she was not as fragile as I first thought. She held me for a minute or two, her green eyes flickering around my face.

A pleasant smile appeared.

"She is beautiful inside and out. She has a pure heart," she said, looking directly at Kai.

"I know."

Grandmother Kateri's voice became serious. "Tell me about the shadows you have been seeing."

"They are more than shadows," I answered. "I've seen them hiding in the forest since the day I arrived. I blindly followed one because a strange force pulled me to it. They look like lawn chess pieces made of shiny stone. At first, they hid in the shadows, but now I see them more clearly. Last night I saw two of them completely emerge from the forest. I showed them to Kai."

"I saw them, Grandmother. They are real."

Grandmother Kateri drank in the details, then gazed thoughtfully toward the ceiling, not saying a word. We waited in silence. Kai squeezed my hand, and I placed my other hand over his.

She took a long, deep breath. "I think the pukwudgies are interested in you. Maybe because of Kai but probably because of your swan spirit. Swans can block invoked evil because they are pure and they are protectors."

She leaned in close. "Please listen to me. Stay far away from these creatures. They possess very strong magic and can appear and disappear at will. They have been known to attack people, kidnap them, blind their victims with sand, even lure them to their deaths. We believe that long ago, Pukwudgies were once friendly to humans, but they turned against us. Their stonelike appearance could mean dark magic. They are best left alone." Her voice trailed off.

She was convincing. Feeling queasy, I rubbed my temples, trying to commit what she told me to memory. Kai kissed the top of my head. "I'll be watching out for you."

Before we left, Grandmother Kateri spoke quietly in Kai's ear. His expression told me he did not like what she was saying.

"Is everything all right?" I asked when we climbed on the motorcycle.

"Don't worry about it." A hard edge had entered his voice.

Kai sped over the limit on the way back. He seemed highly irritated. Taking off his helmet in the parking spot in front of the cabin, he shook his head like he had a bee in his hair.

"What time is it?" he asked sharply, wearing the same look as when he'd had words with Ben.

"It's 12:20. Are you going to be late?"

"Sorry, I have to go," he said curtly. He gave me a quick peck and shook his head again. His eyes looked strange. He blinked rapidly, and I could have sworn his pupils stretched into a vertical line.

"What's wrong with your eyes?"

He shrugged and looked away, shoving his helmet back on. His hands were clenched into fists.

"I have to go!" Anger flared in his voice. I kept my mouth shut, afraid to press the issue. He kicked the bike to life, squeezed my hand, and drove away.

I couldn't help but fume. *What just happened?* I wasn't cold before, but now goose bumps spread across my arms. The shift had happened so fast. *What was going on with his eyes?* I didn't understand his haste. Maybe he thought I was some kind of freak who attracted dangerous creatures. Maybe his grandmother didn't like me.

Kai's leaving in such a tizzy felt like rejection. I bit my bottom lip to keep it from quivering and tried to push down the unnerving thoughts.

CHAPTER 17

THE LAND ROVER rolled up the driveway, trailing a cloud of dust in its wake. Berly sprang off the deck to greet her family, and I followed, thankful for the distraction. I needed to keep my mind busy and stop ruminating on Kai and the creatures of the forest.

Berly was dead-on in her description of her family. Davis, her father, was taller than I imagined. His posture exuded confidence. When Berly introduced us, her dad revealed a matching set of dimples. Dressed in crisp, preppy clothes, he performed a full-perimeter inspection of the property.

Vivi looked like a movie star. She was stunning and had the perfect figure to wear exquisite designer fashions.

Miles, Berly's stepbrother, looked to be around my kid sister's age. He was at that awkward, lanky stage. So full of energy, almost mischievous, he immediately started checking the internet for things to do. He talked Berly and me into going out on the kayaks. We played cornhole and finally ended up in the game room. He chattered nonstop. I didn't think he would ever run out of energy until he announced he was starving.

A tantalizing aroma met us as we climbed the stairs. Berly looked over her shoulder. "My dad is a gourmet chef, and he loves to cook. You had better change into your stretchy pants now." My stomach growled.

Vivi handed us each a glass of wine. Berly smirked at me with a look that said, "I warned you." I smiled and nodded my thanks, taking a sip.

"This is delicious."

Vivi raised her glass.

Dinner was amazing. The family discussed what they wanted to do for the next few days as I half listened. Vivi wanted to go downtown, and Miles hoped to visit the Olympic Village.

Berly's dad booked a helicopter tour and a boat tour of the rivers for Wednesday. Not wanting to intrude, I politely declined the invite, saying I needed to finish a project for school.

Berly had proven to be more than a friend; she was like a sister. Our friendship was effortless, equal, and uncomplicated. I had no doubt that she would stand up for me as I would for her. I had finally found a friend I could count on. It felt like I was already a part of their family.

CHAPTER 18

WEDNESDAY MORNING, I meandered along the stream. Gray mist floated in and out of the trees, but the rest of the forest was motionless and noiseless. I got an uneasy feeling that I should have gone on the helicopter ride.

Nervously rubbing the cool, sleek pink stones in my pocket, I scanned the forest for shadows. I tried to concentrate on the calming sounds of the river. It splashed and burbled over the rocks, curving gently through the forest. A gust of wind rushed through the trees, stinging my face like the slap of a hand—a slap that knocked some sense into me. *How will I ever finish four years of college here if I act like such a weakling?* My fright quickly turned to determination. *Be fierce!* the voice in my head commanded.

I picked up my pace, reaching a spot where the river was not too deep or wide and the current was steady. This was the perfect place to study the river's flow. Sunbeams struggled through the trees, and the dappled light cast shadows all around me.

I took out my notebook to record the data and drew a grid to track the results. Stepping into the river in the high rain boots I'd borrowed from the mudroom, I stabbed four stakes into the riverbed, then set up three more sets farther down the path.

The air was brutally cold as I knelt on the riverbank, staring intently at the stakes. A shadow crept across me. I froze. I could not look up.

A splash startled me and jolted my senses. A baby raccoon had fallen into the river. It was thrashing about, trying to keep its head above the surface. I grabbed a stake and ran down the path to save it, forgetting all about the shadow.

The raccoon slowed itself by grabbing a rock. It tried desperately to hold on, but the rapid flow pushed it back into the turbulent water. I ran farther ahead and stepped into the river, holding out the wooden stake to stop the poor creature from getting swept downstream. The raccoon bobbed up and down and clawed for air. Soon it was close enough to see the panic in its eyes. I stretched to reach it, and it seemed to understand what I was doing, grabbing hold of the wood with both front paws.

"Hold on. You're going to be fine." I gradually pulled the stick toward me until I could pick the raccoon up by its scruff, like a cat would carry her kitten.

I backed out of the river and knelt to set it softly on the ground. The raccoon was panting rapidly and appeared stunned. I was worried it would have a heart attack or had hypothermia as it lay on its side.

After a minute or two, it finally lifted its head.

"Come on, buddy. You'll be fine."

It slowly stood on wobbly feet. A bit unsteady, it shook off the water. The black mask around its eyes and the white fur surrounding it gave the raccoon a quizzical look. It still seemed dazed.

A gust blew my hair back, and a shudder passed through me, bringing the feeling of impending danger. A loud pop sounded in my left ear. I squeezed my eyes shut, afraid to look, afraid not to look. I opened my eyes, gazing down. A puff of dust floated over my left hand.

Beside my hand was a pair of black feet. They were smaller than my hand and looked carved from stone. Each foot had three long toes and sharp, pointy toenails resembling talons. I raised my eyes to see a short, expressionless, stone-faced creature beside me.

Fear washed over me. Remembering what Kai's grandmother had said about looking directly at pukwudgies, I jumped up and bolted down the trail. I ran frantically with no plan, only knowing I had to get away. I tried to scream, but no sound came out. I was struck with déjà vu—except, this time, I wasn't dreaming.

My heart leaped when I glimpsed someone at the bottom of the trail pass through a cave opening. The figure looked like Kai. *He'll know what to do.* With relief, I followed him into the cave. A light, raspy sound escaped my lungs when I tried to call his name. Breathing heavily, I waited for my eyes to adjust to the light.

The cave opening I had slid through was a narrow hole between two rocks, so I was stunned by the massive cave before me. Stalactites hanging from the ceiling and stalagmites protruding from the floor looked like large teeth ready to take a carnivorous bite out of me.

I squinted, frantically searching for Kai in the darkness, and grew alarmed when I heard a giggle and rapid footsteps. Two young girls tumbled out into the cavern and froze. Grabbing hold of each other, they screamed.

I forgot how to breathe. They did not look normal. They had snouts and the ears of a pig. A woman darted out of the same opening, stopping cold when she saw me. She had the same piglike features. The girls ran to her and clung to her skirt.

I stepped back, blinking tears from my eyes. A tall man arrived through another opening. He was dressed in white, and half his face was covered with bees. Behind him emerged another man with oddly shaped legs, the legs of a goat. His hooves sounded strange on the stone floor.

A dull buzz sounded in my ears, and it wasn't from the bees. I wanted to wake from this dream.

I screamed, and this time sound came out. I turned to run but spotted Kai to my left, in the shadows. I called out his name and rushed to him, clinging to his arm. My heart was in my throat. I could not breathe.

Kai had his hoodie drawn over his head and would not look at me. Through deep breaths, I pleaded, "Please tell me what's going on."

His head was tilted low. He answered in a low, broken voice, "I am so sorry. I never wanted you to see me like this. It is a curse. I am so sorry!"

I was confused. Kai reached up and pulled back his hood.

"This is what she made me." Shame choked his voice, and his eyes glistened—eyes that looked like marbles. The pupils were shaped in a vertical slit. Green scales covered his chest and neck.

A sound like a mosquito buzzed in my ear as everything faded into thickening darkness.

CHAPTER 19

I WOKE TO KAI shaking my shoulder and cradling my face with his other hand. Gravel was stuck to my cheek. "Lily, are you all right?"

I couldn't collect my thoughts. Everything in my brain was fuzzy. I tried to answer, but no words came out. Kai placed his arm behind my back and helped me sit up.

"Lily, please say something."

I wiped the sand from my cheek, aware of how close his face was to mine. It made me feel safe, but flooded with memories of snake eyes, I struggled to think clearly. Kai's look of concern held steady while I searched for words.

"How did I get out here?" I mumbled.

"Ben and I walked up the trail and found you lying on the ground."

The other ranger hovered behind Kai. Ben's worried expression was much more friendly than the scowl he'd worn the first time we met.

"Found me on the trail? What? But I followed you!" Anger built in my voice. "A pukwudgie appeared beside me, and I looked it in the eye. I ran. I followed you into a cave. The girls . . . the girls looked strange, with a pig's snout." I pointed to Ben, and in an accusing tone, I said, "You were there too. Bees, lots of bees, and another guy. Kai, your eyes . . . your eyes . . ." I stopped myself, realizing how ridiculous I sounded. I sobbed. Kai cradled me in his arms, and I let the tears flow freely.

"It's nothing more than a bad dream. You probably hit your head when you passed out." His voice sounded shaky.

I wrapped my arms around his neck and held on with all my might. His familiar scent made me tremble. My voice was barely a whisper. "It was the worst nightmare ever. I was so scared. I think the pukwudgies made me hallucinate."

"Shhh." Kai kissed the top of my head.

"I looked it in the eyes," I said, my voice quavering. "Grandmother Kateri said not to look them in the eyes."

"It's okay. I'm here now. You had a bad dream. Everything is fine." He glanced back to Ben. Ben nodded, and Kai stood, pulling me with him. "Let's get you out of this forest."

Feeling weak and dizzy, I was grateful Kai was supporting me. We walked in silence. I was glad for it because I didn't think I could answer any questions coherently.

When the house came into view, Kai asked, "Is anyone home?"

"No."

He looked back to Ben. "Should we take her to Grandmother Kateri's?"

"No, I'll be fine. I just need to rest," I protested, not wanting to be treated like a child.

Kai stopped at the bottom of the stairs to the deck. I leaned on the rail. "See, I already feel better." I was pretty sure I didn't sound convincing. "Berly and her family should be home in a few hours." I hadn't realized that Kai and Ben were wearing their work clothes. "Besides, you two are working. Go. I'll be fine."

"Are you sure you are feeling all right?" Kai asked in a tender voice. "Come. I am not leaving this house until you are settled inside." He walked me upstairs and inside to the couch. "Stay here and rest." He brought me a bottle of water and orange juice. "Drink this. It will make you feel better." The warmth of his hand on my shoulder already made me feel better.

Ben cleared his throat. "Kai, it's time to go," he said. His scowl had returned.

"Sorry, we have to get a move on." Kai leaned down for a kiss. "I will call you in a few hours to check on you."

"Thank you."

"Bye, my love. Get some rest."

The last thing I remembered was the sound of the door closing.

*　*　*

I awoke shaky and disoriented, shocked to discover it was 3:20 p.m. *Did I really sleep over three hours?*

I went upstairs and took a long, hot shower, trying to recall my bizarre morning. Then I remembered. *My notebook!* I had left it on the trail. All my calculations for the semester were in it. I had to retrieve it.

Hurrying to get dressed, I grabbed my phone and ran toward the door. My pace slowed as I remembered my earlier terror. But I pushed my concerns out of my head and told myself, *Suck it up and go get your notebook.* I stomped down the outside stairs and stopped dead in my tracks. My notebook was sitting on the bottom step. My hands shook when I cautiously reached down to pick it up. Kai or Ben must have brought it.

I hugged the binder, unlocked the door, and hurried back into the house. My hands were shaking when I opened it. A squeal escaped my mouth when I reached the page with the grid I had drawn this morning. The calculations had been filled in. My head spun. *Who filled in this data?* I set the notebook on the table and turned on every light I could find. I reviewed the data; it was correct. Goose bumps covered my arms. I yelped when my phone rang.

"Hello."

"Hi, my love, how are you feeling?"

"I feel much better. I slept and took a hot shower." I tried to hide my panic. "Did you drop off my notebook? The one I left on the trail?"

"No," Kai answered. "Why?"

"It's here. Someone or something placed it at the bottom of the steps." I paused. "Someone completed the data grid . . . and it's correct."

"That is odd."

After a few more seconds of silence, I recognized that was the only response I would get.

"This whole day has been odd. Do you think the pukwudgies knocked me out? I slept for three and a half hours. Did they return my notebook? Who did the data entry?" I asked, my cheeks hot.

"I don't know," he said plainly. He was being decidedly unhelpful, but I didn't know what response I wanted from him, so I just sighed.

"I don't either. Nothing makes sense."

The sound of a car engine approaching calmed my nerves.

"Berly and her family are pulling in now." I needed to let my anger go. *I shouldn't direct it at him.*

"Good, I don't want you to be alone. You had me worried."

"Sorry, I don't mean to snap at you. I think I'm still unsettled."

"Lily."

"Yes?"

"Promise me you will stay out of the forest."

The forest was the last place I wanted to go. "I promise."

"Bye, love. Enjoy your Thanksgiving. I will see you on Saturday."

Berly and her family piled inside, and the house was instantly filled with activity. I welcomed the company and the noise.

CHAPTER 20

I ENJOYED SPENDING THANKSGIVING with Berly's family—watching her father navigate the kitchen like a French danseur, getting to know Vivi and her wine, and laughing at Berly's dry sense of humor and Miles's endless energy. They were a great distraction. But I was ready for a full day with Kai. He finally had a Saturday off, and I needed answers.

A familiar tingle rushed through me when I heard a vehicle approaching. I grabbed my stuff and ran outside, halting uncertainly when a truck pulled up. I was about to run back inside when Kai climbed out, flashing his perfect smile. He must have noticed the blank look on my face.

"It's me!"

"When did you get a truck?"

"I've had it for years. I use it during the winter months."

Another thing I didn't know about him. I stepped toward him, my eyes on my feet, annoyed with my reaction. His arms went around my shoulders, and he buried his face in my neck. "How are you?"

I instantly felt calm, safe. "Better now that you're here."

He tucked a lock of hair behind my ear and absently dragged his fingers down my back.

"What's first on our agenda today?" I asked, trying to ignore the sensation from his fingertips.

"We could head downtown, shop, grab a bite to eat. And there's an art festival in the park. How does that sound to you?"

"Sounds great, as long as we get to go into some of my favorite stores."

He grinned. "It is a deal."

The streets were bustling. Kai and I held hands as we navigated the hive of activity.

"What did your grandmother say to you before we left the other day?"

Kai looked away. "She just told me to be careful."

I got the feeling he wasn't telling the truth.

"Did you tell her about my encounter?"

"Of course. She told me to remind you to stay out of the forest and away from the pukwudgies." She didn't have to warn me; I was not going near them.

Soon we landed in front of the Salty Swan. Our eyes linked. The pleasant sound of the wind chimes tinkled as we slipped into the store. Incense filled the air. But the familiarity ended there. The place was busier than I had ever seen it. We could hardly move.

"I think this was a mistake. It's way too crowded to shop."

Kai squeezed my hand. "We can come back another time. Let's head to the art festival."

"That sounds like a good idea."

Turning to leave, I heard a familiar laugh. Customers parted as Wanda approached us.

"Hi, Wanda, good to see you again."

Her eyes scanned us from head to toe like she was assessing a thoroughbred. "Your connection is like no other." Her voice resonated. She stepped around us. "A force like magnets—apart the force is strong, together the force is power."

Kai's grip tightened. Wanda fell silent, staring straight ahead. She leaned closer, a steely edge to her voice. "Don't be afraid, swan. They need you."

I felt like there was something I wanted to ask, but my mind went blank. She glided away through the crowded store. In a synchronized move, Kai and I exited. I searched his eyes, trying to understand what she had said.

"She's so cryptic. What did it mean?"

"I think she approves of our spiritual connection. But who is this 'they' she referred to?" he wondered.

I could barely hear him over the wind and crowd. Cupping my hand to the side of my mouth, I said, "We're going to have to find a better place to talk."

He nodded in agreement.

A cold breeze prompted me to zip up my coat. My neck was bare. I pointed toward the boutique. "Can we run in here so I can buy a scarf before we go to the festival? The Floridian forgot to wear one."

"Sure." Kai's cell phone rang after we entered. He could not hear over the dozen customers, so he signaled he was leaving and leaned against the wall outside to take the call.

I quickly purchased the first scarf I found, coiled it around my neck, and headed out, pausing on the steps because I did not want to interrupt his call.

Benton and his two footmen were traveling up the street behind Kai. The cretin called with a sneer, "Hey, lover boy! Are you lost?"

Kai glanced back, his brow furrowed, and he ended his call. Then Benton purposely knocked shoulders with Kai as he passed, swaying Kai against the wall.

"So sorry I bumped into you. I must have misjudged the massive size of my shoulders," Benton said with a self-satisfied smirk.

Kai's nostrils flared, and redness spread across his face.

Benton looked entirely too smug. "Oh, but it seems you're a lover, not a fighter."

Kai jerked forward and grabbed the front of Benton's shirt, dragging him close as if Benton weighed nothing. The ranger let out a guttural hiss that blew the college boy's hair back.

"Keep it up, and you will make me angry," Kai gritted out, pronouncing each word slowly, deliberately.

Benton's eyes widened. After tugging his shirt free, he held his hands up and backed away. "It's cool. We're cool."

I had never seen Kai act so ruthlessly. I was not sure I liked it. I cautiously stepped off the steps once Benton and his pack had beat a hasty retreat. Kai's unblinking eyes signaled that everything was under control, but his heavy breathing suggested otherwise. Stepping forward, his chin up, he offered me his hand, and I accepted. He kissed the back of my hand as we continued onward.

"He asked for it," he said, struggling for a lighter tone.

"I know. I saw the whole thing."

A smile tugged at the corner of his mouth. "He really says the dumbest things. 'I misjudged the massive size of my shoulders,'" he mocked before bursting into laughter. I shed my anxiety and joined him.

The festival was even more crowded than downtown. We shuffled past a few booths with the crowd, often turning sideways to squeeze past other shoppers. I felt like we were being swept away like that raccoon on the river. The walls of people made it almost impossible to stop and look at anything. Kai tilted his head toward a coffee shop. I nodded, eager to escape this sea of bodies.

Seated outside the coffee shop, I held my mug with both hands, watching the steam swirl out and breathing in the rich aroma of fresh-ground coffee. Warmth spread through me with every sip. We had managed to score the corner table—a perfect place for people-watching.

We leaned our heads together so we could hear each other.

"Who do you think Wanda was talking about? 'They need you.' Who is 'they'?" I wondered, knowing he did not have the answer.

Kai flexed his jaw. He opened his mouth but closed it again, staring blindly into the passing crowd. "Together the force is power," he muttered under his breath.

I started guessing. "My family, my friends, teammates, puk—"

Someone called out Kai's name and Ben jogged toward us, his face warm and friendly. Behind him was a guy I hadn't met.

Ben and Kai shook hands and patted each other's backs with their free hands. I got the feeling they had done that handshake a thousand times.

"Hey, bro, I knew I would find you here." Ben looked directly at me. "Hi, Lily. It is good to see you again." He leaned in unexpectedly and kissed my cheek.

"Good to see you again, Ben."

"Lily, this is Wade. Wade, Lily."

Wade extended his hand and shook mine vigorously. Wade looked younger than Ben and Kai; I would say seventeen. His glossy black hair was shaved on the sides and the rest pulled into a top knot. His large, dark doe eyes gave him an innocent look.

"Nice to meet you." His voice was deeper than I expected.

"Nice to meet you too."

"Care to join us?" Kai asked, gesturing to the open seats.

"Sure, I could use a coffee." Ben and Wade didn't bother going to the entrance, instead electing to hop over the railing. Wade sat on my left, and Ben settled across from me. "What's up? Did you buy anything stupid yet?" Ben asked Kai.

Kai playfully punched his arm. "Not yet. We were hoping you could give us pointers."

Wade's face brightened when he asked, "Have you seen Tate? He's following that nurse from the quarry around like a puppy. I bet she's talking him into buying some stupid shit." His cheeks reddened, and he turned to me to explain, "He's my brother. I've never seen him so starry eyed."

He immediately launched into a completely different subject. "What do you think about the Bronco Sport? I'm saving my money for one. Did you know they have four-wheel drive? When I turn eighteen next month, I'm getting my commercial license to get a job driving trucks at the quarry. That's where the real money is."

I didn't know whether it was nervous energy or he just liked to talk, but Wade's innocence was endearing.

Suddenly, Kai's body went rigid. Ben followed his gaze into the crowd, and Kai's Adam's apple bobbed up and down.

"Wade, please take Lily inside. Now!" Kai barked. Wade jumped up, pulled back my chair as I hesitantly stood, and placed his hand on my back to escort me inside.

"What is it?" I strained to peer over my shoulder, trying to see what they were looking at.

"Go, Lily. Do what he says," Ben hissed. He stayed seated.

I walked slowly, reluctantly, hearing a lady's voice behind us.

"I hoped I would find you here. Enjoying the full moon, are you?"

Inside, Wade and I peeked out the window. The short lady with the long dark hair and oversized sunglasses Kai and I had seen by the lake overlook was standing at the rail in front of our table, flanked by two men in uniform.

"Who is she?" I asked Wade quietly.

"That's Rosella, a hotshot businesswoman with a lot of money. She owns half the town." He rolled his eyes. "Do you want a cookie?"

"Um, yeah, sure." I handed him a twenty, saying, "My treat."

Wade seemed easygoing and honest. It gave me an idea.

I watched the interactions outside intently but could not figure out anything they were saying. The lady ran her finger across the table. A wave of delight passed through me when Kai leaned away from her. Ben sat like a statue.

"Chocolate chip or white macadamia?" Wade asked when he returned with a selection of cookies.

"Chocolate chip," I answered in a cheery voice. I pinched off a piece and popped it in my mouth. "Um, this is delicious. Thank you." Trying to lull Wade into answering my questions, I said, "I like the Bronco Sport. They're rugged and a smart choice for this weather."

"You do?" His eyes lit up. "I think I want a black one."

"I would get a black one too. Go for it." I kept my voice light and charming. "Hey, when you said that lady owned half the town, what did you mean?"

"She owns the mine, the quarry, and the trucking company."

"How does she know Kai?"

"She's been trying to get him to work for her for years. She offered him a lot of money, but he won't do it. She is evil, pure evil." His hand went to his mouth. "I probably shouldn't talk about that."

"It's okay. Kai already told me she was evil. I was just curious. What evil things has she done?"

Wade took a big bite of his cookie. "I probably smoodn't tell you this." He chuckled because his words came out garbled. He held up a finger and swallowed. "I heard she practices dark magic." Those words in his deep voice made me shudder.

"Do you think it's true?" I asked, intrigued.

"Just look at her. She's scary with that wild hair and those beady eyes."

Rosella was talking heatedly, gesturing with her hands, shaking her manicured finger in Kai's face. She snapped her fingers at her guards and swiftly marched away, her wavy black hair and long black coat swaying behind her. The guards followed with stiff discipline.

CHAPTER 21

KAI'S MOOD HAD flipped like a light switch. We rode back in silence. I was dying to ask what Rosella wanted, but judging by Kai's clenched jaw, I wouldn't like the answer.

We slowly climbed the stairs at Berly's cabin, the silence hanging heavy. A note on the counter read: Gone to the airport to pick up Martin and Max. Don't wait up. We're going out.

"We have the house to ourselves," I said, trying to sound cheery and bring him out of his funk.

"We have a lot to talk about." His tone was cold.

I kissed the back of his hand. "Let's go to the loft," I proposed, swallowing a knot in my throat. I was afraid he wouldn't tell me the truth. But more than that, I was afraid of the truth and worried he would push me away. His silence hinted at the latter.

Up in the loft, Kai covered his face with his hands. I waited in silence.

"What's wrong?" I finally blurted out. "You're scaring me."

He leaned his head back and dropped his hands. "You deserve better. I'm no good for you. I don't know what I was thinking. I'm damaged goods."

It felt like someone had dropped a brick on my stomach.

"Forgive me, I must start from the beginning so you can understand everything." His voice lowered, and so did his head. "For many years, itinerants would stay in the old white house by the marsh, performing rituals and casting spells, curses, or other forms of magic using crystals and potions. Grandmother thinks the pukwudgies turned against humans because these mystical travelers tried numerous times to harness the forest creatures' powers. These travelers would only stay for a few months at a time. One of the travelers was Rosella. When she was sixteen years old, she discovered a way to use black tourmaline to control people's minds."

"Is that the lady you were talking to today?" I asked casually, acting like it was normal to discuss witchcraft as a real thing.

"Yes, it is. Rosella was determined to find a way to access black tourmaline. Our little village was built around a coal mine at the base of the mountain. Most people from the village work either in the mines, quarry, or shipyard. The owner, an extremely wealthy businessman, built a massive mansion above the mine entrance. He fortified the eighty-five acres of land with a tall stone wall.

"He was the first person Rosella targeted. She needed his wealth to gain her power. She manipulated him with her mind control, and he gave her everything she wanted. She took over his fortress and moved him into a small servants' cabin on the property.

"She used her power to influence the workers to mine black tourmaline from the mines instead of coal. The more crystals she acquired, the more minds she could control to do her bidding. After you shared what you'd seen of the pukwudgies, Grandmother learned that Rosella found a way to trick them with black tourmaline. She used dark magic to place the pukwudgies under her spell so she could harness their powers and use them as spies. Pukwudgies can communicate telepathically, and they use raccoons as their eyes at night.

"Her power became stronger, and her abilities must have increased when she started channeling the pukwudgies' magic. Eventually their appearance changed. They used to have a cheery, light-gray complexion, with soft, round, ruby cheeks and large crystal-blue eyes. Now they look like they are made from black tourmaline stone themselves. Their faces are stern, like an angry mask made of stone."

"How can she do that to them?" I had been terrified of the creatures, but after rescuing that little raccoon, I experienced the slightest shift in how I perceived them.

"She is evil, Lily." He looked directly into my eyes, placing a finger under my chin. "These creatures have been watching you since you arrived. We don't know the reason why, but she controls them. They are dangerous."

A mixture of hatred and fright gurgled like froth in my stomach. I replayed what Kai had said: *"I'm no good for you."*

I leaned forward until our foreheads touched, placing my hands on his chest and feeling the beat of his heart. "What does she want from you?"

"She wants me to work for her. She is relentless."

"What? Why? Don't do it."

The full moon cast golden shadows on his black hair. He moved away slightly and looked down at his feet. "She likes to recruit forest rangers so she can use them as guards, especially ones who are young and fit."

His voice cracked. "She came after me when I turned eighteen. I was about to graduate the forest ranger program when she approached me." He paused. "Rosella is petite and pretty. She uses it to take advantage of people. You would never expect that this small girl could hurt you until her coal-black eyes lock on you like a laser-guided missile. Her voice is soft and seductive. It anchors to your soul as she lures you under her influence.

"At first, I felt flattered, almost honored. But something deep inside me gave me clarity. I knew it was a ruse. A few weeks later, after graduation, the rangers were celebrating in the village square. Rosella appeared again. She came to me, brushed her fingertips across my jawline, and blew black tourmaline powder at me—though I only learned what it was later. Gray smoke swirled around my head, and she ordered me to report to her fortress on Monday, to be her personal guard. Lily, her demand felt binding."

Kai continued, unsmiling, "But something kept her influence from taking me over. I refused to be a part of her web, locked inside a compound to do her bidding. I fought her manipulation and searched for people who could resist her influence.

"Two of my best friends, Ben and Tate, joined my cause. We traveled to the mine and quarry to wake the people from the trance she held over them. We discovered a handful of people who also had doubts and sought clarity. Some were initially afraid to resist, but they joined our mutiny."

Staring sightlessly at his feet, Kai rapidly concluded his explanation. "Rosella's spies learned of our plans to rebel. She cursed each of us, deforming us in different ways. She ensured we would be too terrified to be seen in public or recruit more people against her. We had to move into the caves because people feared what we had become."

He held his steepled hands to his lips and kept his eyes on the floor.

I straightened. "The caves? What kind of deformity? I didn't imagine that?" It felt like he had punched me in the stomach. "What other lies have you told me?"

He swallowed and licked his lips. "Have you ever wondered why I only visit you between ten and twelve in the morning or the evening?" He glanced at me through wet eyelashes. "Her magic does not work the hour before or the hour after 11:11, the most mystical time of the day."

Kai's deep voice was unsteady as he explained, "The curse is also weakened during a full moon, which is why I can spend the entire day with you during the three days of the full moon. We all largely limit our outings to these days and times, but of course, my ranger work requires me to be out and about. That is why I wear such dark sunglasses and a dark helmet."

His cheeks glistened with tears now. He brought his balled fist to his mouth. "I am so sorry I brought you into this. It's all my fault. I just could not stay away."

I felt a spasm of sorrow. "I didn't want you to stay away."

Kai choked out, "When I met you in the forest, you made me come to life. For the first time in two years, I felt the desire to be normal again. Your pure spirit gave me hope. Ben warned me it wasn't a good idea. My mother told me to end it before you got hurt."

I let out a resigned sigh, bracing myself. *This is it; he never wants to see me again.* I recoiled at the very thought.

"I understand if you hate me. I do not regret any of the moments we had together, but I am truly sorry. I hope you understand why I couldn't tell you the truth. Whatever happens, I promise to look out for you and keep you safe." He took my hand and clasped it between his. "You are a beautiful treasure, and I am a beast."

I realized I had two options. The first was to walk away, forget Kai, and move on with my safe life. The second was to accept the danger, fight for him, fight for us. An alarm went off in my head. *They are the ones who need me.*

Deep down I knew I only had one choice. It was him. A fierce feeling sparked within me. I wanted to protect him, save him whatever the cost—even if it meant my swan song.

A tear tracked a path down my cheek. I wrapped my arms around him, pressing my cheek against his chest, and let my tears flow freely. His soft, silky hair smelled of fresh air. I felt his rapid breath gradually calm.

Locked in an embrace, I was afraid to let him go. I could not bear the pain. I whispered in his ear, "We must find a way to break this spell."

After what felt like an eternity, Kai pulled back.

"I could not bear it if you were harmed. This is incredibly complicated. She is a dangerous woman."

I looked him in the eyes. "Have you ever known me to abandon anyone or anything in danger? There is no way I could walk away from this." My voice softened. "As for me walking away from you, it's inconceivable. I knew that the first time I looked into your eyes."

"You could change your mind."

"No, I don't think I could."

A smile flickered across Kai's face before he kissed me softly. He spoke in a hushed voice. "How was I lucky enough to find you?"

CHAPTER 22

WE STAYED IN the loft and talked. Kai revealed everything about Rosella and the curse as the full moon pulsed above us. Bright stars dappled the sky like a field of fireflies.

"Ben thinks I should accept the offer to work for Rosella. She will lift my curse if I do. I could spy on her from inside the compound."

Fear swirled in my gut. Fidgeting with my necklace, I murmured, "Do you think that's a good idea?"

"I can't decide. Working for her goes against my moral fiber, but working inside the compound could help us find a way to defeat her."

Kai stroked my hair from head to waist, softly listing the pros and cons of that decision. I felt safe and complete in his arms, listening to the soft hum of his voice, and had difficulty concentrating as my thoughts drifted in and out like swirling fog.

I awoke sluggishly to the melodious sound of birds singing their dawn chorus. When I opened my eyes, the silver shine of the moon had been replaced by the sun's warm, golden glow.

Kai and I were intertwined. Trying not to disturb him, I eased over until I could see his face. Kai stirred, opened his eyes with a flutter, and blinked to gain clarity.

His eyes moved down to my face. A sly grin emerged. "This is a nice surprise. Good morning, my love," he said groggily.

I snuggled into his warmth. "Good morning indeed."

He kissed the top of my head and cradled me against him.

"Lily, you can still leave. You know I would understand. This is much more than you bargained for." He sounded grave.

"I'm not going to change my mind," I retorted.

"Are you sure?"

I rolled my eyes, and he finally seemed to relax.

"I'm so happy I revealed my secret to you. I love you and want to share everything with you. Come with me," he said, lacing his fingers with mine. I had no time to absorb his declaration of love before he added, "I want to show you something."

※ ※ ※

We exited the cabin and walked hand in hand down the path by the river. I didn't know who else was in the house, but it was early enough that I didn't feel rude leaving.

My pace slowed when we reached the cave entrance. A mix of emotions arose—fear, excitement, anger.

Kai slipped through the narrow crack, and I followed, quietly taking in the details of the massive cave before me. I expected it to be daunting, like before, but it had the opposite effect this time. It was beautiful.

Water trickled down the far walls, flowing over rocks and into a pool that fed a stream. Sunlight creeping through openings at the top of the cavern made the water sparkle like crystal. A rich, earthy smell filled the air. I stood with my hands clasped in front of me to hide my tremors.

"Lily, are you all right?"

"Yes, I'm fine," I said, trying to sound self-assured.

With a spring in his step, Kai rolled aside a man-sized boulder to reveal a passage.

"This way." He took my hand and stepped through.

The natural cave entrance was beautiful, but this cave was stunning and twice the size. Solid rock walls surrounded tall, cavernous ceilings.

Natural light drifted in from various holes in the rock, and a large waterfall cascaded down one side, landing in the same underground stream as at the entrance. A fireplace made of river rocks dominated the back wall.

The room was furnished in a modern style. The builder had cleverly incorporated the natural rock by carving out bookshelves, storage, and seating. I expected the cave to be dark and stagnant, but the renovations transformed it into a light, comfortable home. It had a tranquil feeling, supported by the soothing splashes from the waterfall. The entire place was striking.

"Welcome to my home."

"It's . . ." I had no words. "How?" was all I managed.

Kai's eyes brightened. "Ben is a wiz; he did all the electrical work. Tate and I installed the plumbing. The kitchen, laundry room, and bathrooms are fully equipped. Jon did most of the interior designs, and we worked together on the furnishings. We added two rooms last year for Tanja and her two daughters."

"Are they the ones with the"—I waved my finger in a circle—"noses?"

Kai's eyes dropped, as did his voice. "Yes."

I hoped I hadn't offended him.

"Where is everyone?"

"It is still the full moon. During the full moon, we often take the opportunity to visit our families, shop, and seek out some kind of normalcy."

"Oh. How many people live here?"

"Right now, seven. The number has varied through the years."

"Why?"

He inhaled deeply. I tried to determine whether he was frustrated or reluctant. "A few of them gave in. They went back to work for Rosella to be free of the curse."

"Do you see them anymore?"

His expression grew puzzled. "Sometimes. Why do you ask?"

"Are they happy?"

He stared blankly.

"With their decision?" I clarified.

"I don't know."

"You should ask them," I said, sounding more direct than I intended. "Maybe it will help you make your decision."

He considered what I said. "Maybe I should. I should." He nodded, then met my gaze. "Shall I show you my room?"

As I followed him into his alcove, I surveyed the space. All the furniture was crafted from natural wood, and the room felt appropriately rugged and manly. A smaller stone fireplace made it cozy. The paper boat I had made was on his nightstand.

I picked up the boat. "You saved it."

"Of course. It reminds me of you."

He pressed his lips to my forehead. My heart thudded against my chest as he moved to my mouth and kissed me tenderly. He tasted like sweet tea and smelled musky, intoxicating. I found it hard to control myself. I slipped my hands under the back of his shirt, my fingers exploring his warm, smooth bare skin. His muscles flexed under my fingertips. His sturdy build seemed indestructible.

We started moving with urgency. Kai's hands skimmed across my body, a current of electricity following his touch. He dragged his warm tongue down my neck and firmly cupped my backside, pulling me closer to him. I felt his hardness, and a moan escaped me.

I shivered, yelling, *Stop!* in my head, but I didn't slow my actions. Desire ruled my actions. *He said he wanted to share everything with me. Could this be what he meant?* I found the courage to pull back. "Wait, please wait," I panted. My rapid breaths filled my ears. I resisted the urge to run out of the room.

"What is it? What is wrong?"

I diverted my eyes to the floor. My stomach tightened.

"Lily, talk to me."

"I just got nervous." My eyes welled up. "Sorry, it just got so real.

I mean, I have never been involved with . . ." Heat rose everywhere. "With anyone. You are older, more experienced. I'm not sure what you're expecting." I feared I sounded childish.

Kai chuckled, which was not the reaction I was expecting. "Do you really think that is why I brought you here?" He chuckled again. "Lily, my love, I brought you here because I want you to know everything about me. Everything means no more lies. I will not lie to you, ever."

"I'm so sorry," I said with a pang of guilt. "I think I was more afraid of what I was feeling and doing."

"You have no reason to be sorry. This"—he pointed a finger back and forth between us—"is all new to me too. I'm as scared as you are."

"Really?"

"Really," he assured me. "I have never felt like this before. You ignited my heart."

"I know the feeling."

"When I told you it would be complicated, I'm sure you never dreamed of how complicated I really meant."

CHAPTER 23

IT HAD BEEN five days since Kai told me about the curse. Five days since I'd pledged to fight for him. Five days, and my mind hadn't quieted. I stared blankly at my computer, wondering what was wrong with me. What had changed in me? The vehement desire to harm Rosella raged inside. I used to avoid risky behavior, but now I just wanted to fight.

I avoided Berly all week, telling her I had a ton of homework. She was observant and would notice my erratic behavior. I didn't want her asking questions, because I would have a hard time lying to her.

I trudged through the snow to the scarcely populated library, choosing a table in the back corner for privacy. I was in no mood for small talk.

After a few hours, the lights flickered above my head, returning me to the present. I leaned back and stretched my neck. Nate was sitting at a table across the room, surrounded by papers. He had one pen behind his ear and another in his hand. He tapped it nervously on the table. I got the feeling he was either studying intently or having a hard time grasping the material. He dropped the pen and placed both hands over his face. I figured my second assumption was correct. He took an exasperated breath and dropped his hands. When he spotted me, a grin stretched across his troubled face, transforming him into the friendly Nate I was familiar with.

He popped up and strolled over to my table. "Hi, Lily. How was your holiday?"

"Good, and yours?"

"It was too fast. I could have used another week." His eyes looked incredibly blue in this light. He had let his hair grow longer. It looked good. My life would have been much simpler if I had fallen for him instead of Kai.

"What are you working on?" I asked.

"Studying for a bio exam. What about you?"

"I'm catching up on some homework." I didn't add that I had finished an hour ago and was wasting time because I wanted to be alone. But now it was time to escape.

I glanced at my watch. "I had better get going."

"Wait, it's dark. I'll walk you to your dorm to make sure you're safe."

We walked in awkward silence until Nate launched into a story about a bear chasing him and his cousin in the woods over break. After we reached the dorms, I leaned against the doorframe, waiting for him to finish his animated story. Nate wasn't as tall as Kai, but he was close. I had to tilt my head back to watch his expressions. I fidgeted with the cool stone in my pocket. He placed his hand on the wall beside my head and finished his story.

"That is incredible. I'm glad you're all right." I ducked under his arm. "Thanks for the escort." I slipped inside, praying Aspen wasn't visiting.

Berly was on the phone, so I hurried into the bathroom. She was under the covers when I returned. I slipped into bed and turned out the light.

She yawned loudly. "I feel like I haven't seen you all week."

"I know. It's been crazy. The teachers are piling it on. I don't think I'll ever get caught up." In fact, I was way ahead of my schoolwork.

"They always do before final exams. I can't believe there are only three weeks left. Martin wants me to go to England with him during the break."

"Are you going?" I shrieked.

"Yeah, I'm flying in after Christmas to stay with him through New Year's. Him meeting my parents over break kind of cemented our . . . thing," she said, gesturing vaguely.

I admired her self-assurance.

"It sounds like you two are getting serious."

"You could say that. How's it going with Kai?"

I suddenly wanted to tell her about Kai, the curse, and everything that had happened, but I bit my lip. This was not my secret to tell, and I didn't want to jeopardize our friendship.

"It's good. Complicated, but good."

CHAPTER 24

I PACED BY THE stone wall, waiting for Kai. Time loomed over me like a guillotine. This would be my first time seeing Kai in his cursed form since the day I fainted in the cave. Kai would not be released from this form for four more hours, but he wanted to visit his grandmother, the person he trusted more than any other.

Kai climbed out the truck and took my hands in his. He wore his uniform and dark sunglasses. I'd never noticed the navy-blue scarf he wore around his neck and tucked under his collar. He kissed the back of my hand and my cheek.

His hands were shaking. "Are you sure you want to do this, Lily?"

"Yes, I'm sure. Why?"

"I'm nervous about you seeing me like this. I worry you might faint again, or worse, you might change your mind."

I took his hand. "I see more of you than what's on the outside. But I must understand. I have to get used to it, just as you did, until we figure a way to end it."

"I could end it by going to work for Rosella."

"That's not the safe option."

Kai's hand trembled when he lowered his sunglasses. His eyes had thin vertical pupils like a cat's, surrounded by emerald green with streaks of gold marbling. They looked like large glass marbles.

His voice was low, tone uncertain.

"Do I scare you? I understand if you need to take a moment—or even leave."

I squeezed his hand. "It will take a lot more than this to keep me away from you."

He removed the scarf, revealing the green scales on his chest and neck, and flinched when I brushed my fingers across them. I felt his heartbeat beneath the cold, pebbly surface. His eyes locked onto mine, and I knew for certain: my feelings had not changed for him.

"This is not who you are. This is what *she* did to you. I still see the person I fell in love with."

He closed his eyes, and when he opened them again, they were full of tears. "I'm so sorry." He buried his face in his hands. It hurt to see him this way.

"I'm not."

* * *

A radiant fire burned in Grandmother Kateri's fireplace, dispersing orange hues across the rich cherrywood floors. The sun dropped gradually into the horizon, filtering through the stained glass and illuminating the room in a rainbow of color.

Grandmother Kateri handed me a cup of coffee and placed her hand on my knee. Her deep-set eyes studied my face. The silence in the room was unnerving. I placed the coffee on the table for fear my hand would start shaking. Kai excused himself.

Grandmother Kateri leaned toward me with a knowing look after he left.

"I knew you could see more than what was before you the moment I met you. Thank you for believing in my grandson and fighting against this injustice. Most of all, for loving him for who he is, not fearing him for what someone did to him."

I was flattered into silence, then hesitantly raised my eyes to meet hers. "This is more than just fighting for him. I feel like we're connected on a whole different level. I don't want to live without him."

She patted my shoulder. "That is why you are here, my sweet. The spirits have a plan."

Kai returned to the room. "What are you two talking about?"

Grandmother waved him off. "It is only girl talk; you would not be interested." She winked in my direction.

"Grandmother, Rosella wants me to come work for her."

"And?"

"She would lift my curse. It would be better for Lily and me."

She stirred her coffee, and silent seconds ticked past. "Do you really think that would remove the danger"—she paused—"or plant you deeper in danger?"

Kai dropped his head and shook it. "I don't know."

"It is good to keep your friends close and your enemies closer. But Rosella is a dangerous enemy. That will be a tough decision. What does Sakari think about it?"

"She is not talking to me."

"Who?" I asked.

Kai sighed. "My mother."

"Why isn't she talking to you?"

"She doesn't agree with me dating you. She thinks I'm being selfish, foolish. That I'm putting you in danger."

Heat flushed my body.

"Sometimes I think she is right," he muttered.

Grandmother let out a deep cackle. "Son, you know what is right for you and what is worth fighting for. The spirits have a plan. Give her time; she will come around. Right now, we need to figure out a way to stop Rosella for good. Tell me what you and the boys have been working on."

CHAPTER 25

THE WEEK BEFORE final exams was called "dead week" for a good reason. No matter how much I studied, it never felt like enough. It totally drained me. I had not seen Kai all week, although my mind never left him for long. I was more anxious about being away from him than about my exams.

I shuffled down the hall past expressionless students dressed in comfy sweats. I felt the heightened irritability and saw the sleep deprivation. The library was an extended torture zone, like solitary confinement littered with coffee cups, energy drinks, and junk food. Everyone seemed to exist in a deep fog.

Procrastinating from studying, I started researching black magic, curses, mind control—anything that would help us break the curse. The message coming through loud and clear in each article was that power used for selfish purposes was associated with the devil or other evil spirits. Grandmother Kateri was right. Rosella was dangerous.

On Thursday, our professor in Ecological Restoration told my lab group that we had scored an A on our project. Thanks to Kai's measuring system, my grade was secure. I could get a C on the final and still earn an A in the class—not that I would settle for a C.

After finishing my paper for Environmental History, I was looking forward to soccer practice. Brooklyn ran over to me when I stepped into the gym.

"Hey, girl. I haven't seen you all week. How's everything?"

"Insane," I answered honestly. "Finals, study groups, papers due. I'm mentally exhausted."

"I'm excited for practice. It always clears my head."

Aspen appeared at her side and unceremoniously asked, "Hi, Lily, how's it going with you and Kai?"

I wanted to say something snarky but resisted. "Good. He's great."

"Have you seen Nate and Troy lately?"

"No, why?"

"We're going to Poncho's for margaritas. I wanted to ask them to come."

"Sounds fun."

Aspen's eyes narrowed. "Do . . . you want to come?"

Her hesitation told me all I needed to know.

"No, I have plans with Kai. Thanks anyway."

Her expression changed instantly. The coach blew the whistle. I was glad for the distraction.

CHAPTER 26

I STROLLED TO THE parking lot, keeping my eyes on the wet sidewalk. The snow was no longer a feather-white blanket of down covering the ground. It had transformed into gray slush, matching my mood. Kai was introducing me to his mother. He also planned to introduce me to the other cursed people living in the cave. I wanted to show I could handle it but worried about how I would come across.

Kai jumped out of his truck, wearing a dazzling grin and his dark glasses. I picked up my pace. He caught me in his arms, lifting me while we kissed. I loved this routine.

"I missed you."

"I missed you too," I said. My jittery voice betrayed me.

"Are you nervous?"

I sighed.

"It will be fine. She needs to meet you, to understand what I love about you. And to see how strong you are."

I wasn't sure he was right. My nails were already bitten to the quick, and my pulse would not calm. We were both silent for much of the drive.

"Do you think this is a mistake?" he finally asked, sounding distressed.

"What if she doesn't like me?"

"Lily, you have it all wrong. She's not iffy about liking you or not. She is only concerned with your safety."

When we arrived at Grandmother Kateri's house, I lingered by the truck, rubbing the polished stone in my pocket. Kai hugged me from behind and murmured, "You are a part of me. She will love you." It warmed me that he was worried about my discomfort.

Kai's face lit up when his grandmother opened the door, accompanied by his mother. He moved his hand to the small of my back as we greeted them.

Kai kissed his grandmother on each cheek. "My guiding star, it is always good to see you."

Laugh lines spread from the corners of her eyes. "My heart."

He embraced his mother with a tender hug and kissed each cheek. "Mother, it's been too long. I have missed you."

His mother looked at him with heavy eyes. "My treasure, I miss this face."

I awkwardly kissed Grandmother Kateri's cheek and said, "It's good to see you again."

Then Kai gripped my shoulders and presented me.

"Mother, this is Liliana Swan Makris. Lily, I would like to introduce you to my mother, Sakari."

I held my breath as her eyes met mine. Her face was somber, guarded; she seemed determined to come across as unworried. She had the same high cheekbones as Kai, but her face was rounder, and her eyes were a tender golden brown.

Sweetness dripped from her voice. "You are beautiful, like the swan."

"Thank you. I am so happy to meet you."

Grandmother Kateri motioned for us to sit. "Let us talk."

Kai settled next to me, taking my hand in his and removing his sunglasses with the other. I was getting used to the marbled look of his eyes, but the shiny scales on his neck and chest still had an impact.

"Mother, I know you think this is wrong. I want you to understand why Lily means so much to me. I was a fool to think I could hide this curse from her, but I have told her everything. She has accepted it. She has accepted me as I am, cursed. I have never felt this way before. She is my world. She has renewed my hope."

"Does she know the danger you are putting her in?" Sakari snapped.

"She does." His voice rose. "She understands."

She turned to me. "Are you willing to live the rest of your life in hiding, carrying the burden of a curse lingering over your head? Never living a normal life again? What will you tell your parents?" she demanded. "Look what Rosella has done to my beautiful son. Think of what she could do to your lovely face. She will curse you too if you are not careful."

Kai stared at her sullenly.

"This was my choice!" I protested. "Kai gave me every opportunity to back out, to leave and never look back. I chose to stay. I choose to stay! I love him. I want to fight for him, fight for us." I didn't recognize the fierceness in my voice. The room fell silent, and I found myself breathing rapidly.

Kai rested his hand on my back and kissed my cheek. Grandmother Kateri's eyes twinkled.

A half smile appeared on Sakari's face. It was the first trace of happiness she had shown. It was genuine, real, and it brightened her essence.

"Are you sure about this?"

I nodded yes.

"I see," she said, looking down. She seemed softer now.

Thankfully, Grandmother Kateri changed the subject. "Any progress on weakening Rosella's power?"

Kai sat forward. "Jace found some odd piping alongside the buildings. He thinks she may be pumping gas through it. We're going to test the air. Elan is collecting samples of the water supplies in the mines and quarry for testing too. Rosella has been visiting the mines more than normal. We are worried she is up to something."

Grandmother probed, "What about your other decision?"

Kai licked his lips. "About working for Rosella?"

She nodded, saying, "I consider that the easy way out. I'm not sure I agree with it."

Kai dropped his head. "It is easier for Lily and me. We are considering how valuable it would be to have someone working on the inside."

We? Am I included in that we? I suspected I was not.

Sakari looked shocked. "You have people on the inside! Jace controls the gate towers. Elan works in the mines. I work in the payroll office for the entire compound."

"I know, but it is not enough. We must destroy her power before she finds a way to harness more. Ben thinks I should do it, Tate thinks I shouldn't, and Jon is undecided."

"This is a bad idea. You need to stay far away from her."

I wondered whether Sakari was speaking about Rosella or me.

"We have to try something," Kai said heatedly.

Grandmother cleared her throat. "Kai, if you want to do this to find a way to break the spell, I agree. If you want to do this so you can date Lily openly, I disagree. Rosella will control your life, your schedule. She is obsessed with power, and working for her will be dangerous for both of you."

"I understand. I will weigh my decision carefully."

"The spirits will guide you."

As Kai shared the rest of the details with them, Sakari continued to study me from across the room. I was too nervous to add much to the conversation and relieved when Kai suggested we leave.

We stood.

"Thank you, Mother, Grandmother. We will talk again soon."

"Good to meet you, Lily. And please be careful, my son."

CHAPTER 27

THE WIND WAS biting on the short walk back to the truck. Kai and I hopped in and snuggled together while the truck warmed. Kai smelled intoxicating. My hands were tangled in his hair, and his explored my back. I closed my eyes and forgot all about the curse—until my finger brushed the cool scales on his neck. I leaned back in my seat with a sigh.

"Do you think she liked me? Did we convince her we're doing the right thing?"

"I think she'll come around. Mother is rightfully scared for the both of us. When you stood up for me, for us, it was the first time in years I have seen a spark of happiness in her eyes. I love you so much."

"I love you too." I caught my breath. In the moment, I yearned for the easy way out.

"Are you ready to meet my other roommates?"

I nodded nervously. It had to be easier than meeting his mother.

***

The cave entrance was much darker than before without sunlight filtering in, but Kai walked surefootedly across the ground, guiding my way.

The main room was well lit by the raging fire in the fireplace and the various lamps spread around the room. Ben entered first. He looked the same, except bees clung to his arms and neck.

"Hi, Lily, welcome to our home."

I hesitantly shook his hand.

"Don't worry. They won't bother you unless you provoke them."

"Good to know."

The man named Tate clopped into the room, the sound coming from his cloven hooves. Kai placed his hand on the small of my back.

"Tate, this is Lily. Lily, this is Tate."

"Nice to meet you." Tate's hand quivered when he extended it, and his cheeks were bright red. He didn't seem comfortable with an outsider seeing him this way.

"Nice to meet you too."

Kai called out. "Jon, Tanja, Sky, Mia, I would like to introduce you to my girlfriend, Lily."

The two little girls with pig features skipped into the room, seeming utterly unself-conscious. Their mother shuffled in behind them, bearing the same piglike features. "Wait up, girls. We don't want to scare her."

I knelt so I was eye level with the girls.

"Hi, I'm Lily. Do you remember me?"

The smaller girl looked up to her mother. "Is she a stranger?"

"No, Mia."

"Is she danger?" Mia asked coolly.

"She is Kai's friend."

"Good." With that, Mia ran over and hugged my neck. "I'm Mia, and that's Sky, my sister, and that's my mom. We don't have many friends. Would you like to be my friend?"

"Of course."

She hugged me again.

"Mia, give her some space. Hi, I'm Tanja."

"Nice to meet you."

Kai helped me to my feet as Jon stepped into the room. He was wearing a cable-knit beanie, and I wondered what could be hiding under there since I saw no sign of the curse's effects on him. "Lily, this is Jon. Jon, Lily."

Jon extended his hand. "Pleasure to meet you." He chuckled at my expression as I shook his hand. He followed up by pulling off his beanie and pushing up a sleeve. Fur covered his arm. He pointed to his ears. "Wolf ears and arms. It's not so bad, easily hidden with a hat and long sleeves. It's ironic, when you think about it. This goes away during the full moon. Do you think that makes me an un-werewolf?"

He winked, and I knew straightaway that I was going to like him.

I wondered why Rosella's curse took so many different forms. The effect on Ben, for instance, seemed entirely different. She hadn't messed with his features. Maybe Rosella cursed him with some kind of pheromone that attracted bees. Maybe there was a Tower of Babel thing going on.

One thing they had in common was that the natural magic of the full moon and the synchronicity of 11:11 weakened the curse's hold, so her power could not be but so strong. *But what damage could she do if she becomes stronger?*

We settled in the great room, and each person began sharing the tale that led to their curse. Tanja excused herself to put the girls to bed.

I asked them the same questions I had asked Kai. "Do you know if anyone who went to work for Rosella is happy with their decision? Are they safe?"

A lively debate erupted, and I found it hard to keep up with the names of people I'd never met.

"Anita's brother is glad to be rid of the curse but unhappy working for that witch," Jon said bluntly.

"What about Jason or River? Has anyone talked to them?" Kai asked.

No one had.

"What do you think about Kai going to work for Rosella?" I boldly asked.

"I think we need a spy inside the fortress if we want to defeat her," Ben stated with conviction.

Tate shook his head. "I don't like it. I wouldn't want to be anywhere near her."

"Her influence does not work on me. I will just have to fake that it does."

"Her curse still worked on you. You are not immune, Kai!" Tate's alarmed voice interjected.

"Has anyone gone to work for her and changed their mind? Did she replace the curse or worse?" I asked. No one answered; apparently, this was unknown territory.

Tate shook his legs a few times. I did a double-take and realized they had become human legs. Kai shivered, and Ben stood up. The bees were gone.

"Ah," he sighed, rubbing his neck. "It's finally 10:10."

They would be curse-free for the next two hours.

Jon popped his beanie back on. "We have a lot to think about. This doesn't have to be decided tonight. I'm going out for a burger. Does anyone want to join me?"

The three of them left Kai and me to our own devices. Kai poured me a glass of wine and opened a beer for himself, then placed one sturdy arm around my waist. Dropping my head on his shoulder, I asked, "What do you think Rosella would do if she caught you working undercover?"

"I hope we never have to find out."

Kai's reply did nothing to assuage my worries.

CHAPTER 28

THE NEXT WEEK, when finals stormed upon me, I fidgeted constantly with the heart-shaped stone in my pocket. The immense pressure to close the semester with good grades was taking its toll on the students. Lack of sleep, excessive stress, and anxiety had them resembling the pukwudgies with their stony, stern expressions.

A pall of angst hung over the classroom where I took my last exam. The clock ticked a constant reminder that time was running out. Then, when I answered the final question, a wave of relief hit me. I was done! I glanced around the room in triumph. Many students still wore tormented expressions as they hunched over their papers.

My head cleared as I crossed the campus toward the parking lot. The butterflies in my stomach came from knowing Kai was on his way. I was free, and it was a full moon. Kai would be curse-free for the next three days, which meant we would have two full days together before I flew home for the Christmas break. The thought of it made me dizzy.

My heart thumped unsteadily when his dazzling face came into view. I jumped into the truck. As he wrapped his arms around me, I clung to him like a magnet.

"Hi, my love. How did your exams go?"

"Nerve racking, just as I expected." His manly musk overtook my senses. "I am so glad they're over. And thank goodness it's a full moon!"

Kai's smile faded.

"Did I say something wrong?"

"The curse," he muttered. "This is no way to live."

I was a little frustrated that he kept returning to something I did not consider an obstacle to our relationship as a whole. I accepted him for who he was, curse or no curse.

"Tell me what you learned about Rosella this week," I asked, eager to get him talking again.

"Jace tested the air and found traces of powder in it. He also mentioned that Rosella has erected a new warehouse on the property over the last few months. Those things might be related to the uptick in production she's been demanding."

"Didn't you say she blew some black tourmaline powder at you before she ordered you to work for her?"

He nodded, looking thoughtful. "Perhaps that warehouse is the key. Ben is working on upping our surveillance to get a closer look."

On the path to the cave entrance, a deep growl sounded behind us. Kai turned to the noise and instinctively pushed me behind him. A black bear stood on the trail, growling and exposing its teeth. Kai stepped slowly backward, guiding me with one hand and waving the other in the air.

"Do not turn your back or run, or he will charge. Wave your arms so you look bigger."

I cautiously stepped back, waving my hands over my head. The bear stood on its hind legs and sniffed the air. I took a few more steps back. The bear dropped to all fours and made a chuffing noise as it ambled into the trees.

"Now, Lily, go! Get to the cave."

When I turned to run, one of my legs slipped into the river, and I landed on my stomach. I hadn't been paying attention to the trail when I'd backed up. Kai gripped my elbow to help me up, never taking his eyes off the bear, then guided me to the cave entrance. As we slipped inside, adrenaline surged through me. I now fully understood why Nate had been so animated when he told me about his bear encounter.

Kai rested his hands on the sides of my face. "Are you okay?"

"A little muddy, but I'm okay." I smothered a laugh. "One of the dangers of the forest?"

"Yes, my love. I tried to warn you."

"You're fearless. You didn't even flinch. I was all weak kneed and fell into the river."

"It's part of my job," he said with a wink.

We stepped into the great room, and Ben leaped out of his chair. "Good, you're here. Come see how I adjusted the cameras."

Gesturing to my wet clothes and muddy hands, I asked, "Do you mind if I clean up?"

"Please use my room," Kai offered.

I emerged from the shower to find a pile of clothes neatly folded on the bed. The joggers were a bit long, so I rolled them at the waist and tied the T-shirt in the back. Kai's clothes smelled like detergent and something musky, noticeably masculine.

I returned to the great room feeling completely refreshed. My mouth watered at the smell of garlic.

Kai rose and kissed me on the cheek.

"Just the sight of you makes my heart beat wildly. Now it's my turn to rid myself of this grunge. I'll be back in a few."

I went to the kitchen to offer my help. Jon was stirring a large pot on the stove.

"This is my famous sauce," he said with a mysterious undertone.

"It smells delicious. What can I do to help?"

"Can you chop a salad and help with the garlic bread?"

Jon rattled on about the different types of tomatoes needed to make the perfect sauce, then handed me a glass of red wine. "You have to drink wine when you cook Italian."

"I shall comply."

We clinked our glasses. "Cheers."

Giggles accompanied the return of the girls about fifteen

minutes later.

"Well, there you are. I was wondering where you were," I said. They ran in from the great room and hugged me from both sides.

Mia, the talker, said, "We spent the day with our dad. Do you want to meet him?"

"Of course. Let me wash my hands."

Jon and I left the kitchen as Kai returned from his room, looking sharp with wet hair and crisp, clean clothes. My chest rose in a long, deep breath as I soaked in his raw beauty. My eyes were glued to Kai when Sky took my hand.

"Daddy, this is Lily."

I turned to greet him. Sky's dad had a caring face, and I wondered if he suffered the same affliction as the rest of his family or if it took a different form. Then I shook away the thought and addressed him human to human.

"Hi, I'm Lily."

He grabbed my hand, pulling me toward him for a one-armed hug.

"I'm Elan. Thank you for being so kind to my family."

I was dazed by his comment.

Kai moved quickly to my side. A pleasant, lemony aroma drifted around me when he slid his arm around my waist. "She is kind. That is what first attracted me to her."

Tate came into the room with his brothers, Wade and Jace. Wade bounced over to me for a hug. "Hey, Lily, so good to see you again." His voice was full of life. "This is my other brother, Jace."

"Nice to meet you, Jace." Jace only nodded in my direction. He seemed shy, reserved, and businesslike, with shorter hair than his brothers. I got the feeling he was a listener.

The volume rose as we sat down to dinner. Clinking, pouring, crunching, and the rich sound of laughter ringing out made the place feel even warmer than usual.

Wade leaned toward me. "I passed the test. I applied for the truck job at the quarry and start in January, after my birthday." Excitement danced in his eyes.

"Congratulations," I said genuinely.

After dinner, conversation continued flowing like the wine. I settled on the floor with the girls, helping them weave threads into bracelets and necklaces. Tanja, sitting with her husband, offered us suggestions and tips.

"The water tested from the compound came up clean," Elan said.

Kai asked Jace, "What about the air?"

"I think I found a way to block it, but it's not going to be easy with all her spies around."

"What about the new building?" I asked.

"It appears to be empty," Ben said. "I'm assuming she thought she'd be filling it up with black tourmaline."

"Rosella is demanding we dig for more, but we're only finding coal. It's making her anxious," Elan said.

Wade tapped my arm. "I'll find out for sure what Rosella is doing in that warehouse after I start my job," he said smugly.

The talk about work dropped off after that. I made eye contact with Kai across the room, and he winked. Jon refilled my wine while I focused on completing a bracelet.

Pleased with my work, I placed the finished pieces on the table. My legs were unsteady when I stood to join Kai on the couch. He held out his hand as I approached, and I leaned in for a kiss and snuggled down beside him. His warmth was rewarding.

Kai touched his head to mine. "Legs a little wobbly, my love?"

"I think I sat too long on the stone floor. The wine might have a little to do with it," I giggled.

With his face so close, it felt like we were in our own bubble.

"I thank the gods every day that you came into my life. I can't imagine why you would stay with me after you learned of this horrid curse, but I'm glad you did. You are brave. You never looked at me like I'm hideous."

"I see you, all of you."

He placed his finger under my chin. "Stay here with me tonight. I would love to wake up with you in my arms again."

At first, I tensed up, but the serenity in his eyes calmed my fears.

"Of course. I would love to."

The activity in the room had dwindled, and people were peeling off to their separate areas, so Kai and I retreated to his room.

He lit the fireplace. The crackling fire cast orange light across the rock. Before he added more logs to the fire, he handed me a new toothbrush.

"Thank you."

My mind raced along with my heart as we settled into bed. The other night, we'd slept together by accident. Tonight, it was by choice. *What if he expects more from me than I'm ready for?*

I rested my head on his chest. His scent was intoxicating.

"Relax. I can feel your pulse pounding," Kai said quietly. I concentrated on calming my breathing. "Trust me, you are safe with me. I do not want you to feel uncomfortable. Plus, I have no idea what Rosella has done to my DNA. I would never risk anything like that."

"Have you ever . . . you know?"

"No, I have never wanted to." His sincerity made me trust what he said. "Until now." He blushed. "My father, a firefighter, was killed on duty when I was fifteen. I was mad, depressed, irritated with the world. I was not good company. I avoided relationships. I couldn't bear being hurt again, and then, for the last two years, I've lived with this curse."

"I'm sorry to hear about your father. I haven't either," I sheepishly admitted. "Or wanted to, until now."

In his embrace, I watched the fire reflect in his eyes. My attraction to him was like nothing I had ever imagined. My heart ached for him; his pain felt like my pain. I did not want him to suffer anymore. I was more determined than ever to break this curse, to help save him. I just didn't know how.

CHAPTER 29

I AWOKE DISORIENTED. The room was dark and unfamiliar and smelled like wood and minerals. I couldn't push the fog from my brain until Kai stirred. He slowly opened his eyes, unfolding a sweet grin. A warm feeling washed over me like a fluffy down blanket. He pulled me close and kissed me with passion and urgency. After a bit, my head moved to his shoulder. Our hair was twisted together, draped across his chest.

"Good morning, my love," he said.

"Good morning, my heart." I pointed to our hair. "It looks like the yin and yang symbol."

Kai glanced at where I was pointing. "So it does, the symbol of perfect harmony."

He lightly rubbed his fingertips up and down the length of my back, underneath my T-shirt, sending chills down my body. He was staring at the ceiling.

"You, my love, are the yin to my yang. I wish I could wake up with you every morning."

I moved up to kiss him. "If you do not stop rubbing my back like that, we will never get out of this bed."

"Tempting. But we have a lot to do today."

"What are we doing?" I reluctantly asked, selfishly wanting more time together.

"We are trailing Rosella."

I gulped. "Will it be safe?"

"She will not even know we are near." When I stood, Kai's eyes went to my bare legs. "First, we need to get you some clothes."

※ ※ ※

Kai drove me back to campus so I could change my clothes and pack a bag. Thankfully, campus wouldn't be shutting down for a few more days.

Back in the truck, I asked, "Do you think Rosella is obsessed with power, control, or money?"

"I think she is driven by greed. She tasted power and wants more. She gained control of a few people and wants more. She stole a fortune and wants more."

"Greed. Interesting. One of the seven deadly sins. As my grandfather used to say, the root of all evil. What do you think she ultimately wants? Why the warehouse and the sudden drive for more black tourmaline?"

"I don't know." He seemed too distracted to offer more, so I fell silent.

Kai parked at the bottom of the mountain, near the mansion compound. We waited until a long black sedan rolled out of the gate and then followed at a safe distance on the short trip down to the mines. Kai parked off the road before the gravel lot, and we hurried along the tall, dark fence. I shivered in the cold as gravel crunched beneath our feet. Kai stopped abruptly, steadying me with his hand when we heard voices on the other side of the fence.

"Have you been successful?" the hateful woman demanded. Her voice was cold and condescending.

"Not yet, ma'am. It will take time. We must dig deeper." It was Elan's voice.

"When you do—which I know you will because your job depends on it—I expect you will inform me, pronto."

"Yes ma'am."

"I don't care if you must work all night and day. Find my tourmaline! Don't disappoint me." I heard the snap of fingers. "Don't just stand there. Move."

Kai grabbed my elbow and hurried back to the truck, pulling me along with him.

"Elan was right. She is impatient. As far as I know, she has never shown this level of urgency. She must be planning something."

We followed Rosella downtown, where she stopped at the Salty Swan. One of her bodyguards went inside and came out with two heavy-looking totes.

"It looks like she resorted to purchasing black tourmaline."

"Do you think we should ask Wanda to take it off the shelf? Make it unavailable for her?" I asked.

"We could, but it might put Wanda in danger. Rosella will curse her if she gets mad enough. Besides, Rosella would find another source."

Next, we followed the woman to Mirror Lake. She pulled to the front of the parking lot, and we stopped back near the restrooms. Rosella marched out onto the viewing dock, her bodyguards trailing behind.

"I do not think we can get close enough to hear what she is saying without her recognizing me."

"I'll go." The words were out of my mouth before I realized what I was saying.

"What? It is not safe."

"Think about it: she doesn't know me. She only saw the back of my head, briefly. I will tuck my hair under my coat and wear my beanie."

"Are you sure?" Kai's voice cracked.

I patted his hand. "Don't worry. I'll be fine." I struggled to believe my own words. When I reached the walkway, I glanced back at Kai's perfect face, and a deep ache throbbed in my gut. *How could she do this to him? To all of them?*

Unfortunately, the viewing platform was not crowded. The most popular times for viewing were sunrise and sunset. I had to think she chose this off time on purpose. With the cold wind whipping across the lake, I zipped my jacket higher and walked close to a family, acting like I was a part of their group. I kept one eye on Rosella and another on the walkway. I assumed she was meeting someone.

Rosella moved to the far edge of the platform, away from other people. Her mouth moved. I couldn't hear what she said but sensed from the beat of the words that she was chanting. She sprinkled some powder into the lake, snapped her fingers, and whirled around to leave. I froze when she looked directly at me. Her dark eyes resembled those of a raven. I remembered Kai had said her eyes locked onto her victims like a missile. It felt more like a look from Medusa. She swept past me. Her guards shuffled dutifully behind her.

I waited until she was at her car before I headed back to Kai. The sedan pulled away before I made it off the platform.

The worried uncertainty in Kai's expression as he jumped out of the truck made him look younger. He cupped my elbows in his hands. "Did she see you?"

"Yes, but she seemed to have no idea who I was. She chanted some words and spread powder in the water. I'm assuming it's the same powder she's been using for mind control." I kept my voice even, trying to shake the nausea prompted by my eye contact with that evil woman.

Kai tugged me to him and tightened his arms around my shoulders. I felt his chest expand with each breath. "I hate her. I don't want her to harm you."

I slipped my arms around his waist.

"I'm fine." Something occurred to me and made me feel queasier. "Do you think she's contaminating the lakes and the city's water supply to gain more control?"

Kai shook his head. "The village water supply comes from Lake Placid. Mirror Lake is small in comparison."

"Maybe she's testing a theory. Maybe that's why she's desperate for black tourmaline."

"We need to tell the others about this. Let's go."

I gripped the grab bar to pull myself into the truck just as a crow landed on the hood. It looked at me with shiny eyes and cawed loudly. The burst of sound startled me, and I lost my grip and fell backward. Kai steadied me with one arm. I turned and clung to his chest. My heartbeat pulsed in my temples. That one look from Rosella had utterly unnerved me.

Kai patted my head. "It's okay. He flew away."

I placed my hands on my cheeks to cool them. "Sorry, it was so loud and unexpected." I didn't tell him about the feeling I'd gotten from its black, lifeless eyes—the same evil eyes as Rosella.

CHAPTER 30

KAI SAT STILL as a statue, staring at the fire. I settled behind him and rubbed his neck. I wanted to ask him what he was thinking but didn't want to interrupt his thoughts. Or maybe I didn't want to know what thoughts lay behind his expression.

Ben, Jon, and Tate strode in.

"What did you find out today?" Ben asked without preamble.

Kai told them what we had witnessed.

"We need to figure out her plans for the lake," he finished firmly.

"How are we going to do that?" Ben asked with a hint of a whine.

"I don't know. But we must find a way. Jace would have the best opportunity. We need to talk to him about it."

Jon let out a howl like a coyote. "Enough talking; it's still a full moon. Do you want to go to Tequilas or Big Bison?"

Enthusiastic replies came from all directions.

"To the tunnels," Jon yelled.

"What?" I asked, mystified.

"The tunnels. You haven't shown her the tunnels?" Jon asked Kai.

"We created passageways to travel undetected in our cursed forms. We have entrances hidden beneath the lean-tos on various trails and under sheds behind stores, homes, and downtown," Kai explained. I was astonished to learn of the impressive labyrinth they had dug. Because they all had connections to the mine and quarry, they'd had access to the necessary machinery. It suddenly made sense how they'd managed to create the caves where they lived.

"Remember when I left a present for you on the Black Pond Trail?" Kai asked.

I touched my bracelet. "Yes."

"You told me what trail you were jogging that day. I took the tunnels to the lean-to beside the dock and placed your gift there right before you arrived."

"Wow, okay. Let's do it," I said, laughing.

Jon waved his hand. "The clock is ticking. Follow me."

He opened a hidden door behind the mudroom attached to the kitchen, and we navigated single file down a narrow set of steps.

"Be careful. They're very steep," Kai warned with one hand on my hip.

Our feet stirred up a musty smell as we landed on the platform below. My eyes took a minute to adjust. A series of minecarts on a track sat before us, leading off into the darkness.

"Wow, this is amazing."

We climbed into a cart and took off so quickly that I was forced back into Kai's chest. Ben rattled on about the cart system and how to navigate the tunnels by reading the different signs. I strained to hear over the hum of the cart. We slowed at the main platform, where six tracks united. After moving to a cart on a different track, we set off once again. Ben stopped the cart at another small platform, and we all clambered out.

Jon skipped over to a ladder. "This way," he sang. He clambered up in an instant. I followed, with Kai close behind me. Jon offered his hand to help me out of the tunnel. Then we were standing in a small four-walled structure. Jon raised one finger, placing it over his lips while he slipped out the door.

"All clear," he called.

Kai led me out of the shed and onto a sidewalk.

"Pretty cool, huh?" he said with a smirk. I nodded, scanning the buildings surrounding us. We were downtown, and it had only taken a few minutes to get there.

"You are still full of surprises."

A smile tugged at the corner of his mouth.

"Margaritas at Tequilas?" Jon asked.

"I'm in," Ben cried out, reminding me of Berly.

The place had live music and was very crowded. Kai wove between the people and tables as if navigating a ski slope. I teetered behind him, trying to keep up. Jon secured a table near the dance floor. His cheerfulness was contagious. Soon we were all laughing, drinking, and dancing. Unsurprisingly, Kai was light on his feet, making me feel clumsy. We danced for hours. When we finally took a break, I caught sight of myself in the window. My cheeks were bright and my eyes lively. This was the look of happiness.

"Quick, will you dance with me, Lily?" Jon pulled me back onto the floor.

"Who are you hiding from?"

"The girl in the red sweater."

I glanced around.

"Don't look at her," Jon hissed.

I tried to use my peripheral vision to no avail. "Who is she?"

"Crazy Krista. She's nuts."

I had to ask, "What makes her crazy?"

"I went out with her two times in high school. Two times. She started planning our wedding, how many kids we would have. She is bat-ass crazy." I giggled. "She continues to stalk me. Do you think Kai would punch me if I kissed you?"

"No, but I might."

"Never mind. Kai would pulverize me."

I glanced at Kai. He wore a satisfied look. A tall girl approached him and leaned down, saying something in his ear. He brushed her hand off his arm and shooed her away. I giggled internally.

Jon expelled a large breath. "That was a close one. I think

she's gone."

We danced until the end of the song. Meanwhile, another girl approached Kai. I had the urge to punch her before he skillfully redirected her attention elsewhere.

Kai pulled me onto his lap when I returned to the table. I was delighted with our new seating arrangement. *Now the vultures will see that he's taken.* I thought about Aspen and released some of my resentment on that front. Territoriality came more naturally to me than I thought it would, making me more sympathetic to her jealousy over Nate.

Kai brushed his lips across my cheekbone.

"I leave you for one minute, and girls are swarming all over you," I joked.

"What girls? You're the only one for me."

Throwing both arms behind his neck, I kissed him.

"It looks like someone lifted his no-dating rule." A girl's snarky comment was followed by snickers. I didn't bother turning to see who had spoken.

Ben plopped down. "I got us another round."

Jon howled again, causing Tate to burst into a deep laugh. When he had calmed somewhat, his round cheeks were red.

We lifted our glasses. "Cheers."

I looked around the table at their young, carefree faces. *This is the life they should all be living, not a life in the shadows.*

***

Kai's silence burrowed under my skin during the ride back to the cave. His friends were lively and loud, yet Kai's jaw flexed as he fidgeted with his bracelet.

"Did you have fun tonight?" I asked to break the silence. He seemed surprised by my question.

"Yes, I always do when I am with you. Why do you ask?"

"You're acting distant." I couldn't think of a better word. "What are you thinking about so intently?"

He hesitated. "I was thinking about my life. Tonight, I forgot about the terrible parts. It felt good. But I'm selfish. This is not good for you."

"I love you. I chose to be with you."

Kai didn't seem to have anything to say to that, so I hoped the subject had been laid to rest.

"I'll light the fire," Ben announced when we emerged from the tunnels.

Kai sat on the great room's couch and brought his steepled hands to his lips, not making eye contact with anyone. "I need to talk to you—all of you."

I sat next to him; my skin prickled.

"I'm going to go to work for Rosella," he said bluntly.

"No, you can't!" I shrieked. I hadn't known until that moment how much I didn't want him to take that risk.

Kai placed one hand on my leg. "Lily, please understand. She cursed others because of me. I refused to join her. I talked others into rallying against her." He brought his hand to his heart. "I of all people have to do everything I can to break this curse, for all of us."

I swallowed to focus on steadying my breathing. My heart ached because I knew he was right. I also knew I would have done the same thing if I were in his shoes.

"I don't like it, but I understand. We need someone on the inside," Ben said.

I interlocked my fingers, placing them over my mouth. I could not control my racing pulse or the heat rising in my cheeks. I struggled to hold it together.

Tate's face was bright red; even his ears were red. "Bro, you need to think this through. What if she finds out you're spying?"

"I cannot sit back anymore. If we want to live a normal life, we must get rid of her. I will do whatever it takes to stop her or die trying."

"He's right," Jon said. A lone tear trickled down his cheek. I was somewhat relieved that the others seemed equally upset.

Kai wrapped his arms around my shoulders. "Lily, everything will be all right."

I buried my head in his shoulder with a sob. "What if she hurts you even further?"

"I'll be extra careful. She will never know I'm not under her influence. But we must act now before she gains more power."

My voice was barely audible. "I'll go crazy worrying whether you're safe or not."

He kissed my forehead. "Trust me, I will be safe."

But I couldn't trust him on that. I knew he knew the dangers. His promises of safety were just words.

I rubbed the stones on my swan necklace, listening to the men discuss Kai's decision. I had never imagined that this last night with Kai before leaving for Florida would be riddled with overwhelming anxiety.

Later, as we lay in each other's arms under a plush mountain of blankets, Kai assured me over and over that this was a smart plan and he would be successful.

"My love, our life will be less complicated if I do this."

I wanted to believe him but knew we would always be far from normal.

The fire crackled. The flames lapped toward the ceiling, spreading warmth and color. I usually loved watching the reflection of the fire in his eyes, but tonight it reminded me of evil lurking in the shadows. Sleep evaded my busy mind.

CHAPTER 31

I SHUFFLED THROUGH THE airport to my gate and later from the plane to the luggage carousel like my shoes were full of cement. Oblivious to the hustle around me, I rubbed the heart-shaped stone, thinking about Kai's decision. His conviction helped me shove down my fear, but I barely remembered the flight home.

My family was overjoyed to see me after an entire semester apart. My mother had made numerous plans for the holiday, but I found it hard to be cheery. Nothing felt the same; even my room felt foreign. I sat on my bed and cradled my knees to my chest, feeling incomplete, sort of like hunger pains. All my thoughts were of Kai.

Kai left the forest service and was accepted as part of Rosella's guard not a day after I left. In exchange, she removed his curse. Kai said Rosella was gratified that he'd apologized. I figured she was just eager to use his strength and size.

Despite the busy holiday schedule, time moved at a sloth's pace. I was unable to sit still or pretend to focus on conversation. The only thing I looked forward to was Kai's nightly text, promptly at 11:11 p.m. I shivered in delight at knowing he was thinking about me.

"Why are you so distracted?" my mom asked several times.

I evaded the question as best I could, but I finally broke down.

"I met a guy, and we've kind of sort of been dating."

I hoped that would be enough.

"Where did you meet him? What's his name? Is this serious?" she asked, steaming with curiosity.

Despite my immediate regret at saying anything, a smile oozed across my face.

"I met him on a hiking trail. His name is Kai, and he is amazing." *Why did I say that?* Fidgeting with my necklace, I added, "The relationship is still new. We have a hard time getting together due to our busy schedules."

Mom could have no doubt from the gleam in my eyes that I was head over heels for him. The obligatory response was incoming: "Be careful, honey. You are so very young. This could just be a crush. Don't let him get in the way of your studies. And are you being safe? We are not ready to be grandparents."

After this machine-gun barrage, I sighed heavily, heat rising across my body. "Mom, please stop. You're right. I'm crazy about him, but it's probably just a crush. And no need to worry about grandchildren; we are far from that."

She kissed my forehead. "Are you happy?"

"Very much so."

Kai could not text or call when he was working, and I hated the radio silence. Dead week and finals had been torture, but they were nothing compared to this. I paced my room like I was in solitary confinement, checking my phone and rubbing the stone in my pocket. I muddled through the holiday festivities with my family, putting on a brave face and watching the minutes tick by.

When Kai did call, we talked for hours. Just hearing his deep voice made me dizzy. This small connection lifted my spirits and made me feel whole again. He said Rosella seemed to trust him and was giving him more responsibilities daily.

My sister, Lydia, and I went to the mall to exchange some presents after the twenty-fifth. Chimes rang when I stepped into a shop called the Crystal Cave. I floated directly to the pink tourmaline. This store had an entire bin of polished heart-shaped stones. I had nearly worn mine down from rubbing it so much.

I counted out twenty-five, wanting to buy one for each of my soccer teammates and one for Berly. I also found a men's wallet with a swan branded on the cover and four strips of pink tourmaline sewn onto the tail. It was very similar to the swan on my necklace and bracelet.

As the rich smell of Italian leather swirled up my nostrils, the clerk passed behind and chirped, "Red tag is sixty percent off today."

Déjà vu swept over me.

While I waited for Lydia, I peeked into my bag to make sure I'd received everything I had purchased. Everything was inside—along with another item. It was a bookmark. FIND YOUR FIERCE was printed in bold letters. A light grin prickled my face.

Lydia came bounding toward me. I could tell she was happy with her purchases.

After the brief foray, it was back to brooding. I had slept the entire two and a half weeks in the intoxicating scent of Kai's T-shirt. I couldn't wait to get back to New York—back to Kai. My last three days at home felt like tracking a hurricane, anxiously waiting for it to hit land.

CHAPTER 32

THE SUN HAD yet to rise as my parents drove me to the airport at the end of winter break. I'd booked a 7 a.m. flight back to Lake Placid, telling them it was the cheapest option. Of course, I was simply impatient to get back to Kai. There were no direct flights, unfortunately, so I had to suffer five hours on what felt like Pterodactyl Airlines. When we finally landed, I could not get off the plane quickly enough.

My heart sputtered as I raced through the airport. I leaped down the escalator, catching my breath when Kai's face came into focus. I ran the final few steps and landed in his warm embrace.

He picked me up, crushing me to him. My fingers dragged through his hair, and I clutched him closer to me, breathing in his familiar scent. My feet were not even touching the ground while we kissed, ignoring the sizable crowd. I tingled under his touch.

Walking hand in hand to the baggage carousel, we found my suitcase already circling the belt. Kai lifted it easily with his free hand.

The drive from the airport was a blur. Kai parked in front of a house I did not recognize.

I must have looked puzzled.

"This is my mother's house. I live here now," he said and casually winked.

I winced, imagining running into his mother. Kai led me inside and held one finger over his lips.

"You'll be staying in the guest room," he said rather loudly.

I played along. "It's quite lovely, thank you."

We stepped into the laundry room on the backside of the house, where a small door led to the underground tunnels.

"This way, my love," he whispered. My heart fluttered as we descended. "We can't risk Rosella finding out about the caves. If she spies on me, it will appear that I live here."

Kai placed my bag in the cart and helped me in.

I hadn't realized how much I missed the peaceful splash of the waterfall and the natural light until we reached the caves. Kai's room brought me even more peace. We hibernated in his room for hours, and I finally felt whole again.

Kai shared everything he had been doing inside the fortress. I did not have much to share about my trip home except how painful it was to be apart, though I did give him the wallet.

"It's not much, but I hope you like it."

"How did you find this?" he asked, turning the wallet over in his hand. His eyes scanned my face. "I love it. Thank you. You are so sweet."

He pressed his lips to mine, and I eagerly accepted the kiss.

"I got this for you," he said. He handed me a large, heavy package, and I carefully tore the paper, revealing a navy-blue blanket with tiny white swans embroidered all over it.

I hugged it to my chest. "Oh my, I love it. It's so heavy."

"It's weighted. Sakari had it made for me."

I looked up with wide eyes. Kai chuckled.

"I think she is coming around. She is happy the curse has been removed."

An alarm buzzed in my head. *Sakari will blame me if anything happens to Kai.*

The alarm blared louder at his next words: "Rosella asked me to accompany her on a special assignment tomorrow."

I steadied my voice. "Do you know what the assignment is?"

He waved his long fingers in the air. "I'm not sure. She said we are going to Mirror Lake because she had something special to show me, and if it works out, she wants to consider me for other special assignments."

Special assignments? What does that mean?

"Do you think she's going to show you she's putting black tourmaline in the water? Maybe she'll explain why?"

"We can only hope."

My stomach twisted. This sounded dangerous. There was no room for jealousy, though it loomed over me. I snuggled in closer, brushing my fingers across the ripples of his abs.

Kai must have felt my unease. He pressed his forehead to mine. His rich voice filled the room. "You are my world; you are my reason to live."

Calmness flooded me, and my heart did a backflip.

"I'm sorry. I just worry about her intentions. I don't want her to hurt you."

"I can handle her. What I can't handle is how beautiful you are." He pulled me closer.

We emerged from his room only when my stomach started rumbling. It was good to see Kai's roommates and get caught up on their progress over the last two and a half weeks.

Ben passed me some bread. "Jace snuck me inside the compound. I was able to install a camera directly on the doors to the warehouse."

"I was on guard duty at the front gate," Jace explained. "We waited until the other guard went on his lunch break. Ben is a genius. He had less than an hour to install the camera, and he did it in twenty minutes."

I liked this lively side of Jace.

"That sounds dangerous," I commented.

"It was, but now we can watch whatever she's doing inside the structure," Ben said smugly, swatting a bee from his eye.

"We know Rosella is putting powder in the lake. Have you thought about installing a camera at Mirror Lake—or better yet, the water treatment plant?" I asked.

"Good idea," Jon exclaimed.

"I'll see what I can do. It may be hard to access the water treatment plant."

"I could drive by it tomorrow and check it out," I suggested, surprising myself. "Kai's working, and I have nothing to do."

Kai looked alarmed, but when he met my eyes, I poured my resolve into my gaze, and he simply nodded. "You can take my truck. I'll ride to work with Jace."

※ ※ ※

The next morning, Kai and I surfaced from the tunnel and followed the rich aroma of coffee to Sakari's kitchen. Kai's mom kissed him on each cheek.

"Good morning, my son." She nodded to me. "Good morning."

I wanted to melt into the floor. It was obvious I had spent the night with Kai.

"Good morning, Mother," Kai said.

I touched her hand with my own "Good morning," thankful when she didn't pull it away.

She motioned to the coffee. "Would you like a cup?"

"Yes, thank you. It smells wonderful," I replied with a bit too much enthusiasm.

She raised her eyebrows at Kai.

"No thanks," he replied. "I need to get going."

I walked with Kai to the front door. He turned and pulled me against his hard chest. My face flushed, but he seemed unaware his mother might be watching. He kissed me as if we were alone.

"This is going to be the longest shift I have ever had to cover. My mind will be on you, my love," he whispered in my ear. "Please be careful and stay safe. I'll meet you back at the cave at 5:30."

He turned and headed outside, his beautiful black hair whipping from side to side.

I returned to the kitchen with my cheeks hot. Sakari handed me a mug.

"Thank you," I said. "What are you doing today? Do you have to work?"

"Yes, but I don't have to go in until ten."

I took a chance. "Do you want to grab some breakfast?"

Kai would be happy I extended an olive branch.

"I would love that," she said, surprising me. She looked at me with a slight tilt of her head, her eyes twinkling, and she reminded me of Kai. "Why don't we go to the Treetop Cafe and get some of those donuts?"

"Deal," I said hastily. "Do we have time?"

"Yes, if we hurry." She sprang to her feet as I hastily sipped at my coffee. "Give me a minute to get ready."

※ ※ ※

At the restaurant, our conversation quickly shifted from pleasant to serious.

"Don't hurt my son," Sakari said bluntly.

Grandmother Kateri was right: Sakari was evaluating me and my intentions.

I had to clear my throat to speak. Anger replaced my initial shock.

"That is the last thing I want to do."

"He has had enough pain in his life. If you have any doubt that you will not be able to handle this, leave him now. I don't want to see him suffer further."

"I don't want him to suffer either. Just for the record, I didn't want him to work for Rosella. To me, shedding the curse is not worth the danger."

She raised her head, and the light from the ceiling revealed the dark circles under her eyes. "You didn't?"

"No, I didn't. I don't trust her. I have seen her up close. I have seen the evil in her eyes. I'm afraid of what she might do if she finds out he's spying."

"She could curse you. Could you live like that the rest of your life?"

"I am more concerned with breaking the curse."

She selected a donut and cracked a half smile. After that, we talked freely and openly with no awkward pauses. I got the feeling she might have been beautiful without the sorrow lingering in her eyes.

"Oh, look at the time. I had better get going. I don't want to be late."

"Thank you for coming to breakfast."

"Thank you for asking."

*　*　*

I cautiously approached the water plant. The place was constructed like a fort, with tall brick walls and few windows. The only windows were at the front door. The water tanks in the back were surrounded by the same high brick walls. The only option for a camera was in the parking lot, which meant we would be able to see whether Rosella visited the plant but not what she did inside.

The lot was vacant except for two cars. It would be easy to install a camera here.

I drove east, heading back to Kai's mother's house. The words on a sign took me by surprise: Mirror Lake Lookout Point: 2 miles. I impulsively turned right.

I drove into the parking area, keeping an eye out for long black sedans, and parked in the far back corner like Kai and I had done before. Slipping out of the truck, I ran into the restrooms for cover.

I placed my hands on the side of the sink and stared at my reflection. It was only when I splashed water on my face that the voice in my head warned me of the obvious: *Stop! This is moronic. If Kai sees you, he might react, blow his cover. Not to mention she'll probably recognize his truck. You could ruin everything. Get out of here now!*

I peeked out the door. Still no long black car. I ran back to the truck, fumbling for the keys. As I steadied my hand and started the truck, a black figure stepped out from the trees. The creature looked my way, raising its arm. He cupped his hand and held it up like he wanted something. My hands were trembling on the steering wheel when I sped out of the parking lot. I had not seen any pukwudgies since Thanksgiving.

And why haven't I? I suddenly wondered. I had been seeing them at least once a week before that. And then I had saved the raccoon . . .

Kai would not be home for five more hours. I drove to the Salty Swan, hoping Wanda might have answers.

*   *   *

The familiar wind chimes tinkled, and the thick aroma of incense wafted around me. I did not recognize the clerk behind the counter, so I wandered the area with the pink tourmaline displays.

When Wanda came from the back room and spotted me, a knowing smile crossed her face.

"Hello, swan. What brings you in?"

"I wanted to ask you a question."

She nodded encouragingly.

I shuffled my feet and stared down at them, trying to find the right words without sounding crazy. "I have seen things—things in the forest."

"What kinds of things?"

"Small, dark creatures. They look like they are made of stone."

"Stone?" She appeared innocently curious.

I lowered my voice. "I think they are pukwudgies."

Her eyes lit up.

"Let's go into the back room so you can tell me everything." She signaled her employee. "I'll be in my office."

Once we had settled into a pair of chairs in the nondescript office, she asked, "Would you like a water?"

"No, thanks."

"Tell me what you have seen."

"Sorry to come to you with this, but I knew you would believe me. Possibly help me."

"I'm listening."

"From the first day I moved here, I have noticed dark shadows moving in the forest. I followed one during my first few days. It was like a strange force drew me toward it. Then it disappeared right in front of me. That was the day I met Kai, my boyfriend. He scolded me for following it. He said the forest was full of danger and made me promise to stay out of it.

"At first, the stonelike creatures appeared about once a week and stayed mostly hidden. Around November, I started seeing them almost every day, and they made themselves more visible. I tried to point them out to people, but no one ever saw them. You told me once, 'You know in your heart what you cannot see.' Is that what you were talking about? The pukwudgies?"

She gave me a comforting smile. "Lily, all my life I have been able to pick up signals, gain information about an object, person, or a location. It's called precognition, the ability to perceive or predict future events. When I meet people or run into individuals who seem to have gained the attention of the spirits, I often see a vision or hear words that are important to that person. I am often not sure of the meaning behind the words, but it is my duty to deliver them to the person who triggered it."

"So, you don't know what it means?"

"No, I don't, but I know it is important. Where did you learn about pukwudgies?"

My pulse quickened. "You believe me?"

"I do. They have been a legend around here for a long time."

"They are real," I said, whispering without intending to.

"However, pukwudgies are not typically stonelike. They are described as resembling goblins or leprechauns, with humanlike features."

"These are not. Kai's grandmother thinks their complexions have been changed by an unnatural power. Rosella has learned how to control them, and she is using their magic. We assume they look like the black tourmaline she uses to ensnare them."

Wanda sat back, rubbing her chin. "That is an interesting theory. Rosella has been a problem in our town for years. She practices dark magic, powerful magic, a kind of magic that comes at a price."

She fell silent, so I tried to push the conversation forward.

"I have not seen any pukwudgies in over a month. What do you think that means?"

"Whatever it means, pukwudgies rarely show themselves. There is a reason they are showing themselves to you. We need to figure out that reason. I have always wanted to see one."

She leaned back, closing her eyes. There was rapid movement under her eyelids. She said, "Your pure heart needs a clear mind. Fear is their fuel, yet your heart is kind."

"A vision?" I asked.

"Yes, dear."

"Maybe a clear mind would help me figure out why they show themselves to me."

"You must be careful. They will use your fears against you."

It felt like someone had punched me in the stomach. "Umm . . . okay." So much for a clear mind. Now I was racking my brain for my worst fears. "Thank you for sharing this with me."

She patted my knee. "No need to thank me. You have given me a lot to think about. Here is my number if you think of anything else."

I fought the urge to cry after I left. I had hoped for answers, but instead I was leaving with more questions.

※ ※ ※

Even with the key, I felt like a criminal as I let myself into Sakari's empty house. I hurried to the laundry room and into the tunnel.

The cart buzzed along the track. At the end of the line, the earthy smell of the cave soothed my nerves. With a few more hours to kill, I completed some prework for my classes and started making hamburger patties for dinner.

Jon was the first one home. He hopped into the kitchen, his cheeks still red from the cold. Somehow, the cold weather had not bothered me since I returned from Florida. Maybe I was getting used to it, or maybe I was too distracted to fret about the weather.

"Hi, Lily. How was your day? Something smells good."

"I hope you like it. I was bored, so I cooked."

"The cook needs wine," he said, wiggling his eyebrows. He opened a bottle and poured us each a glass. "I'm going to go change."

He stopped in the great room and added wood to the fire.

I heard a footstep and glanced back, expecting to see Jon. It was Kai. He reached me in two long strides, and I fell into his welcoming arms and breathed in his musk. He kissed me hard.

"I missed you way too much today."

"You have no idea how much I thought of you, my love," he said. He kissed me again, producing a loud buzz in my ears. Kai pulled back and discovered Ben standing at the door. The buzz was coming from him. Heat blazed in my cheeks.

"Hi, Ben," Kai said, unashamed.

"Sorry to interrupt."

"No problem. I just got home."

Jon came back into the kitchen from the other side. "Evening," he said, holding up his wine in a toast. He wore a short-sleeve T-shirt, exposing his hairy arms.

"I hope you don't mind. I made dinner," I told the new arrivals.

"Smells great," Kai said, kissing the top of my head.

We moved to the great room to eat, and everyone started talking at once. Ben went on about the security cameras, and Jon launched into a story about some rowdy campers.

After the meal, Kai mentioned Rosella had been aggressive today.

"What do you mean by aggressive?" Ben demanded.

Kai shifted in his seat. "First thing this morning, Rosella summoned me to her private rooms. It was mostly white marble and was stiff and unwelcoming. Mirrors covered most of the walls from floor to ceiling, so all in all, it was a really weird effect. She walked around me, twirling my hair between her fingers, and said she looked forward to our special assignment. I stayed as still as possible, pretending to be under her power. I answered that I was reporting for duty, like she requested." He grinned, but it didn't reach his eyes. "I 'ma'amed' her."

Ben let out a short chuckle.

A red flag immediately went up in my head. *This horrid witch has her eyes on my man.* Her intentions concerned me. "What was the special assignment?" I asked with an edge to my voice that I couldn't prevent.

"She took me to Mirror Lake. We walked to the end of the viewing platform, and Rosella paced, chanted, and generated some smoke around her. It slithered slowly over the water. She placed her arm in mine, saying, 'Mirror Lake is my favorite. See how the image reflects perfectly? It's hard to know where it starts or where it ends. I find it powerful. It is nature's mirror. The largest, most powerful mirror you could ever wish for. Do you like what you see?' I stood as still as stone.

"She pointed to the water, saying, 'Mirrors are important to me. Especially when a reflection as captivating as yours is standing arm and arm beside me—reflecting what could be.' She is more of a narcissist than I imagined.

"She asked me if I was happy with my new position. I nodded, purposely keeping my face emotionless. She said, 'I could really use a special guard that would never leave my side. Do you think you could fill a position like that?'

"I said, 'No, ma'am, that is the captain's job. He said that his guarding you was imperative, and I'm not qualified for that position.'

"She actually stuttered when she told me she wasn't talking about work. I had to be careful with the way I refused her so she would not realize I was not under her influence. I focused on keeping my breathing steady when I told her, 'I don't believe I am ready for that position. I'm still in training.' She turned with a huff and stomped away.

"I have no idea if the other guards overheard the conversation, but I swear I detected a smile. When we returned to the fortress, she ordered me to guard the back gate. I think the 'special assignments' she had in mind were purely personal," he finished with a grimace.

By now Kai and I were sitting together in an oversized chair, both of my legs draped over his. Kai stroked my hair with his free hand.

Jon's eyes darted from Kai's to mine while he listened. I had already mentally prepared myself for the idea that Rosella might try something like this. I was perfectly confident of Kai's feelings for me. I was only worried about his safety.

Ben spoke slowly and carefully. "That witch does not take rejection very well. Kai, I do not think that will be the end of it. She is tenacious. We need to find a way to end her reign soon."

"I'm just mad at myself for not getting my hands on some of that powder today," Kai said, twirling a lock of my hair between his fingers. "Rosella is pumping her mist into the buildings. Jace showed me where she contaminates the air supply to the mines, quarry, and all buildings on the compound. And now the lake. Why?"

"Oh, the water supply." I turned to Ben. "It should be easy to install a camera in the parking lot. Inside would be tricky, unless you somehow gain access. It's built like a fort."

"Maybe I can install one this weekend. At least we can see if she goes there."

"Do you think Rosella will do anything to you because you rejected her offer?" Jon bluntly asked Kai.

"I don't think so, as long as I continue to play hazy and emotionless."

I shivered. This was a dangerous game, and Rosella would not accept his "no" for long.

* * *

A little while later, I was sitting cross-legged on Kai's bed, mindlessly running my fingers through the soft fur blanket, when the door opened.

"All finished." He must have seen the look on my face. "Is everything okay?"

I shifted my legs so they hung off the bed. Kai sat beside me and wrapped an arm around my back. "I'm just worried about you, about her, about her anger."

He placed one hand on my cheek. His lips slowly moved across my jawline and down to my neck. "Don't worry about me."

I couldn't stop myself from moving my mouth to his, dragging my hands across his muscular back. He pulled me with him onto the bed, and his kisses grew more urgent. I fervently returned them. The intense feeling surging through my body was foreign to me, but my body seemed to know what it was doing. I told myself to slow down and let my mind catch up.

I pulled back enough to look at Kai's face. "I had breakfast with your mother today."

His eyes jumped around my face. "And?"

"I think she was evaluating me and my intentions."

Kai leaned back on one arm. "How did it go?"

"We have a better understanding of each other." The corners of

Kai's mouth turned up. "I also went to see Wanda at the Salty Swan. I needed to ask her some questions."

"You are full of surprises today. What kind of questions?"

"Today a stone pukwudgie stepped out of the woods right in front of me. It held its hand out to me like it wanted something. I realized I had not seen any in over a month, so I asked Wanda what she knew about them and whether she knew why they haven't been around."

He leaned forward.

"Over a month? I hadn't noticed, or I wasn't paying attention. Weren't you seeing them almost every day in November?"

I nodded, and Kai's jaw flexed.

"She told me something else. She said, 'Your pure heart needs a clear mind. Fear is their fuel, yet your heart is kind.'"

He repeated it a few times as if to commit it to memory.

"What do you think it means?"

"I'm not sure. Wanda said her visions just appear. She doesn't know the true meaning herself, but she warned me to be careful." I couldn't ignore the churning in my stomach and blurted, "Rosella will not take no for an answer. She wants you for more than guard duty. She wants you as a lover."

"I do not care about her wants or desires. You are the only one for me."

This is not going to end well, I told myself.

Kai kissed my cheek. "Do not worry, my love. I will handle her."

Sleep evaded me. Flashes of a petite, dark-haired, beady-eyed woman haunted me. I tossed and turned, thinking of the danger Kai was risking for us. Kai must have sensed my emotional distress because he spooned me tightly against his body. His quiet breaths brushed the back of my neck, and eventually, I drifted to sleep.

CHAPTER 33

THE CLEAN, FRESH snow under our feet reminded me of potato chips, producing a loud crunch with every step. The stillness on campus felt peculiar. The last time I'd walked these paths, they were flooded with anxious students, but now the place was as quiet as a crypt. Our footprints were the only ones.

I halted and released Kai's hand, plopping backward and waggling my arms and legs in the snow to form an angel. Kai grinned.

"You are such a Floridian."

"I've never made one," I defended myself.

He dropped beside me and made one as well. We stood carefully to view our creations, the white powder dusting our hair.

Kai chuckled and gestured toward my angel. "Look how your ponytail landed over your head. It looks like a swan's head."

I giggled. "My swan head made me taller than you."

We brushed the snow off each other's backs and continued to the dorm.

Searching for my keys, I said, "You've never been to my room before. Do you have an ID?"

Kai grabbed me from behind as I opened the door.

"Warning, unidentified male contaminating female dorm room." He nuzzled his face into my neck as we stumbled into the room, leaving our wet coats and shoes at the door.

Kai acted like Inspector Gadget, analyzing every detail of the tiny room I shared with Berly. Finally, he stretched out on my bed and clicked the remote with curiosity; he changed the pattern of the lights around the room over and over as I unpacked my suitcase and draped the swan blanket over him.

I finished putting the last stack of shirts away, and Kai lifted one side of the blanket with sultry eyes. "Come here, my golden swan."

The heat rose in my cheeks as I slid in beside him, and the weighted blanket pressed down like a hot stone massage.

Kai smothered me with kisses. I felt my pulse quicken, shocked by the unexpected excitement of having a forbidden visitor in my room. We lost all track of time in each other's embrace.

I flinched when a door slammed.

"Why are you so jumpy?" Kai asked.

"Generally I'm a rule follower, but something about you makes me break all the rules. I must confess, it's kind of exciting."

He planted his face in my neck. "I wouldn't be here if you had not learned to break a few rules."

"So, you admit it? You're the reason I'm a rebel," I said with a grin.

He whispered, "You make a good rebel."

I looked at the time. "The office opened twenty minutes ago. We need to hurry to beat the crowd." I hated the idea of getting bundled up again to brave the cold, but the influx of winter sports enthusiasts would make campus a madhouse by the weekend. I had to get my schedule and books today.

The walkway was now littered with additional footprints, though our snow angels remained untouched. We admired them, arm in arm. I tilted my head up for a quick kiss, and Kai brushed my lips softly like butterfly wings.

The crunch of heavy boots interrupted our moment—Benton and his two buddies stomping up the path. I felt Kai's muscles tense.

"Oh look, the lovebirds made some snow beasts," Benton said in his raspy voice. He and his buddies smirked and shuffled their feet to ruin our snow angels. "Oops, what a shame. Did we ruin them?" He stood directly in front of us in a wide stance, hands on his hips, expecting a confrontation.

Without thinking, I reared back and kicked him in the private parts. He fell to the ground with a guttural groan. Benton's buddies froze. I think they were afraid to move.

I slipped my hand around one of Kai's fists and tugged him with me as I briskly walked away. "Come on, honey."

Behind us, Benton garbled out some threatening remark I couldn't make out.

I whispered, "Quickly, so we can beat them in line."

We picked up our pace.

"Where did that come from?" Kai laughed.

"He is an idiot."

"That was shocking, but he deserved it. I think you found your fierce."

Moving with urgency to avoid running into Benton again, we were able to get my schedule and books in less than an hour.

Kai's stomach growled. "I am starving."

"So am I." We had originally planned on eating in the campus cafeteria, but our encounter with Benton changed our minds. We settled for fast food on our way to Grandmother Kateri's.

※ ※ ※

"Kai, Lily, what a pleasant surprise. Please, come in."

Grandmother Kateri's home was warm and cozy. A fire burned in the fireplace, and the stained glass windows left the room awash in color.

"What is new with you two?"

"I took Sakari to breakfast yesterday."

Kai's grandmother nodded approvingly. "Good for you. How

is she?"

"We definitely have a better understanding of each other."

Grandmother let out a gravelly chuckle. "Her son is the anchor of her life. She will always protect him and dreams only of his happiness."

We sat in front of the fireplace, and Kai shared why we had come to visit.

"Yesterday, a pukwudgie walked out of the forest. He held his hand out to Lily like he wanted something." Grandmother sat forward. "Lily has not seen any in over a month. What do you think that means?"

Grandmother stared at the fire. "Something is attracting them to you, but you are strong enough to resist their magic. They may be attempting to draw you to them."

"I talked to Wanda from the Salty Swan. She wasn't sure either," I added. I pointed my thumb at Kai. "Some other issues have cropped up too. Rosella wants Kai to be more than just a guard. She wants him for her private use."

Grandmother's expression turned hard. "Private use? What did she say?"

"She asked if I wanted a new assignment as her personal guard twenty-four seven. When I said no, she stormed away."

Grandmother shook her head. "That's not good, not good at all. You need to stay far away from her."

We didn't leave Grandmother's house until after dusk. I enjoyed every minute of our day together. Spending time with Kai was effortless, and as energizing as going to a state fair. His kisses were sweet like cotton candy on my tongue.

Despite our wonderful day, in the back of my mind, I felt like we were balancing on a tightrope. The dark curse lingered over our heads like a storm cloud, and I kept wondering when it would burst.

CHAPTER 34

O NCE WE MADE it back to the cave, Kai hugged me from behind. "I need to take a shower. Do you know of anyone available to help me wash my back?"

"I think I could find someone," I croaked, trying to control the electricity coursing through my veins.

He pulled off his shirt in one swift motion. *How can anyone look so perfect, like a bronze statue?* I held up my arms, and he removed my shirt. My heart thumped so loudly in my chest that I was afraid he could hear it. Conscious of the bareness between us, I tried to wrangle my conflicted thoughts.

"Are you uncomfortable, Lily?"

"No, not really," I lied. I was terrified. I'd never longed for someone like this. My hands trembled when I stepped into the shower. I had never felt so completely exposed.

As I ran my soapy hands over Kai's back, his muscles flexed under my fingers. My body tingled wherever he touched it while the water splashed softly over our heads.

"I was thinking," I started to say, but my trembling voice betrayed me.

Kai's fingers rested on the curve of my hips. "Thinking about what?"

I started again. "Well, you know, I mean, it's just . . . umm." I took a deep breath. "Well, Rosella took the curse off you, right?"

He considered what I was trying to say, shifting through a series of expressions.

"Lily, do you really . . . ?" His words trailed off, and his jaw flexed.

Looking down, I murmured, "I don't know. I mean, I don't know what to expect. I have no experience here." Embarrassed that I could not articulate what I was thinking, I finally managed, "I don't think I could ever feel any closer to someone than I do with you."

He pulled me close, letting the water cascade over us for a minute. He chose his words carefully. "Not that I don't want to; I do. But I'm still afraid to risk it. I have waited far too long for you to come into my life." My heart soared; this man was more concerned with my well-being than his own desires. "I think we need to make sure the curse is gone forever before we take that step. I love you. I love everything about you. We can wait until the time is right. Besides, there are plenty of other things we can do." He moved his hand between my legs, and my knees buckled.

CHAPTER 35

THAT WAS THE second night I dreamed of Rosella. I woke up startled, clutching the sides of my head, trying to stop myself from screaming. A high-pitched cry escaped my lungs anyway. Placing my hand over my mouth, I tried to extinguish the vivid images. *What dredged up this crazy dream again?*

The dream had changed. This time, Rosella was chasing me. Clawing at me with long, talon-like fingernails. I ended up trapped in the old house with no exits. My hands were bloody from trying to claw my way out, and a dark shadow was still following me.

I used to think the dream was triggered by feeling trapped in high school. Now I wasn't sure.

Kai's eyes popped open when he heard my cry, and he sat up.

"Sorry, it was just a dream. Go back to sleep."

He rolled over, and I rubbed his back, pushing the dream remnants from my head. Kai's breaths slowed, and his face looked peaceful. The muscles on his bare back expanded under my fingertips with every breath. I was jealous of his flawless russet skin. Mine was white as snow.

I must have drifted off to sleep again. When I opened my eyes, Kai was staring at my face.

"Good morning, my love," he said, his voice thick with sleep.

I kissed his cheek. "Morning, my heart."

"Did I hear you scream last night?"

Heat rose in my cheeks. "Yes, sorry. I had a bad dream. The same dream I always have about being trapped in a house, only this time Rosella was chasing me."

Concern shone from his eyes when he promised, "I will protect you from her."

"I know you will."

* * *

This was our last full day together before my semester started since Kai had to work on Sunday. Casually looking for something to do, we drove downtown and stumbled upon a Three Kings Day celebration. A parade was scheduled at noon, and the town square was packed with people trying to secure a good spot.

We searched for a good vantage point. Kai moved to a short brick wall lining a patch of grass and hopped on top to sit. He effortlessly lifted me by the armpits like you would lift a child.

The sun was peeking through the clouds, and the wind was mild. I sank back against Kai's warm chest. A loud horn signaled the parade's start, and the enthusiastic crowd sounded like a flock of seagulls hovering over a picnic at the beach.

Kai wrapped his long arms around me, securing me in place, and rested his chin on my shoulder. We fit together perfectly.

"How did you manage to come up with this entertainment?" I joked.

"Skills. I have skills and I have connections." His tone was light and cheery. "It only took me a few hours to pull this together for you."

"I'm a fan of your superhuman skills."

"I have lots of skills."

I liked seeing him this way—almost childlike, without a care in the world.

"This thing is huge," I said after watching float after float roll by.

"I think the whole town is here. We should get some cotton candy," Kai said, his voice high and silly.

The parade was a pleasant surprise, a moment of normalcy. Another marching band passed, and soon, only four or five floats remained.

Kai kept nibbling my ear, distracting me. I shivered.

"Are you trying to make me fall off this wall?"

He whispered with another nibble. "I would never let you fall."

Then his whole body stiffened. I heard him swallow and take a deep breath.

"I think we might have a problem," he muttered.

Knowing only one thing could cause this reaction, I lifted my eyes and scanned the square. There she was. A pair of piercing black eyes stared at us from across the fountain. She was flanked by four guards. So many emotions flooded through me in a second. Shock, fear, disgust, anger, ending with a fierce feeling to protect Kai, no matter what. *Why is she here? Why is she staring at us?*

Kai lowered me carefully to the sidewalk and dropped beside me, whispering, "Walk slowly to the truck, and try not to attract attention."

I could not utter a sound as I shuffled through the crowd with Kai. We made it to the street corner and turned right as the last float rounded the fountain. Rosella's guards swiftly moved around us, blocking our path. I stepped back with a squeak.

A soft voice called out from behind us, "What is your hurry, my handsome guard, my Kai?"

My blood boiled. *Who does she think she is?* Kai squeezed my hand, and we turned back to face her.

She approached us and placed one finger under Kai's chin. "This one is quite handsome and so strong." She cut her beady eyes to me. "Don't you agree?" she snapped.

I swallowed but could not speak, so I just nodded.

Rosella sneered and looked back to Kai, jabbing her bony finger at my face.

"So, this . . . this thing, this blondie, is why you refused me? You chose this ordinary girl when you could have had all the power of me—*me*?"

"I love her. We love each other!" he answered boldly. This was it. There was no way he could continue the charade of being under her control after this.

Her vile voice rose louder, drawing a crowd. "Love? You say you are in love? In love with this? She does not even know who you are. *What* you are!"

She turned to me again, and with venom in her voice, she asked, "Do you really think you love him? Love, you have no idea what love is!" She directed her voice to the crowd. There were a lot of mystified faces. "They say they are in love. Do they even know what love is?" She turned to me again. "You, you little twit, you do not know him enough to love him."

"I do love him, with all my heart," I said through gritted teeth.

Rosella laughed in my face. I seethed, hating everything about her. Curious people continued gathering.

Her voice, full of fury, was now directed to Kai. "You chose this skinny little pixie over me? That child over the most powerful woman known? How could you? Why would you? Why would you choose that?"

Kai narrowed his eyes. His face was dark with fury, like he was about to breathe fire. His lips pressed into thin lines, and he held back a response.

She started speaking to the crowd again, jabbing a finger toward us. "She thinks she loves him. They are in love. Do they look in love to you? Love, love they say. Is it true love, or is it lust? Look at them. Can you believe it?"

Several people frowned or raised their eyebrows at her. One or two made eye contact with me and shrugged. I wasn't sure why she was putting on this show. *Why draw attention when she's up to so many nefarious things?*

Rosella let out a malicious chortle and turned to me, waving her finger in my face.

"I will teach you about love. Tell me if you love this."

She waved her hand in a circular motion over her head, and an overpowering acrid smell filled the air. A dark cloud of smoke formed where she had gestured, making a funnel.

The gray smoke swirled over Kai's head and drifted slowly down his body. She twirled her finger again, and the dust and stench faded above his head. Screams erupted as the frantic crowd scrambled to run away. She had transformed Kai's eyes into those of a snake, and green scales covered his exposed neck once again.

Rosella laughed hysterically. "What do you think of him now?"

Her guards remained stern and serious. Our group was now alone in the square.

She cackled, "How do you like your snake man?"

I stepped toward her, making sure I was in her personal space. I looked her dead in the eyes. "I love him. I will always love him. I love him with all my heart."

Rosella stepped back, her eyes flaring with rage. "You are a fool. You love him like this?" Her hands were shaking, and her face was mottled red. Spittle flew from her mouth as she screamed with clenched teeth and pointed at Kai's eyes. "He is a monster. How could you love a monster?"

I tilted my head back and said in a hardened tone, "No, my dear, you are the monster. I love him now, and I will love him forever. This is not who he is. This is what you did to him. I love him. I love everything about him!"

I jerked back when something like thunder cracked above our heads. The ground shook, and tree limbs shed their snow. Kai and I braced together as the wind picked up and whipped our hair about. It whistled through the trees and stirred up the powdered snow, creating a crystal-white twister that swirled around the town square—and then dropped with a plop.

Silence replaced the uproar. I glanced back to Kai, and he no longer had scales or snake eyes. *Is her spell broken?* The shock on Rosella's face quickly turned to fury.

"Love wins over hate!" I screamed fiercely.

Her nostrils flared, and her eyes burned right into my soul.

"Love will never win while I am around."

She chanted in a language I did not recognize.

Wind blasted past us. My heart lurched. I looked into Kai's eyes for strength, but Ben's voice haunted me: *"That witch does not take rejection very well."*

A sound like fireworks erupted from every direction. I involuntarily jumped with each pop. Kai squeezed my hand until they subsided.

Smoky gray dust floated around my body, and suddenly creatures with emotionless stone faces and sharp, talon-like feet surrounded me, emitting a low-pitched hum. The pukwudgies reached for me like they had in my dream.

Their cold stone hands landed on my legs, arms, waist, and back, and the disturbing hum grew louder, until an explosion rang in my ears. The muffled sound of Kai screaming my name faded as darkness engulfed me.

CHAPTER 36

MY HANDS AND knees slammed to the ground, stirring up dust clouds. I coughed, sputtered, and blinked away the grit. Leaning back on my heels, I brushed the dirt off my hands. The musty smell made me sneeze.

My chest tightened as I gazed down at familiar wooden planks. I raised my head. Sunlight cast streams of faint yellow light through the slits in the windows.

I surged to my feet in an eruption of dust. My heart racing, I grabbed for the window, pulled and tugged, but it was nailed shut. I ran to the other window. It too was nailed shut.

Is this really happening? Am I dreaming? As I gasped for air, the voice in my head screamed, *Wake up!*

I could not see anything outside through the dust obstructing my view. The constant tick from the clock synced to my pulse. It was impossible to tell whether minutes or hours were passing. I rushed to the door, snatched the handle, flung it open, and again the doorway was bricked over. My ears hummed.

I tried to scream but only managed a barely audible cry. I was trapped, confused, and full of rage.

Where is Kai? What did she do to him? Where are the stone creatures? Adrenaline coursed through my body. I had to calm down, search for a way out. I rubbed my temples to clear my mind like Wanda had said. The creatures were using my fears against me.

Footsteps sounded behind me. A dark shadow elongated across the wall.

I breathed deeply, chanting internally, *Remain calm. Think, think, clear your mind.* I shivered, unable to forget the sensation of those cold stone hands grabbing me.

I had to get away. I flung myself up the stairs, opening the first door—but found no windows, no way out. The heavy footsteps drew closer. Room after room provided no escape. The pukwudgies had to be getting closer because the hum in my head grew louder.

I dashed to the last door. Behind it rose another staircase. Slamming the door behind me, I fled up the stairs, leaping them two at a time.

I made it to the top. Just like in my dream, the staircase led to nothing. It seemed like the house itself was alive. I pushed on the walls, banged on the roof. It was all solid. "Nooo!" I cried. This time, sound came out and rebounded against the walls.

I heard a click, and at bottom of the stairs, the doorknob began to turn. I had nowhere to go. I sat on a step, resting my elbows on my knees, and buried my face in my shaking hands. Then I remembered. *Why am I running from these creatures? I need to face them, find out what they want.* I stood and tried to feel brave as I fearfully inched down the stairs.

The door creaked open. My heart skipped a beat.

Kai was on the other side.

I sobbed with delight and ran to him, almost knocking him over.

He spoke in gasps. "Follow . . . me. I have . . . a way out."

I followed him in a cloud of unbridled bliss. He led me to the kitchen, where he had broken a few floorboards to get in. Stepping through the hole in the floor, he reached for me.

"Be careful, stay close to me, and keep your hand on my leg as we tunnel our way out. It's very dark. I must know you are still with me."

Easing into the hole, the boards creaking under my hands, I

coughed. It was hard to breathe under the dusty house. The darkness was unnerving. I felt around for Kai's leg and grabbed hold of his calf.

"Follow me," he rasped after a cough.

I crawled inches behind Kai, shivering and brushing cobwebs from my face. My eyes stung. My mood lightened ever so slightly when I saw rays of sunlight through lattice panels.

Clearing the crawl space underneath the old house in the marsh, Kai turned to help me out. I slipped my hand into his, crawling out of the darkness. Kai clasped me to him.

"I love you." His lips pressed against my ear.

Tears streamed from my eyes, and my breath erupted in convulsive gasps.

I coughed out, "How did you know . . . where to find me?"

"I was in a panic after you vanished with the pukwudgies." His voice was deep and gritty. "Rage overtook all my senses, and I tried to tackle Rosella. She laughed and grabbed one of the pukwudgies, then disappeared with a crack. She placed the curse back on me."

He coughed a few more times, never releasing his hold on me. Once my sobbing quieted, he wiped my wet cheeks with his thumbs. "My love, you are safe with me. We have got to get moving."

Kai moved quickly to the path. I had to scramble to keep up with his long strides, still pawing at myself to shuck off lingering cobwebs.

His voice sounded clearer as he shared the rest of what had happened.

"The townspeople were appalled by what they had witnessed. It seemed their initial reaction was more about the magic revelation than my appearance. When Rosella vanished, for once they looked at me with sympathy, not fear. But I no longer care what I looked like in their eyes. You are way more important to me than that bitch's curse."

"How long have I been gone?"

"Hours," he replied. I gasped, noticing the low sun on the horizon.

It had felt like minutes to me.

"Ben was certain she had you in her warehouse. He's searching for you on the security cameras. Grandmother Kateri suggested I go to the Salty Swan to get help from Wanda. Then it hit me: Wanda told you that *fear* is their fuel. I knew you feared the creatures in the forest, and the marsh. Jon and the other rangers are leading search parties around here, but I headed to the spot where the pukwudgies lured you into the forest the day we met. When I passed the old house, I remembered your recurring dream.

"I spent two hours trying to find a way inside. It seemed impregnable. The old travelers must have placed spells on the doors and windows. Finally, I broke in from beneath the house."

Cold wind swept across our faces.

"Hurry, we have to get to the tunnel, and we cannot be seen by any of her pukwudgie spies." We ran up the trail to Black Pond. The tunnel entrance between the lean-to and viewing dock where Kai left my bracelet was the closest entrance.

We ran at a full sprint when I spotted a dark face in the trees. Terror blossomed in the pit of my stomach. I couldn't swallow, I couldn't breathe, I couldn't think. I slowed and stopped running. She would know I escaped and come after us.

"Come on, baby. We're almost there," Kai urged me on.

"Her spies have found us."

Kai glared into the forest. The defeated look on his face was heart-rending. *What can I do? Think. Be calm. What did the shop owner tell me? "Your pure heart needs a clear mind. Fear is their fuel, yet your heart is kind." Kind. I must be kind.*

"I have an idea," I said quietly.

I cautiously approached the stone pukwudgie. He appeared to be alone. Grabbing my favorite heart-shaped pink tourmaline from my pocket, I tossed it across the trail. It rolled briefly, stopping at the creature's stone feet.

The creature peered down at the stone and back up at me. Past the point of caring, I dared to look directly into his eyes. "Take it. It is a gift."

I motioned for him to pick it up.

"Hurry, let's go," I said, tugging on Kai's arm.

We took off again as the sun dropped below the horizon.

When we reached the tunnel, Kai directed me to slide down the sides of the ladder revealed beneath a trap door. He climbed down after me and closed the entrance securely behind us.

"Do you think the pukwudgie will notify Rosella that I found you?" Kai asked through rapid breaths.

I hugged myself, trying to hold it together. "That's why I threw my heart stone to it. I was trying to be kind, to offer it as a gift. The stone was precious to me. I don't know if it will work, but I had to try something."

Kai pulled me to his chest, and I began to sob again.

"What are we going to do?" I asked in a broken mumble. I doubt he understood me, but he didn't ask me to repeat myself; he just stroked my hair.

The hum of the tram reminded me of the sound I'd heard when the pukwudgies touched me. I gritted my teeth throughout the ride. When we reached the cave, Kai swiftly got on the phone to notify the search parties I had been found. Meanwhile, I closed my eyes, fighting the compulsion to throw up.

Ben and Jon were waiting for us in the great room.

"Lily," Jon shouted, pushing Kai out of the way and pulling me into a bear hug.

"Can't breathe," I wheezed.

Jon released me, and Ben swarmed in, hugging me from the side with one arm.

"Where is everyone else?" Kai asked.

"Most of them are on their way here. Jon and I were just heading to the office to watch the security cameras. Do you want to come?"

I swayed dizzily as exhaustion caught up with me. I felt like I had played five soccer games in a row. Kai scooped his hand under my elbow.

"I need to take care of Lily first."

Kai got me into a chair in the kitchen and set a bowl on the table.

"Please, try to eat something. It will make you feel better."

I stirred the noodles and watched the steam swirl out of the bowl. It reminded me of the gray smoke Rosella had cast around us. It was hard to swallow after screaming so desperately, but the warm liquid soothed my scratchy throat. "This is good. Thank you."

Kai sat beside me.

After I finished, we heard voices in the great room, and Kai placed a hand on my thigh. "Do you think you can handle talking with everyone now?"

I took one more sip of the broth. "Yes."

In the great room, Sakari had joined most of the adults who called the caves home. Jon dove right in, speaking with animated hands.

"Rosella's outburst at the parade has caught a lot of attention, in town and at the quarry. Workers are asking about mind control. Townsfolk are asking some big questions about stuff they used to think was only legend. I doubt it will end up in the paper, but the gossip mill is running overtime."

"Workers walked off their jobs in the middle of their shifts. Most of them were shocked to learn they were being manipulated," Kai's mother said.

I gasped. "What if she curses them?"

Sakari looked worried. "I talked to as many of them as I could. She might decide to keep a low profile for a while, but I explained what she is capable of and urged them to continue working for now."

Tanja paced from the chairs to the stream. Elan was still down in the mine and had no idea what had happened.

When it was my turn to talk, I rubbed my tense shoulders and gathered my courage. Kai placed his hands beneath mine, taking over massaging my shoulders. I did not even recognize my own scratchy voice telling the story of being trapped in the house, but I made sure to repeat the warning from the shop owner: "Your pure heart needs a clear mind. Fear is their fuel, yet your heart is kind."

I struggled to clear my throat. "Search deep inside yourselves to recognize any real fears you have. You should share them with someone else in case she attacks this way again. I would still be stuck if Kai hadn't guessed where to find me."

My pulse quickened when I got to the part concerning our encounter with the lone pukwudgie. "I looked directly at the stone pukwudgie. To be kind, I offered it a gift. It wasn't much, just a polished stone I carried in my pocket for luck, but it was dear to me. Why shouldn't we show them some kindness? The myths say they were once friendly with humans. Rosella has tricked them. She uses them. I would be furious with humans too, if they controlled me and stole my magical abilities." I was beginning to ramble.

Sakari shut me down. "They are dangerous tricksters. They will lure you to your death," she said flatly, flushed.

"I wouldn't trust them," Ben said honestly.

"Neither would I," Tanja said, shaking her head.

I wanted to defend my actions but fell silent at Sakari's expression. She had already decided against it, and I didn't want to create more friction between us.

Kai dropped his hands and shook his head. The time was just after ten. The curse would be lifted for the next two hours.

When Elan arrived, Tanja and Ben filled him in on what he'd missed. Before Kai's mother left, she and Kai conversed tersely near the tunnel entrance. Sakari's face was red. She punctuated every word she spoke with a tap on Kai's shoulder. His lips flattened, and he stood with his arms crossed, silent. Finally, Sakari kissed his cheek and swiftly exited through the tunnel.

"What was that about?" I asked.

Kai averted his eyes. "Don't worry about it. Let's get cleaned up."

Kai and I retired to his room, dragging our feet. I was grateful we had already moved past the awkwardness of showering together because I wasn't sure I could stand on my shaky legs without his support. My reflection was atrocious. My clothes were dirty, cobwebs matted my hair, and dirt smudged my face. My knuckles were bruised and split. I should have been embarrassed, but I was too tired to care. We washed each other's hair twice, trying to rid ourselves of the sticky webs and grime we had crawled through. The hot water revitalized my weary brain and body.

Afterward, Kai added a few logs to the fire in his room, sending sparks dancing upward. I slipped into some joggers and one of Kai's shirts. I felt safe amid the manly smell of musk, rock, and wood.

Resting my hands on his hips, I pressed my forehead to his chest.

"I'm so sorry. I messed everything up."

Kai lifted my chin with his fingers. "Lily, you did not mess anything up. You stood up for me. You risked your life for me."

The sorrow in his eyes was unbearable. I closed my eyes so I wouldn't have to see it.

"What about your job? I ruined your undercover operation."

"You ruined nothing. It was my decision to work for her. We will find another way to defeat her."

"Do you think she'll come after me?"

"No, I don't." His eyes begged me to believe what he said. "Too many people witnessed her outburst. She will have to repair the damage to her reputation first and deal with any rebellion after."

"Do you think she'll curse anyone else?"

"I hope not, but my mother is very concerned that she will. She is meeting with the town leaders tomorrow to explain how Rosella had been influencing people with the use of spells and dark magic. They have no idea of the power she has harnessed with the use of the pukwudgies' magic. She wants to convince them to join with us and try to minimize any problems." Kai pulled on a long-sleeve T-shirt. "But I only care that you are safe and that she did not curse you. I won't let her hurt you."

His lips found mine, and I forgot everything else.

His long fingers rested briefly on my shoulders before he slipped them lightly down my spine, eliciting a shiver. He stopped at the small of my back, where I was the most ticklish, and moved his fingers in light circles. My body betrayed me.

"I think I have found your weak spot," he whispered in my ear, sending more chills through me.

Remembering the feel of the cobwebs, I squealed and squirmed to get away.

"What's the matter, Lily. Are you ticklish?"

"Stop, please stop," I pleaded, giggling and crying at the same time. "No, no, yes, it tickles, it tickles. It's making me think about cobwebs. It's creeping me out."

Kai rolled back, chuckling. I rolled on top of him and pinned his arms over his head, saying, "No more tickling."

Kai wore a devilish grin. "So, you think you have me trapped?"

I kissed his neck. "Yes, I do. You are my prisoner."

We both laughed again, heartily. It felt good to laugh.

His good mood suddenly faded. He shook his head with dread in his eyes, and I glanced at the clock. It was 12:11. The curse was returning. That was why he put on long sleeves.

Kai kissed my forehead and turned away. "Let's get some rest."

I clasped my arm around his waist. "I love you, my heart."

"I love you, my swan." He sounded sad.

*　*　*

I expected my night to be filled with restless sleep and was surprised when I awoke feeling refreshed. Light was drifting over the top of the door when Kai opened his eyes. He pulled me onto his chest and kissed me firmly.

Then he stopped abruptly and pulled back. "Sorry."

"For what?"

"For being a monster," he mumbled.

"You have nothing to be sorry for. Come on, Kai. I can handle this."

"I can't."

My stomach dropped, and for a moment I felt like everything inside me was shattering.

"You can. We can."

Kai placed his hands over his face. "I feel so foolish, defeated."

"You saved me! Doesn't that count for anything?"

Kai rose slightly to press his forehead to mine. "You are the only thing that counts." Then he stood, taking my hand. "Let's get some coffee and see if anyone has come up with a plan."

I knew he was just distracting me. Kai's mood remained dark and detached.

Out in the great room, I stirred my coffee, silently watching the interactions around me. Sakari called Kai and updated him on her meeting. I could not hear much of the conversation. I only heard, "They understand," and Kai asked her, "How many more?" before they hung up.

"When does Wade start?" Kai asked.

"Monday," Tate answered.

Jace was studying blueprints of the compound and reviewing them with Tate.

"I think we can block it or even divert it here. What do you think?"

Tate studied the document, tracing the area with his finger.

Kai and Ben entered a deep conversation about the security cameras and the large warehouse. "Now that the people have seen the pukwudgies, she's openly using them to guard the warehouse. We need to find a new way to get inside."

"That is why I was asking about Wade. If Rosella gets the supply of black tourmaline she has been asking for, they will most likely store it in this structure. Wade needs to be on that delivery," Kai said before his phone rang again. He stepped out of the room to answer it.

A few thoughts circled my head, mostly centered on the pukwudgies. No one seemed to care about the poor creatures because they were dangerous, yet so much of Rosella's influence seemed to rely on their abilities. Without them, how much power did she have?

Kai's hand landed on my shoulder. I had not noticed him return.

"That was the chief of the forestry department. He heard what happened and gave me my job back."

"That's great news."

Ben patted him on the back. "Welcome back."

A little after ten, the curse lifted, and the energy in the room did too. I was glad to see Kai's mood had lightened.

The ride back to campus was quiet. So much had changed over the winter break. I couldn't imagine how I was going to return to school and act like everything was normal. The revelations of the past few weeks filled my mind.

After Kai parked, we sat in silence, huddled in the truck. Kai mindlessly traced his finger down my arm, over each finger, and back up my arm again as I ruffled the silky hair at the back of his head.

"You're driving me crazy the way you are rubbing my head. If you don't stop, I won't be able to let you go."

I cut my eyes to his hand. "Likewise."

Contentment radiated through me. Kai gave me strength I didn't know I had. I was determined to fight for him, no matter the cost.

I had to learn to balance both worlds.

CHAPTER 37

I TOOK A FEW breaths before I opened the door to the suite at the dorm, bracing myself. Aspen and Berly were sitting on the couch in the common room, cradling coffee cups.

"Good morning," I said as Kai followed me in. "Or should I say, rough morning. It looks like we missed a bit of fun last night."

Berly tilted her head back over the couch cushion with a half grin and disheveled hair.

"I guess you could say that. Although it was more than a bit, and you would not miss the way my head feels right now."

"It looks like you could use a greasy breakfast," I said cheerfully. Aspen moaned, and Brooklyn shuffled into the room in wrinkled clothes. I hugged her clammy neck. "Morning."

She grunted and made a beeline for the coffee maker. Kai and I searched the pantry and refrigerator. "You have a few options: oatmeal, peanut butter crackers, or a cup of soup. Otherwise, it's time to head to the cafeteria," I said.

Berly held up her hand. "Crackers."

I threw her a pack, and Kai motioned to my suitcase.

"Should I put this in your room?"

"Yes, we should." When I reached for the door to my room, it popped open, and Martin emerged wearing British-flag-print pajama bottoms and a fluffy pink robe that was too small for him. His hair looked like a chia pet.

"Me noggin' is achin'. Must have some bacon," he said groggily, stumbling around me. He kissed Berly on the top of the head and plopped next to her on the couch. "Hiya, love. Hide me if the dorm cops come in."

Berly chuckled. "I'm sure they'll think you're one of us."

Kai and I went into the bedroom, and I shut the door behind us. Kai set my bag on my bed. I folded myself into his arms. When he leaned back, his serious expression was alarming.

"I'm sorry I got you mixed up in this." His voice was velvety, and the golden flecks sparkled in his human eyes. "I love you. I cannot—will not—let her touch you ever again. You are my world."

My chest constricted. "I love you."

"Call me immediately if you see any signs of Rosella around here."

I suddenly felt all alone and abandoned. I gripped Kai tighter, pressing myself against him. I wanted to pull him closer, but we were already as close as magnets. Gripping his back, I kissed him with urgency. He was so solid. I needed his strength right now.

He didn't resist but pulled away after a few moments.

"Lily," he whispered against my cheek.

"I'm scared," I admitted. "I don't want you to leave."

"I'm sorry, but I need to go. It is almost noon. You must be brave. Brave like a swan."

"I know. I will," I said, attempting to pull myself together mentally so I would not fall back into my wimpy flight-not-fight mentality.

After Kai left, Max arrived and was soon dancing around the common room.

"Tallyho, mates, it's time to rally. Hair of the dog will cure your bangin' head."

Berly shook her head, but Martin looked like he could be persuaded.

"It's our last night of freedom," Max added.

"Food, I need food. Please, can we just go to the cafeteria?" Brooklyn pleaded.

"Jolly good! We can start with a cuppa and go from there." Max grinned, full of glee. It was hard for anyone to be in a bad mood around him. He had a natural way of lifting people up.

It was time for me to toughen up, lighten up, and readjust to this half of my crazy life.

"I'm in! You know I'll always eat," I announced.

Max patted my back. "Atta girl. Chop-chop." People scattered to change. Max and I sat on the couch. "How was your holiday?"

"Really nice. It was good to see my family and spend time with Kai." My answer sounded scripted, almost robotic, but what else could I say? "What about you?"

"It was brass monkeys outside most of the time." He prattled on and ended with "She was bonkers."

I had difficulty keeping up with the story because his accent had become much stronger. Thankfully, the others returned, and we headed to the dining hall.

On the walk, Aspen crept up beside me. "How's it going with Kai?"

"Great, why do you ask?"

I knew the reason—I just wanted to see her squirm.

"I was just wondering. You make such a cute couple."

"Thanks."

"Have you seen Nate and Troy?"

"Not yet. I just got back to campus."

"Didn't you come back last week?"

"I did, but I only picked up my schedule and books. I didn't stay here."

"Oh. Oh!" It must have clicked in her brain where I had been staying because her mouth dropped open and she slowed her pace.

I chose that moment to catch up to Berly.

"How was London?"

She flashed her dimples. "Bangin'! You must come with us next time."

"I'm so glad you had fun."

"How was Florida?"

"Warmish."

She pulled at her scarf. "I'm jealous."

The dining hall was packed with students.

"Wow, look at this place. Bring on the winter sports," I said, trying to sound normal.

Berly leaned toward me. "We'd better stock up on breakfast items. This is going to be insane in the mornings."

"Agreed."

The swarm of people was a great distraction. Going through the motions was easier amid the mindless chatter. People really didn't want to know what I did on break; they were just waiting to tell me what they did on theirs. So I asked questions and tried to sound interested. Then I grabbed more food to take back to the dorm.

Max persuaded a few guys to meet him at the recreation hall, but none of our group seemed willing to join him. Berly and Martin went to the bookstore, and I excused myself.

"I'm heading back to the dorm. I need to get unpacked and ready for class tomorrow."

I took a long, hot shower. It wasn't long enough. Resisting the urge to call Kai, I reviewed my class schedule and organized my books. Then I opened my laptop and searched the internet for information on Mirror Lake as it related to magic. The first thing that popped up was a book: *Curses and Magic Spells of the Ancient Romany Gypsies*. Some of the topics listed on the preview of the table of contents included how to invoke curses or blessings, conjure or channel spirits, and develop skill with illusions. *Rosella is invoking curses. Can she conjure spirits or cast illusions?*

My being trapped in the house for hours had certainly not been an illusion. Kai saved me, so it had to be real.

Next, I searched for spells that used black tourmaline. As a grounding stone, black tourmaline could help a person relax, especially during stressful moments or even panic attacks. *Does she calm her victims before she manipulates their minds?* I wondered.

I searched pukwudgies again. They could be dangerous, but only to people who treated them with disrespect. Every entry stated that they had strong magical powers. The only similarities between the stone figures I had encountered and the pictures on the internet were the height, hands, and feet.

The door popped open, and Berly stepped in.

"I snuck away." She giggled. I quickly shut my laptop. "Whatcha working on, Lil?" She was slurring a little. It appeared that Max had gotten his way.

"Nothing, really. Just getting ready for classes tomorrow."

She flopped on her bed. "Ugh, tomorrow. Max is crazy. You were smart to stay away. I need an aspirin, a shower, and a good night's sleep. Then I'll be ready to slay this semester."

I loved her confidence. Berly was the best roommate and best friend I could have dreamed of. I admired her general attitude.

Kai called while she was in the shower.

"Evening, my love. How was your day?"

"Good, I guess. I'm ready for tomorrow. Did anything happen after I left?"

"Not much. It looks like Rosella wants to be inconspicuous for a while. Jace said she never left the compound today."

"That's good news, right?"

"For now. We pray people will show up for work tomorrow so she does not seek vengeance."

"Where are you working tomorrow?"

"The chief wants me to stay inside at the control center. I'll be monitoring the security cameras with Ben. Ben thinks it's too dangerous for me to be out in the forest."

"Good."

"Jon will be on the trails near campus tomorrow. Call us if you see anything strange. Stay safe, my love."

"You too."

I received a text at 11:11: "Missing you, my love."

"xoxo," I replied.

CHAPTER 38

The next morning, I layered up before trudging across campus to my first class. The crisp wind chilled my bones. The walkways were crowded with students wearing jackets with logos for winter sports. It made me feel silly about my soccer scholarship. Winter sports were clearly more popular in this area.

I settled in a seat near the front of the classroom.

A deep male voice asked, "Is this seat taken?"

I looked up to see Nate smiling at me shyly. He had let his sandy-blond hair grow out, and it looked good curling below his ears.

"So good to see you." I stood and gave him a light one-armed hug. "How was your holiday?"

"It was fun but extremely cold. My brothers and I did a lot of fly-fishing, hiking, and camping. What about you?"

"Florida stayed pretty warm. I spent some time at the beach but mostly hung out with family."

"Must be nice."

The teacher entered, and students quickly found seats. Every desk was taken. Nate leaned over and commented, "I don't think we'll be able to swap any classes this semester."

I was surprised when the class ended. It seemed like we had only been seated for a few minutes.

"Where's your next class?" Nate asked.

"This building."

"Mine is next door. I'd better hurry so I can secure a seat. See ya."

Nate zipped up and dashed outside.

After lunch, I had two more classes. Luckily, they were both in the same building again. Somehow, I had managed to arrange a great schedule without trying. I found my last class easily and secured a seat in the middle, near the front, my favorite spot.

"Is this seat taken?"

I turned back to see Nate wearing an uncomfortably large smile.

"Be my guest." I motioned for him to sit.

"I can't believe we have two classes together. This will be great for studying," he said with enthusiasm.

"Yeah, it will," I hesitantly agreed.

Near the end of class, my stomach growled loudly. Nate cheerfully handed me a power bar.

"Here, eat this. I always keep a few with me for times like this."

Heat rushed to my cheeks.

"Thanks."

We left the classroom together after class. Nate chattered about the lecture and assignments we needed to complete, making it easy for me because he was basically having a one-sided conversation. Suddenly, I choked on a piece of the power bar and began coughing uncontrollably.

Nate patted my back. "Are you okay? Lily, can you breathe?"

I couldn't answer. Tears rimmed my eyes. I was mortified that he might try the Heimlich maneuver on me. Instead, he said, "Come on, let's get you something to drink."

He took hold of my elbow and steered me to the coffee bar. I was still coughing lightly when he handed me a cup. The first sip soothed my throat, and I gulped down the rest.

"Thank you so much," I managed to say after the hacking subsided.

"No problem," Nate said, looking pleased with himself.

"I'm a mess. First you feed me, then I gag to death, and you must save me again."

"It's what any gentleman would do." He placed his hand on my arm again. Brooklyn and Aspen picked that moment to enter the coffee shop, and Aspen's eyes cut right to Nate's hand.

I quickly moved my arm, my aggravation rising.

"Hey, you two. How was your first day?"

"Brutal. That's why we're getting coffee. I already have a ton of homework," Brooklyn answered.

"Same here," I commiserated.

"What brings you here?" Aspen asked Nate directly.

"Lily was choking, so we got her some water."

"Leave it to me to choke on a power bar." I stood up. "Thanks again, Nate."

"Are you going to meet Kai?" Aspen asked, blatantly seeking to remind Nate that I was dating someone.

I focused on keeping my voice calm. "No, I need to get to the library."

"Can I come with you?" Brooklyn asked.

"Sure."

"Just give me a minute to get a coffee."

"What are you doing the rest of the day?" Aspen asked Nate after her sister headed to the counter.

He glanced at his watch. "Troy is meeting me at the forestry cabin for practice in twenty minutes."

"Why don't you stay and finish your coffee?" Aspen said, her eyes flicking toward me above a smug smile.

"As you wish," Nate answered like a proper gentleman.

But he looked at me with sadness in his eyes. I wished he wouldn't look at me like a puppy being left at home. He was so nice and helpful. It was hard not to like him.

★ ★ ★

By the end of the week, I had gotten into the swing of things and was well ahead on my homework. School was a great distraction. I talked to Kai every day, and he confirmed Rosella was lying low, probably waiting for things to blow over. She had demonstrated openly to the townsfolk that she could conjure up a curse, and she exposed the pukwudgies, which before were only a legend. She needed for the tale of what had happened to pass into rumor and legend rather than something a crowd of rational people had objectively witnessed.

Nate and I left class together on Friday afternoon.

"Any plans for the weekend?" he asked nonchalantly.

"I'm going out with Kai tonight. Shopping with Berly tomorrow, and I have no idea about Sunday." His sad look made me feel guilty and then annoyed. "What about you?"

"Troy and I are training for the next lumberjack competition, so I'll probably be at the woodsman arena all weekend."

"When's the next competition?"

"The end of the month," he answered.

"I can't wait. You guys are too good. You'll crush the competition."

His cheeks turned cherry red, and he kicked a sodden leaf off the sidewalk.

"We'll try."

"Come on, you know you have no competition. You guys are deadly with an axe." His gaze lingered on my face again for longer than I liked. "Good luck with your training." I waved and scrambled down the path to the dorms.

At the parking lot, I brushed the snow off the stone wall and sat on top. My pulse quickened when I spotted Kai's truck coming up the road. He parked and jumped out in one swift movement, locking me in a tender embrace.

"Good evening, my love," he said.

"My heart, I'm so glad you're here. I missed you."

His lips met mine, and I forgot anything I was about to say. Our kisses became unconstrained. When I brushed my hand across his back, I felt the rough texture of scales under his uniform and automatically moved my hand to his hip. Kai instantly pulled back. As he opened the door to the truck, he shook his head.

"Is everything okay?" I asked once inside.

"Yeah, everything is fine." I wished I could see his eyes to determine whether he was telling the truth. "I hope you don't mind eating in tonight." He gestured to his chest. "I'm kind of stuck this way until ten."

"It's perfectly fine with me. I would rather not be seen in public right now anyway."

My head buzzed with nervousness. I was balancing two worlds, the real world and the cursed world. Now I also had to balance between Kai's moods. Things were much simpler when I didn't know anything—and when Rosella had lifted the curse. I hated that he was embarrassed. I hated myself more for pulling my hand away.

"Rosella left the compound today. Jace said she went to Mirror Lake again," Kai mentioned.

"How is Wade doing? Has he made any deliveries?"

"One of the drivers did not return, so Wade has been assigned to local deliveries. He hasn't made any yet, but at least he will be close to the compound."

After my long week, the rich smells in the cave and the fire's shimmering light created a relaxing atmosphere. Ben and Jon joined us for dinner, and we watched an old movie afterward. It was a Western full of twists and turns.

At one point, Kai pulled me onto his lap, whispering, "We are good, you know. I am sorry for this mess, but I'm not sorry for loving you." His breath tickled my neck.

When I turned to kiss him, his eyes were normal again.

"Complicated, but good," I whispered back.

"Shhh," Ben hushed us with one finger to his lips.

By the movie's end, we were all rooting for the bad guy. He had done some terrible things but had charisma and unexpectedly staunch morals.

Kai drove me back to campus just before midnight. He parked and said, "I'm escorting you back to the dorm."

I raised my eyebrow. "What about the campus police?"

"You're already past curfew." He touched one finger to my nose. "It's too late to let you walk alone, and frankly, I don't care about the rules anymore."

We did not pass a single person on the walkways, not even a guard, which was unnerving, though I was sure cameras were recording our every move. When we reached the door, I wrapped my arms around his waist.

"Thank you for the nice night and the personal escort."

"No problem. It's the least I could do. Would it be too much to ask that we do the same thing tomorrow night? It's four days until a full moon."

"It sounds perfect. I'll text you when Berly and I get back from shopping."

"Love you."

"I love you too."

When we kissed, I felt whole. I almost forgot about Rosella and her curse.

CHAPTER 39

SHOPPING WITH BERLY the following day started down by Mirror Lake. According to Berly, the shops there had the best skiing equipment, and she wanted to buy something for Martin.

"This is it!" Hopping excitedly, she held a Burton snowboard aloft mere minutes after entering the first store. "He's been talking about this for months. I can't believe they have it."

I was stunned by the price, which of course didn't faze Berly at all. She then searched for the perfect binders to go with the board and bought a matching Gore-Tex jacket.

"This is the best material. Feel how lightweight, and you can stay outside three times as long."

"Maybe I should get one of those."

"You should. Let's go look at the women's section."

The cheapest one I found was $425, but she was right; their jackets were remarkable. I texted Dad to ask if I could get one, pleading that I was freezing. Of course he said to get it. Berly purchased the crystal-blue one, and I chose one in jade spruce. We had just spent about $1,800 in a half hour.

"I forgot how dangerous it is to shop with you," I said wryly.

"I'm just getting warmed up. We have a few more shops on this strip before we head downtown."

Berly opened the back hatch so the clerk could load her large purchases in the jeep for us. I was standing beside the rear door when

I glanced down the road. A large black sedan was heading straight toward us. Without thinking, I backed up and onto the sidewalk. I knew my face was red because my ears were hot.

"What's up?" Berly asked. I kept my eyes on the car, and Berly turned to see what I was staring at. The sedan had stopped at a traffic light only a block away. The light turned green.

As the car pulled forward, I hurried to move out of sight and fell over a small fence and into a large hedge.

"Ouch," I squealed, landing on my back with my feet waving in the air.

Berly and the clerk ran to me, full of concern. The clerk extended his hand to help me up.

"Are you all right?"

I stood and brushed the dirt off my pants. The black sedan sped past. I couldn't hold in my laughter. "What a klutz."

"What were you looking at?" Berly asked. "You looked afraid."

"It was a bee. Didn't you see it?" I forced a giggle, hoping to convince her.

"No, I didn't see anything except you upside down in the bushes. I wish I had taken your picture before you crawled out of there." She flashed a dimple.

If that was Rosella's car, she wasn't looking for me. She was probably visiting Mirror Lake again. I didn't bother texting Kai.

Berly and I shopped the entire strip before driving to the downtown area. The streets were jam-packed with people.

"Wow, it's crowded," I commented.

"It's always like this during the winter months," Berly said. "People flock here for the winter sports. The Olympic complex has some of the best ski jumps in the world. We must go watch them sometime soon."

"Sure, that sounds fun."

After I said, "Pardon" for the sixth or seventh time as we swerved through the crowds, Berly stopped and stomped her foot. "This is nuts. Do you want to stop for a coffee or something? I need a break from this chaos."

"Sounds like a good idea. The Coffee Bar or Mountain Cafe?"

"Coffee Bar," she said quickly.

"This way." I motioned to the left, slipping my arm through Berly's. We were in the middle of the block when I noticed the black sedan parked across the street. Rosella was leaving the Salty Swan, flanked by two men in uniform.

I halted, my eyes locked on Rosella.

"What's going on?" Berly followed my stare to Rosella. "Who is that?"

"Kai's old boss. She does not like me. We need to go, and we need to go now." I escorted Berly to an old general store, slowly backing up the steps. "Stay behind me. Don't let her see you."

Too late. Rosella's eyes locked on mine. She shouted to her guards and pointed in my direction.

I leaped through the door, dragging Berly with me. The store was huge—three full stories of touristy junk.

"Run!" I yelled. Berly's face turned white, so I grabbed her hand and headed downstairs. Thankfully, the people in the store parted, and we rushed past.

"Quick, through here," I said, pushing open a door marked Employees Only. We sped through the back room to the loading dock.

I waved to the driver like we were employees and slipped outside. We raced behind the stores for a block or two before I realized we were leaving footprints in the snow. I signaled to Berly. "This way."

We slipped along the side of a building until we landed back on the sidewalk.

"Why are we running from her?" Berly demanded, alarmed.

"I'll explain later." We weaved through the crowd, looking over our shoulders until we reached the next block.

I called Kai, and he answered on the first ring.

"She's here!"

"Where?"

Between breaths, I answered, "Downtown. She saw me and sent her guards after us. We're running from them now."

"Where are you? Exactly?" I heard the panic in his voice.

"In front of the Pickled Pig."

"Go one more block, turn left, and go to the shed. Stay on the stones so you do not leave footprints. Go around to the back door and pull the red cord. Once you get inside, lock the door quickly. Call me once you are safe inside, and I will tell you where you should go from there."

"Okay. Thanks."

"Hurry."

My adrenaline surged. Berly was running as fast as she could to keep up with me. Once we turned left, I pointed to the stone path.

"We have to stay on the stones so we don't leave footprints."

Berly nodded, wide eyed.

We stepped into the shed, and I locked the door behind us. It was hard to catch our breath in the musty old shed. The darkness and smell reminded me of being trapped in the house with no exits.

"Kai, we're in the shed."

"Lift up the top on the bench; you should feel a ladder. You can use your phones for light as you climb down, but the tunnel itself will be lit. Take the tram to Sakari's. She's home and waiting for you. Do you remember how to get there?"

"Yes."

"Be careful, my love. I will meet you there as soon as I can."

I helped Berly into the miner's cart. She simply stared straight ahead and did what I told her. When the cart started humming down the track, I took her hand.

"I'm so sorry to scare you like that and to get you involved." Plagued with guilt, I rambled on, "I'm sure she didn't get a good look at you. She will never recognize you."

Berly blinked. "What . . . who . . . why?" She shook her head and covered her face with both hands, clearly overwhelmed. "Involved in what?" she asked, her voice muffled. She dropped her hands to her sides and finally seemed to recognize how strange our surroundings were. "Where are we?"

"In the tunnels," I answered, receiving a blank expression in return. "This is a mining town. Kai and his friends made underground tunnels a few years ago so they could travel from place to place without being seen." It was true, just not the whole reason.

"How long have you known about this?"

"For about a month or two. We use it to go out at night. It's safer and faster than driving."

"Why are you running from that lady?"

"That is a rather long story. I might need Kai's help with the details, but long story short, Kai went to work for Rosella over the Christmas break. She wanted him to be more than a guard, but he refused her advances. She caught us together at a parade and pitched a fit."

I was trying to hide secrets that weren't mine, but I knew that much of what was happening wouldn't make sense if I didn't share the most absurd parts.

"She cast a spell on me," I blurted out, "trapping me in that old, abandoned house in the marsh. Kai rescued me. Now we're afraid she wants revenge."

Berly's eyes were wide, but she wasn't looking at me like I was insane. That was encouraging.

Sakari must have heard us coming in from the tunnel. She rushed to me as we emerged into the laundry room, taking my face in her hands and kissing both cheeks. She hugged me so hard I could barely breathe.

"I'm so glad you are safe." It was not the greeting I expected. "Come in. Let me get you some tea, coffee, hot chocolate."

In the main part of the house, I made introductions.

"Sakari, this is my roommate, Berly. Berly, this is Kai's mother,

Mrs. Sakuna."

Sakari shook Berly's hand. "Call me Sakari. Mrs. Sakuna sounds old. Coffee? Tea?"

"Nice to meet you. Coffee would be great. Would you mind if I used the restroom?"

Berly sounded calm, though her voice trembled slightly.

"Second door on the right." Sakari motioned down the hall, then turned toward me. "How much does she know?"

"Not much, only that Kai worked for Rosella and that she wanted him for more than work. And that she placed a spell on me when she found us together, and the tunnels were made by the guys for easy travel," I sputtered, trying to tell her everything quickly.

"Do you trust her?"

"Like a sister."

"I think we should fill her in on everything. She could be in danger now and needs to understand the severity of the problem. Are you okay with that?"

I eagerly agreed.

When Berly came back, Sakari and I told her the entire story. Berly sat quietly and absorbed all the details. To my surprise, she shared some details of her own.

"Our realtor warned my father about a powerful lady who owned the quarry and mines. She said not to do any business with her."

Sakari kept gently stroking my hair and patting my hand, and for a while she just held one of my hands between hers. Her sudden affection confused me.

"How many people has she cursed?" Berly asked, unflinching and unquestioning.

"Seven that we know of. There were more, but Rosella will remove the curse if you go back to work for her. That's what Kai did." I hung my head, blinking back the tears. Sakari squeezed my hand. "He went to work for her so she would lift the curse and we could be together. Rosella decided she wanted him for herself." My voice cracked.

Berly sat up straight. "This is messed up!"

"I know. I am so sorry. I never meant to get you involved."

"I'm not sorry. In a strange way, I'm glad I know. You shouldn't have to go through this on your own, and besides, that crazy spell-casting witch didn't get a look at me. She was too busy looking at you."

"Berly, she is dangerous, very dangerous. Do not underestimate her power," Sakari warned.

Kai burst through the front door and engulfed me in a hug. I lifted my face, expecting a quick kiss hello in front of his mother, but he surprised me by locking his lips on mine and kissing me until my knees were weak. He pulled back a centimeter.

"Are you all right?" But he didn't let me answer; he just resumed kissing. He sighed heavily before he finally let me go.

"I'm fine. We're fine." I gestured toward Berly.

He picked her up in a bear hug, her feet dangling about a foot above the floor. "Are you okay? I'm so sorry."

"I'm fine, now that I can breathe," she answered after he put her down.

Kai kissed Sakari on both cheeks. "Mother."

"My heart," she replied.

"Thank you for letting them come here."

"Of course."

"Jon will be here in about an hour. He can bring Berly back to her car so she can get home. Lily, we should wait until after dark to take you back to campus." Kai sounded like he was giving orders in the military.

Berly stood with her hands on her hips. "So, what is this curse?" she asked Kai directly.

He looked at me uncertainly.

"It's okay," I said. "Sakari and I told her everything. It's a safety issue in case she ever runs into Rosella again."

Kai let out a heavy breath and removed his sunglasses and scarf simultaneously.

Berly sucked in air, but her expression remained steady.

"That's a bitch. She's a bitch." She stepped closer to study his eyes, her gaze drifting to the wide green scales on his neck. "She is a bitch," she repeated under her breath. Kai slipped the sunglasses back on. "You don't have to put those on for me. I can handle it."

"Thanks, but I would prefer to keep them on," he muttered.

Berly glanced at the clock on the wall.

"What time do you need to be back on campus?" I asked.

"I have reservations for 6:30."

Sakari picked up her coat. "Come on, I will take you back to your car. No need to wait on Jon."

"Are you sure?" I said, placing my hand on Sakari's arm.

"It's the least I can do." A strange smile twisted across her face. "Besides, I don't think Rosella would want to fence with me right now anyway."

I was too stunned to say anything.

Berly gave me a quick hug at the front door.

"Go get to the party," I said. "Be careful. I'll see you back on campus. Wish Martin happy birthday from us."

"We'll be in the rec hall later."

"I'm not in the mood for any party. I'm so sorry we dragged you into this."

"I'm not," she reiterated, her confidence unwavering. "I love you. Be strong."

"I love you too."

Kai placed his arm across my shoulders as Berly and Sakari disappeared into the garage.

"Text me when you get to the car," I yelled, "and when you get back to campus!"

I curled into Kai's chest and let out a sob. I didn't mean to cry, but as soon as he curled around me, I let go. He gently stroked my hair. All I managed to say was "Why?"

I held on tighter, fearing I was about to break apart. He smelled like leather and musk. The familiar scent made me feel safe. But I wasn't.

CHAPTER 40

KAI USED HIS mother's car to return me to campus in case Rosella's spies were tracking him. He gripped the steering wheel, his knuckles white. Silence with Kai was never good, especially when his jaw muscles were clenching.

"What are you thinking about?"

"Just about you and my messed-up life."

I felt uncomfortable—the kind of feeling I typically got before realizing I was about to throw up.

Kai parked the car and came around to my door. Without looking at me, he held out his hand. His expression was grim.

"Let me escort you back to your room."

I slipped out of the car and took his hand. Cold crept up my spine as we neared the dorm. Everything was silent except for the muted crunch of snow. In the distance, music drifted from the recreation building.

Panic was on the verge of overtaking me when we reached the building door. Kai wrapped his arms around me and rocked me lightly. We stood that way for some time. Longer than we normally would. My heart thumped against my chest. I wanted to stay there forever.

When he pulled back, his face looked like death.

"I can't do this to you anymore." His voice grew raspy. "We have to end this."

My head spun. "Don't be silly. It's just complicated, like we said."

"No! It is dangerous, much too dangerous." He sounded so grim.

"I was a fool to think it could work out."

"It will work out." I wanted to sound confident but knew I sounded naive.

"You deserve better. You'll find someone better. Someone less damaged." He hugged me again. I didn't care that I couldn't breathe in his vise grip. I no longer wanted to breathe.

"I will never . . . find someone . . . better than you," I said between sobs.

Tears coated our faces. Kai kissed me hard, one hand at the small of my back, pressing me against him, and the other twisted in my hair. He whispered, "I love you. I will always love you." He let a groan escape. "I must end this before you get hurt. I would never forgive myself. I'm sorry." He kissed my forehead, saying, "Goodbye, my love."

His final tear landed on my cheek.

"No. Please no" was all I could get out between sobs.

Kai turned and walked into the darkness.

It felt like acid was pulsing through my veins. Nothing made sense. I wanted to sleep and never wake up.

***

When the morning light sliced through the windows, I remembered. I didn't want to remember. Agony ripped through me. I wanted it to be a dream. It wasn't a dream. It was a living nightmare.

After closing the curtains, I went back to bed. Berly came in and out of the room a few times, probably assuming I'd had a late night and needed to recover. I just lay there, lifeless, not moving a muscle as time passed.

Berly came back to the room around 9 p.m. with her arms full.

"Have you been in bed all day?"

I tried to answer, but it came out in a croak, and the floodgates opened. Berly dumped her stuff on her bed and sat beside me.

"What's wrong? What happened?" she asked.

"I . . . Kai, he . . ." An ugly moan escaped my throat.

She patted my shoulder. "Did that witchy lady come back?"

I choked out, "He broke up with me. Too . . . dangerous."

"What? No! How could he do that after all you've been through?"

"He doesn't . . . want . . ." I couldn't finish. My sobs became convulsive as I drowned in sorrow.

Berly helped me into a sitting position and rocked me.

"He is a fool, Lily." She paused. "Still, you know he loves you. He adores you. This is only about that crazy witch lady."

I knew she was right but didn't want to hear it. Anger swelled inside me. *To think, I almost gave myself to this man. How could he do this to me?*

"Lily, this whole situation is hard to comprehend, much less navigate. I saw firsthand how scared you were of Rosella. The danger is real. Sakari preached about it on the way to get my jeep—about the danger, about the reasons you two should not be together. I'm not saying I agree, but I understand. And I know you do too."

I closed my red, puffy eyes. Sakari must have finally gotten to Kai.

"Have you eaten anything today?"

I shook my head.

"Come on, why don't you take a hot shower? I'll get you something to eat."

Still numb, I pushed the covers back. "K."

I knew I should be hungry, but food had no meaning. When Berly returned with a muffin and a cup of soup, I merely picked at the muffin and stirred the soup.

"Please don't tell anyone."

"Of course. It will be our secret. Although, what about Martin? I'll need help keeping you busy and away from probing questions."

"Sure." I sighed. "They'll all find out soon enough. I just don't think I can bear it yet."

※ ※ ※

The next morning, Berly laid my new jacket on the end of my bed. I pulled on any clothes I found, not caring whether they matched. Throwing my hair in a ponytail and grabbing the coat and scarf from Berly's cabin, I walked to my first class in a fog.

A cheerful "Good morning" momentarily shook me from my daze as I sat at my desk. It was Nate, bright eyed and energetic.

"Hey" was all I managed to get out before I buried my head in my notebook. Thankfully, the professor gave us a quiz, and we could leave as soon as we finished. I rushed through the quiz to escape conversation with Nate and then hid in the bathroom between classes. I had come full circle, just like in high school when I was too shy to stand up to bullies. How pathetic.

It was inevitable that Nate was going to ask questions in our next class. Trying to prepare myself, I waited until the minute class was supposed to start before going inside, hoping to eliminate the opportunity for small talk. Nate looked happy to see me.

"I saved you a seat." He gestured to the desk beside him.

"Um, thanks."

He leaned over. "Are you okay?"

"Yeah."

"Doesn't seem like it."

Tears welled up in my eyes. I blinked, trying to stop them. This was not a good time to cry. *Get a grip on yourself!* I hugged myself.

When the final bell rang, Nate leaned toward me as we stood.

"Sorry."

"For what?"

"For being frank," he admitted.

"It's okay. I don't mean to be such a"—my voice broke—"a mess."

He placed his hand on my shoulder. "Lily, I'm here if you need anything."

I nodded and bit my thumbnail. I was grateful he did not press further before heading off.

For the rest of the week, Nate saved me a seat in the two classes we shared. He was courteous and only talked about schoolwork. During one class, he offered me a power bar. I declined.

"You need to eat," he said with concern. I took the bar and nibbled on the end before throwing it in the trash when he wasn't looking.

"Some of the lumberjacks are going to Anthony's for pizza after practice tonight," he mentioned during our last class. "Do you think the girls would want to meet us there?"

"Probably. I'll tell Aspen," I answered without thinking.

"What about you?"

I frantically shook my head no. "Thanks anyway." The corners of my mouth tugged down. I ran off to the dorms before I started crying again.

As another week of school ticked past, I went through the motions like a robot. I carried five pink tourmaline stones in my pocket, endlessly running them through my fingers. Painful memories of Kai danced endlessly through my head. It was like a broken rib. I looked normal on the outside, but I was broken on the inside. Everything hurt.

Berly and Martin were nothing but supportive. They dragged me to lunch and dinner. I barely ate anything. Nothing tasted good anymore, so I was living on Cheerios.

Tuesdays and Thursdays were the hardest because I had no classes. I would complete my homework assignments and head to the gym. Running had always cleared my mind. The first week, I ran seven miles each day. By the second week, I was up to ten.

The gym was packed with unfamiliar faces, mostly winter athletes. I started noticing different guys circling the cardio area. Others stood awkwardly around the girls' locker room entrance like sharks circling their prey, no doubt waiting for their opportunity to strike up a conversation full of lies.

Friday, after another refusal of Nate's offer to go out for pizza, I headed to the gym. I was just past nine miles when Benton sauntered through the main doors.

"What do we have here?"

I heard his snide voice over my loud music but ignored him.

"She looks good all sweaty," he said to his footmen. I cringed when he added, "I'd like to make her sweaty."

After I finished my run, I hurried to the locker room. Benton could not follow me in there, and I took the gym's back exit to avoid running into him again.

The slam of the metal door behind me made me jolt. The forest loomed ahead, alive with nighttime activity. Shadowy trees towered over me. Paralyzed with fear, I watched a dark shadow move between two trees. I waited and waited.

Finally, the small figure stepped into the open. For some reason, my fear melted. I had nothing else to lose. *Why was I afraid of these creatures, anyway?* The stone creature held out one hand to me, palms up, just like the one at Mirror Lake. *Be kind*, I told myself.

I plucked a pink stone from my pocket and tossed it to him. "Please take this gift."

The pukwudgie bent down and clutched the polished stone to his chest. White smoke swirled around him. I gaped as the smoke wreathed upward and faded into a hazy, swirling halo over his head.

The creature's transformation was astonishing. The stonelike features were gone, his skin now bluish gray. His features were almost human. He had large, almond-shaped, crystal-blue eyes; oversized, pointed ears; and a long, hooked nose. His black hair was spiked at the top and ran down his back like a war bonnet.

He turned his hands over, studying the change. When his head lifted, his plump cheeks turned apple red, and a large smile spread across his face.

A loud bang alarmed me—the metal door again. Benton and his posse emerged from the side exit and found me alone on the sidewalk.

"Did you get lost? Aren't you afraid that wild animals might get you out here by the forest?" Benton asked, moseying my direction. "Or are you afraid of more dangerous things?" He gestured to his private parts and barked with laughter at his own rancid joke.

"Leave me alone," I spat.

"Why? Don't you want some alone time with me? No lover boy out here to save you. Where *is* lover boy? No lovey-dovey date night?"

His words stung.

"Get lost!" Anger flared in my voice.

The bullies did not notice the pukwudgie. It raised one long, skinny finger, twirling it counterclockwise. A sparkling orange light fizzled at the finger. Like lightning, it arced over to Benton and his friends, coiling around them like a lasso.

Snowy-looking smoke surrounded them for a few seconds. When the smoke dissipated, the three of them wore blank, distant stares. They promptly turned on the sidewalk and trudged slowly back to campus with their heads down.

I looked back at the pukwudgie, placed my hand on my heart, and nodded my thanks. His cheeks were still round and red as apples. He nodded back and bowed deeply as if for royalty.

"Thank you." A small smile worked its way across my face. It felt weird to smile.

The pukwudgie bowed again and disappeared with a pop.

All at once, my mind was racing. *Did the pink tourmaline break the spell on him, or was it the act of kindness—or both?* One thing was for sure: the spell had broken, and the pukwudgie had helped me by getting rid of Benton.

I wondered about the creature Kai and I had encountered near the tunnel. We hadn't waited around to see the effect the gift had.

I pelted down the sidewalk toward the dorms, slipping in the slushy snow as I automatically pulled out my phone. I was about to press Kai's number when I realized what I was doing. Pain ricocheted through me. I threw my phone down in a fit of pique, then dove into the snow to retrieve it.

I dragged my sweaty body into the common room. Brooklyn and Aspen were sitting at the table.

"Hey, Lily, what's up?" Brooklyn asked.

"Not a thing," I answered sourly.

"Where's Kai?" Aspen asked, digging the knife in deeper.

"Working," I replied quickly. "Nate and the guys are going to Anthony's for pizza tonight. They asked me to tell you in case you wanted to go."

"Really?" Her tone was light and chipper.

"Really," I mocked.

"What time are you going?" she asked tentatively.

"I'm not." I didn't bother to explain. "Well, I've got to take a shower. See ya." The smile widened on her face. I resisted the compulsion to slap it off.

An hour later, I walked to the dining hall alone and, ironically, purchased a slice of cheese pizza for dinner. I found a table overlooking the lake. After a few bites, I put the slice down and picked at the crust, wondering whether Kai was walking the trails around the lake. I wondered how many more stone pukwudgies were in the forest.

It was time to put my new coat to the test.

❅ ❅ ❅

I got up early the following morning. Berly, Martin, and Max were going snowboarding. They invited me along, but I declined on the pretense that I was an inexperienced Floridian—though breaking my neck on the slopes sounded better than living with the current crushing feeling in my gut.

I put on my new coat for the first time, adjusting the sleeves and neck scarf and breezing through the instructions to activate the thermoregulating liner and warming pockets. I downed a cup of coffee, grabbed a water and a few power bars, and filled my pockets with the pink tourmaline I'd intended to give to my teammates.

Taking the trail by the marsh, I scurried past the old house. Goose bumps covered my body, even with the liner. I jogged to the spot where I'd first met Kai. Ignoring the trembling in my stomach, I marched off the trail and into the forest, breaking my promise. *What does it matter? He broke his promises to me too.*

After wandering for a good hour, I stopped to rest on a fallen tree. I elected to try waiting for the creatures to come to me and took this break to nibble on a power bar. Time passed slowly. It didn't matter. I had nothing but time.

But after about forty-five minutes, I grew restless. I climbed back to my feet and moved farther into the trees, trying to stay parallel to the trail. The forest grew denser. The sun was barely filtering through the thick canopy.

Gray clouds drifting overhead suddenly darkened, blackening the forest. Cold crept up my spine when I heard a sound. I remembered the bear Kai and I had encountered by the cave, and my heart pounded while I tried to quiet my rapid breathing. Minutes passed. It seemed like hours. I stayed as still as a statue. A small stone creature popped into existence a mere ten feet away.

After the initial gush of panic, I reached into my pocket and tossed it a stone, saying, "Please accept this gift."

The creature picked up the stone. As with the one I'd encountered the night before, white smoke swirled around him, then collected into a churning cloud over his head. The stonelike features were gone. The creature's apple-red cheeks rounded into a smile, and he blinked his large blue eyes. The black stone had been replaced with blue-gray flesh. Small tufts of reddish-brown hair rose from the top of his head.

I stood and bowed to the pukwudgie.

He bowed back, flawlessly.

I threw it three more stones. "If we bond together, I think we can break Rosella's spell. Give these to your friends. It will release them from her power."

I spoke slowly, hoping it understood some English. The pukwudgie picked up the other three stones before vanishing, giving me hope.

Hope dwindled as I searched fruitlessly for the way out of the forest. I had been walking in circles for a good half hour when I heard another pop. The pukwudgie I had just freed appeared in front of me. He pointed and was gone in a snap. I followed the direction his finger had indicated and found the trail within minutes.

Being back on the trail made me more nervous than being in the woods. I did not want to run into any rangers, especially Kai. I jogged the whole way back to campus and was surprised that it was almost 4 p.m. I had spent the whole day in the forest, enjoying being antisocial. Spending the day in the "cursed world" made me feel closer to Kai.

I spent a few hours at the gym before heading over to the dining hall, counting the number of stones I had left as I walked. I pulled out my phone to call Kai and tell him about my day. My heart dropped like a brick in my stomach. *Why do I keep doing that to myself?*

Sitting alone at a small table, I picked at my french fries, the only food in front of me.

I wanted to find more pukwudgies, and I wanted to go to Mirror Lake, though I knew that was dangerous. I couldn't ask Nate for a ride; he might get the wrong idea. Berly would go with me, but that would put her in danger again.

Realizing I had to stay near campus for now, I planned to walk the trail to Black Pond in the morning and search the forestry cabin in the afternoon. I threw away the bulk of my fries and headed back to the dorm.

※ ※ ※

I had no luck finding pukwudgies on the trail to Black Pond, but I didn't stay long. Too many memories rushed back when I passed the tunnel entrance and the dock at Lookout Point. I rubbed my empty wrist.

I had to find a way to get to Mirror Lake.

CHAPTER 41

OVER THE NEXT few weeks, I became a model student. I never missed a class, completed all my assignments, and even did extra credit. But I did nothing else except work out every single day. My clothes sagged off me. I had to wear a belt to keep my pants up. Even some of my spandex pants grew baggy.

I started hearing whispers: "I think she has anorexia." "I heard the guy dumped her." "Maybe she is bulimic. She's always eating, more than most guys." "Oh, she thinks she's a model." Flashes of high school haunted me.

Nate and I were heading out of class on Wednesday afternoon when I overheard someone say, "That girl has to be hooked on drugs. No one is that skinny."

I glared at Nate. "Did you hear that?"

He nodded.

I stomped over to the girl who had spoken. "I'm not on drugs. Worry about your own nosy ass instead of mine!"

Nate grabbed my arm and tugged me away from them.

"Whoa, what was that all about?"

"I'm sick of people talking about me behind my back. It's about time I stood up to them."

"It's all right. Calm down. I understand." He chuckled, then laughed heartily, repeating, "Worry about your own nosy ass?"

That comment broke the tension. I started laughing with him. It was the first time I had laughed in twenty-three days. It sounded weird.

"Let me buy you a coffee and a scone or something," Nate offered. "People think I need to fluff up around here too. I need some winter blubber."

He scooped my arm into his and escorted me to the coffee bar, where he ordered coffees, four chocolate croissants, two muffins, and two scones. Of course, Aspen and Brooklyn walked in during our eating fest.

"Hey, what's up?" Aspen asked in a sickeningly sweet voice.

"We're pigging out," I answered wryly, stuffing another bite of muffin in my mouth. My ability to tolerate snarky people was all dried up.

"Oh?" She rested her hand on Nate's arm. "What time is the competition on Friday?"

I smirked; she knew the answer.

"Seven sharp." He leaned past her and asked me, "Are you going to come?"

"I wouldn't miss it for the world," I said, chomping into the croissant. I pointed to Brooklyn with the rest of the pastry. "Are you going?"

"Heck yeah."

"Cool, save me a seat."

Aspen squirmed.

"Lily, I'm sure Nate will save us good seats right up front," Aspen said, batting her eyes at Nate.

"Yes ma'am," he answered in his gentlemanly Idaho accent.

I motioned to our table. "Why don't you join us?"

"Sure," Aspen answered uncertainly.

Brooklyn snagged a croissant as they sat. "You are a bad influence."

I nodded, taking another bite of my own croissant.

"I heard you and Kai broke up. Is it true?" she asked bluntly.

Aspen kicked her sister under the table.

"You heard right."

Nate sat up a little straighter. Clearly, he had wanted to know whether the rumors were true but was too polite to ask.

"I'm so sorry to hear. Why? You two were perfect together."

"It's complicated," I said shortly, feeling like a blender was churning up my insides.

"Call me anytime. We can hang out, work out, pig out, study, or go to the movies. Anything you need."

"Thanks, Brooklyn. But if we pig out, I'm only eating french fries and ice cream," I said with a grin. Brooklyn was a true friend, even if her sister wasn't. "And croissants, of course."

"Stop! You're making me hungry."

I laughed for the second time in twenty-three days.

***

Friday afternoon, I hated to admit it, but I was excited to watch the lumberjack competition. Even though Benton was competing, at least I had something to do besides study, work out, or wander the forest looking for pukwudgies. I was disappointed I hadn't found more, but I kept the stones in my jacket just in case.

Berly, the twins, and I had an early dinner together before the competition, and I managed to consume a small bowl of mashed potatoes. At the arena, the Axe Men were crushing the competition from the start, but the Oxford M & Ms were crowd favorites.

The women's restroom line snaked out the door during intermission. The men's had no line at all.

"Heck, I'm going in. Who's going to cover me?" I declared.

"I'm in," Berly answered in a millisecond.

We ran to the men's room. I opened the door, yelling, "Anyone in here?" The coast was clear. I was out in no time and guarded the door for Berly, then waved Brooklyn and Aspen over. Brooklyn ran in after Berly, and Aspen followed.

"You are crazy," Berly said.

"No, I'm just finding my fierce."

"I like it."

"I'm going to get some popcorn. Does anyone want anything?" I asked before we headed back to our seats.

I took the back way to the concession stand, hoping to avoid the crowd. No lights were on the perimeter, and the forest menaced from mere feet away. I heard a crack and froze, scanning the forest, waiting for my eyes to adjust. Using my phone for light, I saw a shadow in the trees. I tossed a stone toward it. "This is a gift for you."

I couldn't be certain it was a pukwudgie, but I hoped it was.

With my phone in hand, I typed three or four words to Kai before I stopped myself and deleted the message. Right before I exited the app, a small bubble popped up with three flashing dots. I stared in awe at the message bubble until it disappeared. Kai had been about to send me a message. My heart leaped at the knowledge that he was thinking of me that very second.

I returned to my seat with my popcorn, trying to control the elation percolating in my stomach. It was only a small connection to Kai's world, but it was all I had.

CHAPTER 42

On Monday, as I stomped through the fresh snow on my way to class, I couldn't help wondering how people lived in this mess. The snow was up to my knees and probably up to Berly's thighs.

Bright-red fliers hung from every post. I paid no attention to them as I struggled to navigate the deep powder, but once inside, I stopped to read one: Hearts and Arts Festival: Celebrate with your Valentine on Mirror Lake. Free shuttles all weekend.

I ripped the flier off the wall and shoved it in my pocket. I could sneak to Mirror Lake without asking anyone for a ride. *Valentine's Day.* The pain in my chest was crippling. I had never despised this holiday before. In fact, it used to be fun—candy hearts, cupcakes, and cards. Now it was a painful reminder of what could have been.

Valentine's Day morning, I dressed in all black as if I were in mourning. In my first class, Nate set a box of candy hearts on my desk. The look I shot at him should have burned through him like acid.

He held up both hands. "Wait, don't kill me. Just read them."

I opened the box and poured the candies onto the desk to read a few: You are *not* the father, Go Away, Dead Inside, How About Never, and Love Is Like a Rash.

"Okay, I have to admit, these are brilliant." I picked up a Dead Inside candy and popped it into my mouth. "Thanks for making me feel less weird."

"It's the least I could do."

When the final class ended, I stood and stuffed my notes into my backpack, eager to get to the gym.

"Do you want to get a coffee?"

"No thanks. I want to get to the gym before it gets too crowded."

"I don't think it will be crowded tonight."

My mouth gaped open, and pain twisted through me. I expelled my breath, resting my forehead in my hand.

Nate scrambled to find something to say. "I mean it's—ugh. Sorry." He hung his head.

I was such a mess. He was just trying to be helpful. I feebly patted his shoulder.

"Don't be sorry. I'm the mental case."

"No, you are not."

"I am. See you on Friday." I waved and headed to the gym to change.

* * *

The best part of my day was when I pushed myself to a runner's high and the pain of training transitioned to euphoria. I slipped into this relaxing state around mile six. As I approached mile eight, I figured I might as well push it to ten because this was the only time my emotional suffering faded.

With my music blaring in my ears, I walked a slow lap around the track to cool down, purposely paying no attention to anyone around me. I was just about to enter the locker room when someone grabbed my arm.

"Hey, blondie, where's your Valentine? Did lover boy forget?" I tried to shake Benton's hand off my arm, but his grip was too tight. There was a strange look in his eyes.

"Do you want another knee to your groin?" I growled.

"So, you do want to touch my groin?" With that, he yanked me into the men's locker room, grabbing me from behind so I couldn't kick him.

I screamed and thrashed. "Help! Please, someone, help me! Get him off me!"

He trapped both of my arms along my sides with one of his burly arms and groped my chest with his other hand. Pressing his hot, sticky lips on my neck, he hissed, "Stop fighting. Don't you want to know what it's like to kiss a real man?"

Bile rose in my throat. "Get off me!" I screamed. I managed to get one arm loose and elbowed him in the ribs, but he didn't lose his grip. I had lost a lot of strength along with the weight. "STOP IT!"

Rearing my arm to elbow him again, I froze at the sound of a loud thud. Benton released me, and I fell to the floor. Someone or something else hit the floor with me. Heavy breathing, thuds, and lots of moans followed.

I turned to see Nate standing over Benton, kicking him in the ribs. Blood dripped out of Benton's nose and mouth.

"You are a fucking animal," Nate snarled at him.

Benton spat blood on the floor. "I wasn't going to do anything to her."

"Shut the fuck up!" Nate kicked him a few more times.

"I didn't hurt her. I was just messing around."

"That's not the way I saw it." Nate kicked him again. "You're a pig."

Troy pulled Nate away from Benton. "I called security. They're on the way. Nathan, calm down!"

"I want to kill that son of a bitch." He pointed threateningly at Benton. "You should be glad we're not at the woodsman arena, or you might be dead. Did you hear me, Benton? You shallow little prick." I had never seen Nate mad. I didn't know he had this type of anger in him.

"Nathan, get ahold of yourself," Troy ordered.

I sat against the wall until security arrived to drag Benton to the infirmary. When I resisted going to the security office to give a statement in my current state, they instructed me to call the police and file charges.

Troy knelt beside me. "Are you all right?"

I hadn't realized I was crying, but tears poured nonstop from my eyes. Troy helped me to my feet, and I hugged him. "Thank you." I pulled back and grabbed Nate. I hugged him hard. "Thank you . . . for saving me," I said between sobs.

When I let go of Nate's neck, he dropped his arms.

"You're bleeding," I said numbly, pointing at his hand.

He covered it. "I'm fine. Don't worry about me." Someone threw him a wad of paper towels, and he wrapped it around his hand.

"How were you here?"

"Troy and I came to lift today. We'd been here for over an hour. I tried to wave to you, but you never looked up."

"When I get in the zone, I tune everything else out." I sniffled.

"You were running so hard I thought you were going to break the treadmill. When you finally stopped, I noticed Benton follow you to the locker rooms. That's when I heard you scream."

"I hope you broke his ribs and he gets expelled."

"He broke some ribs, all right. I heard them crack," Troy said with satisfaction.

"Come on. Let us escort you to the dorms."

Troy slipped his arm around my waist to steady me as we walked. Nate clasped the towels to his hand. The three of us hobbled across campus and into the dorm.

One look at my face as we entered the common room, and Berly jumped up.

"What happened?"

"Benton happened," I answered.

"That ape tried to force himself on her," Nate growled.

The twins gasped.

"Nate heard me screaming and beat the shit out of him."

Nate's face turned so red it was almost purple.

Aspen fussed over him. "Are you hurt?"

"I'm fine." He shrugged her off and turned to Berly. "Do not leave her alone tonight. I want all of you to escort her to dinner and make her eat."

"We will," Berly said firmly.

"I need a long, hot shower and some bleach to rub the rancid stank of Benton off my body." With my hand on the doorknob, I glanced over my shoulder at the Axe Men. "Thanks again."

As I sat at my desk and struggled to take off my shoes, I started crying again and picked up my phone to text Kai. I typed and typed, only to delete everything. The small bubble with three dots showed up again. Kai was texting me back. The bubble disappeared. Dropping my forehead on the desk, I let go and indulged in a full-on ugly cry. *Is that what we are now? Wordless texters?* I fell deeper into my hole of agony. Then numbness swaddled my body.

At dinner, we learned that Benton had four broken ribs, a black eye, and purple bruises all over his torso. The bad news was that the school hadn't immediately kicked him out or called the police themselves. His daddy would likely make a huge donation to make the incident go away, but I could still press charges against Benton, and I would.

That night, when I got into bed, I pulled out my phone and waited until 11:11 p.m. to further torture myself. The text bubble flashed onto the screen. I typed and erased words without sending them. *Has he been wordlessly texting me every night?*

I hoped so.

CHAPTER 43

A FEW DAYS LATER, while Berly was still asleep, I took the first shuttle to Mirror Lake. Arts and crafts booths lined the perimeter of the parking area. The large crowd would make it easier to hide from Rosella if she showed up.

The lake looked completely different iced over. The mirror effect was gone. I spent the first few hours following the shore along the forest—sitting occasionally, waiting, hoping a pukwudgie would show itself. One finally did, and I tossed it a stone. He transformed, and I kept moving. From the viewing dock, I watched the ice skaters, toboggan riders, and the dog sled race all at once. I stalked the other side of the lake in the afternoon and encountered one more pukwudgie before the last shuttle was due to leave.

Back on campus, I hurried back to the dorms because it was getting dark. The door creaked when I opened it. Berly's head snapped around. "Where have you been all day?"

"I took the shuttle to Mirror Lake. They had a festival of sorts."

"Lily, you shouldn't go out alone. It's not safe."

"It isn't safe for anyone I bring with me, either. I was looking for stone pukwudgies. I've tossed the pink tourmaline stones to four of them now, and they all transformed. It's like the spell was lifted, and they returned to their normal form."

"Why don't you tell Kai?"

Just hearing his name made me wince.

"I want to be sure it works, that it wasn't a fluke." Cutting my eyes to the floor, I said, "And I'm not sure I can talk to Kai."

"Just call him, Lily!"

"I will. I just want to be sure," I said in a weak voice, trying to persuade myself to do it. "I'll call him tomorrow after I go to Mirror Lake again."

"We're coming with you!"

I sighed, realizing resistance was futile. "Okay."

🦢 🦢 🦢

In the morning, Berly jogged in place on the sidewalk to stay warm. "Why don't we just drive?"

"We can't risk it. What if Rosella learns what your car looks like?"

Martin and Max approached.

"G'day, mate." Martin tapped my hand and kissed Berly on the mouth. I looked away.

Max waggled his eyebrows. "You look smashing today, Lily. Quite lovely."

"Thanks, Max."

"Any ale at this soiree?"

"I don't know, but I'm sure you'll find some," I said wryly.

Nate and Troy exited the dining hall and headed straight toward us.

"Where are you guys off to?" Nate asked.

"Bloody Mirror Lake, some kind of soiree," Max said, pointing to a nearby flier.

Nate shrugged at Troy. "Do you want to go?"

"Why not? When are you guys going?" Troy asked.

"As soon as the bloody shuttle gets here, any minute now," Max answered cheerfully.

Troy tilted his head. "We've got nothing else to do today."

Nate shielded his voice with his bandaged hand and whispered so only I could hear: "Have you seen Benton around?"

"Not once. I think his lawyer advised him to steer clear of me."

"Good. I think he's staying clear of me too."

I texted Aspen and Brooklyn to ask if they wanted to meet us at the festival. This small party was getting a bit too cozy for me. Thankfully, the twins agreed.

The shuttle dropped the rest of us off at the front of the parking area. People were parking in the grass because it was so crowded.

"Why are you fidgeting?" Berly asked me quietly as we headed toward the booths.

I crossed my arms and kicked a rock. "This is not working out as I planned. How can I break away to walk alone by the forest?" I kept my voice low and guarded.

"We'll figure it out once Martin and Max find a beer garden," she replied with certainty.

We strolled around the booths for an hour or so. Just as Berly predicted, the guys found a spot for drinking. I held up my hand. "None for me." I hadn't had anything to drink since the breakup.

I glanced at my watch. The time was 11:11. Grief engulfed me.

"I'm going out on the viewing platform," I announced, hoping to be alone for a while.

Nate sprang to my side. "I'll go with you."

"Will you come too, Troy?" I asked, trying to keep it light and friendly.

"Yeah, sure," he answered hesitantly.

I grabbed Troy's arm and pulled him forward until he was at my side.

"It's much prettier here when the lake is not frozen over. Have you ever seen it?" I asked them both. Troy shook his head. "The entire lake looks like a mirror—go figure. It's fascinating, almost magical."

I babbled on with both hands secure inside my pockets, tumbling the stones between my fingers. The three of us sat on the edge of the dock to watch the dog sled races.

"This is a cool festival. I'm glad you invited us," Nate said.

I was about to respond when he rested his arm across my shoulders. I froze, forgetting to breathe. Anger welled up inside me. I had not invited him. Max did. Nate remembered it differently because he wanted it to be different. I have known for a long time he had feelings for me, and this confirmed it. I sat forward, hugging my knees so his arm would fall away. I did not want to give him the wrong impression.

"Lily . . ." Nate's expression was pained. Troy seemed to be craning his neck unnaturally to avoid looking in our direction.

"Don't," I whispered. "Please. I can't handle it."

"Sorry." He looked down, embarrassed.

Forcing a smile, I tried to sound casual. "Don't be sorry." I stood. "I could use a hot chocolate or a vanilla latte. What about you guys?"

"Sounds like a good idea, as long as we get a few croissants too," Nate answered. The tension had already left his voice.

"I could use some food," Troy said, hopping to his feet.

We circled back to the beer garden to find the others and discovered Aspen and Brooklyn had arrived.

"Hi, Nate, Troy," Aspen said, waving her fingers. After a pause, she added, "Lily."

"Hi, Brooklyn." I paused to mimic Aspen. "Aspen."

I met Berly's eyes, sharing our usual look whenever Aspen acted snarky. Berly flashed a dimple. I could always count on her.

"Fancy a pint?" Max asked the girls, holding up his ale.

"Not yet. Maybe later," Aspen answered.

"This looks like a great festival. What have you done so far?" Brooklyn asked no one in particular.

"The toboggan ride looks fun, but the line is long. We were watching the dog sled races from the viewing platform," I answered.

"Why don't we start with the booths?" Brooklyn suggested.

"Sounds good. We only made it down a few aisles before these two found the beer garden and our progress halted," Berly joked, gesturing toward the Brits.

"We'll keep your seats warm," Martin said.

Nate hesitated, probably wondering whether to stay with the guys or come with us. When our eyes met, he immediately looked away. Pushing the awkwardness aside, I waved him and Troy forward.

"Come on, you two. Someone has to carry our large purchases."

The cute, shy smile returned to his face.

The five of us meandered through the booths. I couldn't stop myself from scanning the forest whenever we drew near.

When the shuttle dropped off another batch of students in the parking lot, Benton was among them. I caught my breath. He was headed right for us. I halted and grabbed Berly's hand. "Keep me away from him." She glanced up to see where I was looking.

My bottom lip quivered when I turned back to Nate. His face was as red as mine felt, his hands balled into fists.

"Troy, come with me," he barked, spinning me in the other direction. "Come on, Lily, we need to get out of here."

Nate took off, towing me with him. Troy was right at my side, and Berly scrambled to keep up with our long strides. Once we made it to the end of the row, we looked back. Benton and his buddies were nowhere in sight.

Aspen and Brooklyn caught up to us.

"It's okay. They turned and went the other way," Brooklyn said. My pulse was racing, and I found myself clinging to Nate.

My face slipped into a frown. "This is stupid. He has to stay away from me. I have a restraining order against him. His daddy will not be able to buy his way out of it if he comes anywhere near me." I peeled myself out of Nate's arms. "Excuse me, I need to go to the bathroom."

"I'm coming with you," Berly said.

Inside the facilities, I splashed water on my face to regain my composure.

"Just give me a minute," I told Berly when she emerged from a stall.

"Take your time. I'll be outside."

When I left the restroom, Kai was leaning against the wall beside the doorway, wearing a scowl. I started to hyperventilate. His arms were crossed over his chest.

I tried to casually walk past him, but he blocked my path.

"What is going on?" he demanded.

I turned and walked away from him. He followed so closely I felt his breath in my hair.

"What do you mean?" I finally demanded, whirling to face him.

"Are you on a date?"

"A what?" I snapped. "Why do you care? You dumped me, remember?"

"It's been thirty-four days. Thirty-four days, and you are already snuggled in some other guy's arms." He was almost yelling.

Exasperated, I rolled my eyes. "You have no idea what you're talking about."

Kai leaned in, inches away from my face. "How can you do this to me?"

"Do *what* to you?" My hand was trembling when I raised it to push him away. I didn't want to push him away. He smelled so good, looked so good. My heart was being shredded through a meat grinder.

"Lily." His deep voice lured me like a trance. He pressed his forehead to mine.

Tears flooded my face. "Please stop. You're killing me. I have to go."

I darted past a surprised Berly, calling out, "I'm taking the shuttle back to campus" and jumping on the shuttle almost as it was pulling away.

Safely back on campus, I disembarked and started running. I didn't know where I was going; I just wanted to run.

I slowed my pace only when I reached the kayak-launching dock. Stumbling to the end, I sank down and buried my head in my knees.

CHAPTER 44

Soft footsteps approached from behind. I didn't have the will to look and see who was coming. A manly musk engulfed me when Kai sat and draped his strong arm around my shoulders. We sat quietly for some time, except for an occasional sob from me.

I finally worked up the courage to look Kai in the eyes. His mesmerizing green eyes.

"Why are you doing this to me?" I demanded, flipping his question back on him.

"I didn't mean to. We came to the lake looking for Rosella. We had no idea about the festival. When I saw you in Nate's arms, I wanted to die."

"He was protecting me from Benton." Kai tilted his head like he didn't believe me. "A couple of days ago, Benton tried to force himself on me. Nate pulled him off me and beat the shit out of him."

Kai inhaled deeply, and his cheeks colored. "Benton did what?"

"I really don't want to talk about it. Nate broke four of his ribs, and I pressed charges. Benton's daddy paid the hefty fine. I have a restraining order against Benton, and he received a year of probation. Nate saved me. He's been overprotective ever since."

"I am so sorry. Are you all right?" I looked down, shaking my head. "I guess I should thank Nate," Kai said sincerely.

I was furious with Kai and didn't want to give in, but something he'd said sparked hope within me. I cleared my throat.

"Did I hear you say thirty-four days?"

Kai nodded.

"You were counting the days?"

His head bobbed again.

"What's with all of the wordless texting?" I asked frankly.

"Lily, I . . ." Kai fiddled with my shoelace. "I—what did you call it? Wordless texting? I wordless text you every single night. I have called you a hundred times a day in my head."

"Why are you doing this?"

"What?"

"You're confusing me! What do you want, Kai?"

"I cannot do it. I cannot stay away any longer. I do not want to stay away. Please forgive me. I am miserable without you."

"Miserable? Miserable is a kind word. More than once, you have told me you were damaged goods. Well, I'm shattered. Shattered. Do *not* make a fool of me! I can't handle it. Besides, your mother hates me." My voice rose with each sentence.

"You are so wrong. Lily, she loves you. She just does not want to see you get hurt."

"Like this doesn't hurt?" I stood up. "I need some air." I stomped off the dock in the general direction of the trails. Kai caught up with me easily and slipped his hand in mine. The familiar feeling of his fingers shot a current up my arm. Before I knew it, we were at the first split on the trail. My anger lightened, along with my pace.

He stopped and pulled me to him. "I am so sorry, sorry about everything. Can you ever forgive me?" His eyes gleamed with sincerity.

There was nothing to consider. I was still madly in love with him.

"I might be able to forgive you."

"Please forgive me. I am so sorry I screwed this up." He cradled my cheeks.

"Promise me you will never do this again."

"I promise." He pressed his mouth to mine, and I didn't stop him. His hands brushed through my hair and down my back, pulling me closer to him. My body melted under his touch.

But I leaned back carefully to look him in the eyes.

"Are you sure? Because I mean it. You can't keep going back and forth on this. Either we're a team, or you need to leave me alone." I could barely say the last part over the knot in my throat.

"I have never been surer of anything." When his lips crushed to mine and he kissed me again, I believed him.

"You look so thin," I finally said when he let me breathe again.

"I couldn't eat. Nothing tasted right." He gestured toward me with one eyebrow raised.

"Same here. I've been living on Cheerios, plain pasta, and french fries."

Kai let out a deep sigh. "I know the feeling."

"What has been going on since, um, thirty-four days?" I didn't want to say it.

"Rosella cursed the driver who walked off the job. He has antlers. It's awful; he can't even disguise them to continue working. He's thinking about asking for forgiveness."

"That's terrible. How can she—"

I cut myself off midsentence when two stone pukwudgies stepped out onto the trail, one noticeably larger than the other. I placed both hands on Kai's shoulders. "Stay here. I need to show you something I've been working on."

Kai grabbed my hand to pull me back. "No, Lily, they are dangerous." His voice was stern.

"Trust me." I ran my fingertips across his palm and stepped toward the pukwudgies. Kneeling in front of them, I tossed each of them a stone. "This is a gift for you. Take it," I said, nodding encouragingly. "It will release you from her spell."

When the creatures emerged from the white mist, the stonelike features were gone. Tender blue eyes and rosy cheeks replaced their masks. The tall one had spiked, inky-black hair, and the little one's black hair was long, cascading down its back.

I stood and bowed, tossing them four more stones from my pocket. "Please give these to your friends. Help us break her spell over your kind."

Both bowed back. They collected the extra stones and disappeared with a pop.

Kai was beside me in a second. "Lily, what did you do?" he breathed in awe.

"I think I figured out a way to release the pukwudgies from Rosella's spell."

"How?"

"Remember when I tossed my pink tourmaline stone to the one on the trail after you saved me from the old house?"

"Yes."

"We didn't wait around to see what happened. Since, uh, thirty-four days, I have been walking through the forest, looking for more of them to test my theory. I have now changed six that I know of and possibly more. I just had to be sure it worked before I contacted you." I paused. "I wasn't sure if I should contact you," I shamefully added.

"Lily, you know that was extremely reckless."

I released an irritated sigh. The true swan bubbled up inside me.

"Everything is dangerous! I was attacked on campus. A campus with police and cameras all over the place." I started pacing back and forth. "Think about it. Even Grandmother Kateri said the pukwudgies used to be kind to humans. If we are kind, we can earn their trust. I was only scared of them because of what everyone else said. And no one wanted to listen when I said we should try to communicate with them. So I decided, what did it matter? I had nothing to lose. I was already dead inside after you left me. I had to find a way to help, even if only from afar—even if you didn't want me. And it worked, Kai. It worked!"

"Lily, you are brilliant." He kissed my forehead, nose, and my cheeks four times. "We have to tell the others." He took my hands in his. "My love, please come with me to tell the others." Oh, how I longed to hear him call me that again. It left me breathless.

"Yes, of course." I squeezed his hand.

※ ※ ※

Kai kept his hands on me in some form or fashion even when he was driving, like he couldn't believe I was beside him.

The woodsy smell of the caves filled my senses. I hadn't realized how much I missed this place.

Jon and Ben came crashing into the great room when they heard us and smothered me with hugs.

"Lily, we are so glad you're back. He's been miserable to live with." Ben gestured at Kai.

I grinned widely. "It's so good to see you."

"Lily has figured out something important," Kai announced before the merriment overtook us.

"What is it?" Jon asked, straightforward as always.

"I offered a gift of pink tourmaline to the stone pukwudgies," I explained. "They transformed back into their original forms. I think it releases them from Rosella's power."

"Are you sure it works?" Ben asked in disbelief.

Kai nodded. "I saw it myself. It was crazy. Lily tossed them a stone as a gift. When they picked it up, they were no longer made of stone."

"How many pukwudgies have you changed?" Jon asked.

"Six that I know of, possibly a few more because I gave them extra stones to give to others."

Ben tapped his chin thoughtfully. "Where can we get more of these stones?"

"The Salty Swan, downtown. It's pink tourmaline."

"We all need them. We need to carry them with us," Ben said

urgently.

"Ben, the pukwudgies are only showing themselves to Lily so far," Kai said.

Ben frowned. "We should still be prepared."

Tate and Wade appeared suddenly from the tunnel.

"She got her first truckload of black tourmaline delivered to the warehouse," Wade yelled as he climbed through. His face lit up when he saw me. "Lily, what the heck?" He barreled across the room for a hug. "How are you? I was tempted to go find you. If this big dummy was stupid enough to let you go, I planned to scoop you up. I'm kind of a catch around here, you know."

Kai punched him in the arm.

"It's good to know I have options." I waggled my fingers. "Hi, Tate."

"Lily made a breakthrough." Jon explained everything to Tate and Wade.

"If we distribute enough pink tourmaline to free the pukwudgies, shifting their power back to them and away from her, we have a chance to defeat her." I glanced around the room. "What do you think?"

Jon sat stone faced, absorbing everything. "I say we fight, but we need to move quickly. She is definitely up to something with that large shipment of black tourmaline."

Ben stiffened. "He's right. We have to act now before she realizes her powers are weakening."

Kai let out an audible breath. "How many pukwudgies do you think she has under her control?"

Nibbling on my thumbnail, I asked, "How many are inside the compound?"

"A dozen or so," Kai answered with uncertainty.

"If she has one or two stationed along every trail, and there are fifteen trails, that's thirty more. Possibly less, with the stones I've already handed out." Counting the remaining stones in my pocket, I said, "We're going to need to get more pink tourmaline."

I reluctantly agreed with the others that the warehouse pukwudgies couldn't be freed until we wanted Rosella to realize what was happening. We considered different ways to get more stones into the hands of the trail-guarding pukwudgies until we had a plan on which we all concurred. Twirling a lock of my hair, proud of my accomplishments, I wondered what else might unfold.

Kai slid behind me, wrapping his arms around my waist and resting his chin on my head. "Look what you've created." I glanced up at him questioningly. "You have given us hope again. Look how determined they are. Like a ray of sunshine, you brought us back to life." I turned around and folded into his embrace. "I can't believe you're here."

As I inhaled his scent, a voice in my head warned, *Don't be foolish. Take it slow.* I dropped my hands and turned to rejoin the conversation. But all I really wanted was to get lost in his embrace forever.

*   *   *

Kai drove slower than usual on the way back to campus, his arm curled around my waist. I imagined his cautious pace was because he was trying to prolong our time together. He turned the truck off, closed his eyes, and flexed his jaw a few times.

"I'm sorry. I'm sorry I hurt you so badly. I will never forgive myself for breaking up with you. I just thought if I stayed away, you would be safe."

"I get it. I hated it, but I get it. Look, I might have done the same thing to you if I was in your shoes." His eyes opened. "Neither of us want to be apart, right?"

"Do you realize how much I love you?" Kai pulled me to his chest.

"If we really want to make this work, we must destroy Rosella's curse over you. That is the only way we can be together for real. That is what really matters."

I assumed that his silence meant he agreed.

CHAPTER 45

EVERYTHING FELL INTO place easier than I thought possible. I shifted back to balancing a cursed life with college life. Nate was sulky and distant, and Aspen was friendly again. Things were normal.

The first two days after Kai and I found one another again fell under the full moon, allowing us to spend as much time together as we wanted, although I declined to stay overnight with him at the cave. After that, Kai manipulated his work schedule to cover the campus trails on Tuesdays and Thursdays so we could search together for more pukwudgies. Wade volunteered to accompany me to Mirror Lake on Saturday to do the same. If something big was coming, we needed to free as many pukwudgies as possible, as quickly as possible.

*   *   *

Wade picked me up early Saturday morning, running around his truck to open my door.

"This way, my lady," he crowed, a grin covering his face.

"Thank you, sir." I felt a surprising swell of joy at seeing him, like having a playdate with your best friend in elementary school. You never knew what adventures would unfold.

When we arrived, Wade hit the ground running. "Are we hiking, sledding, ice skating, or all of the above?" He was so full of life and enthusiasm it was impossible not to get swept up. I hoped I'd stuffed my backpack with enough snacks and food to last us all day.

"Mostly hiking, but all of the above could be fun too."

As we walked, Wade rambled nonstop about his new job, what he ate for breakfast, the best fishing spots, hunting. He changed subjects like a driver shifting through gears.

"Do you want to stop for a snack?" I asked when he paused to take a breath.

"Yeah, I'm starving."

We sat on a log by the tree line. I passed Wade some peanut butter crackers, an apple, a cheese stick, and a muffin. "Take what you want. I have more."

He devoured the muffin and started in on the cheese stick. "Why do you think they come to you?" He pointed the cheese stick at me. "You know, the pukwudgies?"

I stared at the apple in my hand. "That is a good question. I've thought about it for a long time, and the only thing I can think of is my spirit animal." He raised an eyebrow. "My middle name is Swan, and my spirit animal is a swan. Swans are known for their beauty, but they are also fierce. Swans protect the ones they love. Because of their pure spirit and ability to protect, swans can block invoked evil."

He simply nodded casually. "Cool."

A loud pop sounded behind my head. I slowly turned to see two stone pukwudgies less than ten feet away from us.

"Please stay here and remain still," I said, holding my hand out to keep Wade back. His eyes were wide as saucers. I stood and stepped closer to the two creatures, knelt before them, and tossed each of them a stone. "Please accept this gift from me. It will help you." After the smoke dissipated, their humanlike features appeared. I tossed them each a few more stones. "If we work together, we can release you all from Rosella's spell."

The taller of the two wore a large quiver of arrows, many-colored sashes around his neck, and feathers woven through his hair. His large crystalline eyes were surrounded by laugh lines. I assumed he was important, an elder or a chief. He swirled his long finger, and a sparkling orange light materialized, like on the night the pukwudgie had saved me from Benton and his crew. Something dropped in front of me in a puff of smoke.

I bowed my head. He likewise dipped into a low bow. Both creatures then disappeared with a pop.

A small hand mirror lay on the ground in front of my knees. I picked it up and studied the details. The frame comprised an intricately carved swan. The swan's neck and head extended from the mirror, and its wings encircled the frame.

"What is it?" Wade asked.

"A mirror." I stood and returned to his side.

"What the heck?" Wade's surprised look was comical. "Did you see how he was decorated? Do you think he's important?" His voice sounded high, like a little kid's.

"He was impressive. Most wear leather outfits in natural colors. They all have arrows, spears, and knives, but I have never seen one wearing so many colors or feathers in their hair."

"Let's go find some more!" Wade skipped backward along the edge of the forest. I had to scramble to keep up with him.

We encountered three more on the north side of the lake. I tallied the number of pukwudgies I'd released from Rosella's power in my head. With the additional stones I'd handed out, it was potentially close to thirty saved—possibly enough to cover the trails.

Dark clouds rolled in, swiftly covering the lake in shadow. It was only 3 p.m. but suddenly looked like the middle of the night. The wind picked up, whipping across the lake and burning our exposed skin under its icy power.

"We need to get out of here before this storm hits. It's going to be a bad one," Wade said, his face serious for once.

I tightened my scarf. "I think we'd better hurry."

Icy rain pelted us on our way back to the truck.

"This is going to be a blizzard. I hope we make it back before we lose visibility," Wade muttered.

"Did you know this storm was coming?" I asked.

"Everyone's been talking about it at work. Looks like it's coming earlier than expected. We aren't allowed to make any deliveries during this type of storm. It's too dangerous. The good news is it will be the last storm of the year. Sorry we missed our chance to ice-skate." He must have noticed my bewildered expression. "After this storm, the ice will melt on the lakes."

"Oh, good to know."

Wade was silent while he concentrated on descending the mountain in the crazy weather.

We eventually drove out of the storm but saw it roiling behind us as we parked near the caves. Wade rounded the truck to open my door.

"May I escort you inside?"

"Of course."

An intoxicating aroma engulfed us past the cave entrance. Tanja and the girls were at the great room table, bent intently over crafts. Jon was cooking something in the kitchen that smelled delicious. Ben stepped out of the office, bees buzzing on his arms.

"How did it go today?" he asked.

"This chick is amazing. The pukwudgies just appear for her. She gave them a stone, smoke swirled around, and they returned to their original form. We freed five today, and one might have been the chief!" Pride dripped from Wade's voice. "We would have saved more if the storm hadn't stopped us."

"Kai and Tate have already shut down all the trails. They're on their way here now with supplies. Everything is going to shut down for a few days," Ben said.

I heard a click. My pulse raced when I turned to see Kai looking stunning as always. His hands were full of bags. He brushed my head with a kiss as he walked past, and I followed him into the kitchen to help him unload. Before I reached the counter, he was kissing me enthusiastically. I kissed him back until I felt lightheaded.

"How did it go today?"

"Better than expected." When I told him about our successful day, I remembered the mirror. I pulled it from my backpack to show everyone, then handed it to Kai. He inspected it carefully.

"The details are amazing. This is hand carved. They gave you a gift," Kai said quietly, almost whispering. "What does it mean?" He handed the mirror to Jon.

"He looked like the chief or someone important," Wade said. Ben, Tate, and Tanja all inspected the mirror.

I absently pulled a heart-shaped stone from my pocket and rubbed it as if it would grant us the answer. As I passed the stone from one finger to another, it popped out of my hand and rolled rapidly toward the stream.

Mia reacted with the speed of a cat, jumping up and stopping the stone with her foot. She picked it up and skipped over with her hand held out to return it to me.

My eyes widened. I blinked a few times and tapped Kai's arm. "Are you seeing what I'm seeing?"

His gaze fixed on Mia's face. Mia's features were human again.

"Why didn't we think of this before?" I reached for another stone and called for Sky. My hand shook when I handed it to her.

She cradled the stone with fascination, and her pig features faded away.

Adrenaline and hope pumped through my veins. I turned to Kai, reaching for his hand. I ignored the butterflies swarming my stomach and carefully placed a stone in his palm. My heart pounded in my chest as his features shimmered and lightened, but his scales returned, and his eyes shifted back to his cursed state.

I placed a second stone in his hand. Not blinking or breathing, we watched, and this time his cursed features completely vanished.

"The pink tourmaline is blocking the curse! I think you needed a larger stone to counteract the spell. The girls are small, so this size worked for them." We continued to test the theory, passing the stones. The stones had the same effect on all of them.

I frowned at the bracelet on Kai's arm. "It must only be effective when the stone touches your skin directly."

Kai unhooked his bracelet and took it off, setting the stones in his hand on the table. His face shivered and faded, and his scales and snake eyes returned. He then fastened the bracelet upside down so the stones directly touched his skin. In a flash, his fetching features reappeared. "Did it work?"

"Yes, my love, it did," I said joyfully.

Excitement flooded the room.

"We must get back to the Salty Swan to purchase more stones. We must distribute them to all the people under Rosella's influence. Hopefully it will block her mind control," I said.

"We can make jewelry to keep the stones pressed against our skin. Remember the bracelets the girls and I were working on? We can intertwine the stones in the cord," Tanja said enthusiastically.

"Great idea," I said.

Wade suggested, "We're going to be stuck inside for the next few days, so we can all make them."

Kai placed his arm around my waist and pulled me toward him. "I am so lucky you came into my life."

The air in the room felt lighter and energizing. I emptied the stones from my pocket so we could dive into making bracelets.

"I'm glad you're staying with us through the storm," Mia said innocently.

"I can sleep on the couch if you want," Kai whispered.

"Don't be silly. I'm good. We're good."

***

The next morning, I followed Kai into the tunnel and wiped my sweaty palms on my pants before accepting his extended hand and letting him pull me into Sakari's laundry room.

"Are you sure you want to do this?" I asked. Sakari's ambivalence toward me left me in a constant state of uncertainty.

"Lily, she doesn't hate you. She is just worried about you."

I took a deep breath before we stepped into Sakari's house.

"Good morning, Mother," Kai said, kissing each of her cheeks.

"Good morning, my son." She turned to me. "Lily, it is good to see you." She hugged me lightly and kissed my cheek. I tucked a necklace and a bracelet I had made into her hand.

"I made these for you. Please wear them for protection."

"They are a gift from you, so they are a gift I will cherish," she said sweetly. A spark ignited in her tired eyes. Maybe Kai was right and she didn't hate me, but her present demeanor didn't stop my stomach from churning.

She placed her hands on Kai's cheeks. "My son, my beautiful son, it works. It really works."

"Yes, thanks to Lily, the curse is blocked. The pink tourmaline worked on all of us. We need to get it into the hands of every person working for Rosella. But how?"

"I think I can convince Wanda to bring us more after the storm passes," Sakari said. "We'll find a way to distribute them." She slipped her hand into mine and kissed the back of it just like Kai did. "Tell me about the pukwudgies."

I described my various encounters and showed her the mirror.

She inspected the object. "We must show this to Grandmother Kateri." She turned shining eyes toward me. "The spirits guide you. Kai adores you. We have been waiting for someone like you. I am so grateful you found us."

Our eyes met with understanding, and a tingle ran down my spine. "Thank you for accepting me."

When she handed me back the mirror, the puzzle pieces clicked in place.

"Kai, how long has it been since Rosella has emerged from the compound?"

"About two months," he answered with a puzzled look.

"How long does Mirror Lake stay frozen over?"

"It depends—usually a few months. It thins during March and is usually ice-free by the first week in April, sometimes sooner."

"Oh my God, we only have roughly two weeks." I stood and started pacing.

"What are you talking about, Lily?"

I pointed to the mirror in my hand. "The mirror! The pukwudgies gave me a mirror not as a gift but as a clue. Didn't you say Rosella called Mirror Lake nature's largest mirror?"

"She did," he said.

"She's using mirrors to work her spells." I continued to pace. "She hasn't been out because she can't put anything into the lake while it's frozen over, even though she has more black tourmaline. She will use the lake as a mirror to reflect her power and ensnare more pukwudgies. We have two weeks at most to find a way to stop her. Blocking her might not be enough if she can channel more pukwudgies."

✺ ✺ ✺

Kai and I traveled in silence back to the cave.

After dinner, Jon started the conversation. "Her power has to be weakening from the pukwudgies Lily has been freeing."

"She probably hasn't noticed it yet. Think about it; she hasn't left the compound. The pukwudgies inside the warehouse probably provide her with enough magic to hold her spells and curses," Jace interjected.

The lights flickered before going completely out, leaving the fireplace as our only light source. Groans abounded. Losing power to the storm changed the mood.

"It's getting late. Why don't we call it a night?" Kai remained in high spirits. "Want a glass of wine?"

"Sure, that sounds great," I answered, assuming Kai's lighter mood came from no longer being embarrassed by his appearance.

We sat by the fire in Kai's room and sipped our wine until I yawned. Kai offered me his hand. "Come on, love. Let's go to bed."

Kai slipped under the fur covers beside me, cradling me against him. I breathed in his familiar scent.

"It's nice being on lockdown with you," Kai said. He pressed his mouth to mine. Everything felt familiar, natural. Kai slipped his hand under my shirt, moving his fingers lightly and giving me shivers. His hand traveled up my spine, and I kissed him with more urgency. My body surged forward like it was moving on its own accord, and his breath quickened.

A memory of Benton breathing heavily on my neck flashed through my head, bringing me back to reality. I pushed away but kept my hand on Kai's chest. For a second, we just lay there, breathless. "Sorry." I wasn't sure whether I was ashamed or scared.

"Don't apologize." He brushed my hair back.

"I just . . . I'm just scared." I paused. "Scared of myself, really. It's just, I don't trust myself with you. I get carried away, and I don't want to get hurt again."

I wasn't making sense.

"Lily, my love, I will never hurt you again. Trust me. I can never lose you again. Things will be back to normal soon. It's my fault. I get carried away too, and I know we can't. I will behave. C'mere, my love." He enfolded me in his arms. It felt good. It felt safe. "Sweet dreams."

I whispered, "I love you," thinking ruefully, *We never were normal, and if we don't defeat Rosella, we never will be.*

CHAPTER 46

I **WOKE TO THE** sound of running water. Sitting up, I ran my fingers through my hair as Kai exited the bathroom in nothing but a towel. I hugged my bent knees to fight the desire to tackle him.

"Good morning, my love." The rich tone of his morning voice made me think I was dreaming. "How did you sleep?"

"Fine. And you?"

"Perfect. The power is back on, and the storm has weakened. Wanda dropped off plenty of pink tourmaline at Mother's house. We can pick it up before I drive you back to campus."

"I should get ready," I said, slipping out of the covers.

He gestured toward the bathroom. "It's all yours."

A few hours later, we were in the truck heading back to campus. After Kai pulled up to the curb near the dorms, we kissed.

"Bye. Call me after work."

"Stay safe, my love."

The path to the dorm was covered with ice, so I moved carefully to avoid falling. Halfway there, I spotted Nate walking in my direction and gave him a wave.

"Hey, Nate."

"Oh, hey," he replied with little enthusiasm.

"How was the storm here?" I asked.

"Insane. I'm glad it's over." The corners of his mouth tugged down.

"Do you want to grab a cup of coffee?"

He crossed his arms. "Why?"

"Nate, I miss you. You are still my friend, aren't you?" My voice sounded whiney.

His expression lightened. "Yeah, I could use a coffee."

We stayed in the coffee shop for an hour, chatting about our classes, assignments, and the storm. When we stood to say our goodbyes, Nate asked, "So, it's back on? You and him?"

"Yes, it is. I don't think I ever really let him go."

"Are you happy?"

"Yes."

"I am happy for you." His expression hardened. "But if that guy hurts you again, he will look worse than Benton did. I will always be here for you, Lily."

He turned and walked away.

Nate was such a great guy. A normal guy. The realization kind of stung.

* * *

The week flew past. I was bogged down with extra work from the snow day at the beginning of the week.

Kai called Thursday night to ask if I'd managed to free any more pukwudgies. I had gone with Wade to Mirror Lake and would be going with Berly on Saturday and Kai on Sunday.

"A few. For some reason, I haven't seen many in the last few days. Wade suggested it's because Rosella's power is the weakest at the full moon, so she's keeping them close."

Kai was silent. I let a few seconds pass.

"Kai, are you there?"

"A full moon. The full moon." He sounded distracted.

"Yes, the full moon." I was confused; he had lived around the full moon's schedule for the past three years. How could he forget?

"Rosella is going to strike after the waning crescent moon," he declared. "The three days of the *new* moon. That is when she is the strongest. Mirror Lake will be thawed by then. She could reconquer all of the pukwudgies."

"Oh my God, that totally makes sense."

Kai sounded rushed. "I need to talk to the guys. I'll call you back later. Thank you, love."

Berly was sitting on her bed when I walked into the room. "How did it go today?"

I filled her in on the details.

"Now I'm excited for Saturday."

"I really need to figure out how to communicate with them so I can warn them about the new moon," I muttered anxiously.

"Why don't you give them a clue?" she suggested.

I tilted my head questioningly.

"They gave you that mirror, and you said it was a clue about the lake thaw, right? So maybe you need to give them a clue."

Astonished at the genius of her suggestion, I kissed Berly on the head. "You are brilliant." My head was spinning. *What can I warn them with?* "Do you have any colorful scarves, ribbons—anything you don't want?" I asked, frantically digging through my closet.

We accumulated a pile to take with us on our Saturday outing. I called Kai and told him what else I needed.

Berly was up before I was on Saturday, proving her eagerness for our adventure. I threw my backpack into the jeep.

"Jace is working the tower. He'll message us if Rosella leaves the compound," I said to reassure her we would be safe.

Berly and I started on the north side of the lake, covering the territory along the forest. I was about to give up when I heard a crack. A small pukwudgie—maybe the smallest I had seen yet at less than two feet tall—stepped from behind a large tree. I touched Berly's arm and nodded in the creature's direction.

"Move slowly."

We stepped into the trees, and I knelt before the pukwudgie, tossing it a stone. "Please accept this gift. It will help you." The pukwudgie picked up the stone and transformed. She had flowing dark hair with a streak of white and was dressed in a leather outfit adorned with fringe and freshwater clam shells. She carried a bow and a quiver of arrows.

I tossed her three more stones. "Give these to your family and friends."

I pulled out a colorful ribbon and laid it close to her feet.

"This is a gift for your elder, the one who dresses colorfully. I need to speak with him, give him a warning." I bowed my head. She scooped up the stones and ribbon, bowed low, and disappeared.

"What the what?" Berly squeaked, looking delighted.

"Pretty cool, isn't it?"

"Lily, I'm tingling."

"Come on, let's go to the other side to see if we can find another."

Berly and I did not find more that day, but seeing one made her a believer.

* * *

Kai brought the items I had asked for on Sunday morning. We got an early start by the lake and traveled to the spot where Wade and I had freed the chief. I set out my colorful offerings and hung the necklaces on a branch.

Kai mindlessly traced my fingers while we waited.

"I talked to Grandmother Kateri this morning. She said to tell you she is proud of you. Proud that you did not give up on us. She said you are a true swan, and she loves you."

I wasn't sure how to respond. "I never stopped loving you."

It sounded like a firecracker had erupted beside us. I jumped and let out a small shriek. The elder pukwudgie and the tiny female stood before us.

I bowed and waved my hands over the gifts.

"These are gifts for you. Especially this one." I held up the necklace with the pendant of a perfect circle, empty inside, then stepped back to give them room.

The elder stepped forward and brushed his hand over the necklaces. One was the waning crescent, another the waxing crescent, and the one I had specifically shown him was meant to represent the new moon. He blinked a few times, and a look of satisfaction inched across his face.

"Rosella will enact her terrible plan during the new moon. If we work together, maybe we can destroy her power," I explained.

Kai's deep voice echoed my words in his native language. We all bowed, and they popped away with our gifts.

I hugged Kai. "Do you think they understood?"

"I do."

Kai called Grandmother Kateri on our way back to the cave to let her know we thought we had been successful. His call reminded me that I needed to tell my parents I wasn't coming home for spring break. I gave the excuse that I was working on a special project. Not really a lie, just not school related. I could tell they were concerned and disappointed, but they seemed determined to give me my space and accepted my excuses.

A large group of people met us at the cave that evening, including Wanda and Grandmother Kateri. The kitchen area was cramped. There were a few people I did not know, and Sakari made the introductions. One of them was the driver who had been cursed with antlers. I struggled to remember all the names.

I glanced nervously at Kai, and he reached for my hand, radiating warmth and strength.

A mysterious look grew across Jace's face. "I think I know of a way to get us inside and lure her outside at the same time."

He shared his clever idea. It was good, but the timing would be critical.

Across the room, Sakari was talking with her hands. Her cheeks were round and flushed. I had never seen her so animated. She was taking on the role of a leader, handing out assignments and cheerfully interacting with everyone in the room. Kai's eyes beamed like a lighthouse. He placed one finger under my chin, tilting my head toward him.

"None of this would have happened if you had not entered my life. I love you."

I pulled him closer, burying my face in his chest. "I'm here for you. I will always be here for you."

Once again, we were waiting on the cycle of the moon.

CHAPTER 47

THE MORNING CAME upon us like a storm. Neither of us could sleep. Kai sat up, looking serious. The golden flecks glittered in his eyes. "We must be extra careful today. I cannot, will not, let her touch you ever again. You are my world. You've made my life worth living."

"You give me strength I never knew I had. I promised to fight for you, all of you, no matter the cost," I said, secretly praying that normal was just hours away.

We kissed like we were leaving for war. My spinning mind ticked off some internal advice: *Be brave, be fierce, be a swan. I love this man. I will do anything to keep him safe. If Rosella curses me, at least I will still be with Kai. If I must face death, I will gladly face it for him.*

Pacing in the kitchen, dragging my fingers through my hair, I was glad my friends were on spring break and far away from here. Kai stepped into my path with a concerned look. He handed me a fresh croissant wrapped in a napkin, knowing I would never pass one up.

I kissed him for the sweet gesture. He pressed his lips to my forehead.

"Eat, my love. We will need our strength today and our wits. Oh, and put these on."

He handed me some stretchy pink tourmaline bracelets.

By 7:30 a.m., everyone was assembled.

I stood with my arms around Kai's waist, feeling calmer when I was near him.

"Stay safe, everyone. Time to get this started," Ben called out.

❧ ❧ ❧

Most of us convened at Mirror Lake while a crucial few activated the first few steps of the plan. Deep in the dark mines, Elan would pretend to collapse. A few minutes later, his friend Marshall would also slump to the floor, pretending to faint.

Mining policy stated that if more than one person collapsed, all miners had to evacuate quickly to assess the air quality and reduce the risk for other miners. They would have to abandon the shaft for the rest of the day.

Elan sent a message around eleven that the first step was complete. The mine had been evacuated.

Wade was up next, with a delivery of black tourmaline for Rosella's warehouse. He soon texted that the guards approved the delivery and cleared them for unloading. Hopefully he and Jace could turn off the contaminated air flow and distribute the pink tourmaline to the warehouse pukwudgies.

Kai and I rode his motorcycle to the far side of Mirror Lake. We walked hand in hand near the banks of the slushy water, scanning for a stone pukwudgie spy. We needed to be seen together and reported to Rosella. I observed the first spy near the bridge and a second in the brush. Even though they were part of our plan, I worried about what their presence meant—whether Rosella had far more pukwudgies under her power than we had estimated. How had she not felt the loss of all the ones I had freed?

Over the rapid pounding of my pulse, I heard Kai say, "They've seen us. It's time to go."

We grabbed our helmets and sped to the other side of the lake. Kai stayed close to the forest, tree limbs slapping us as we flew past. Grandmother Kateri and Wanda were waiting near the viewing deck. Elan, Tanja, and the girls jogged up to us. Tourists and visitors milled around, unaware of the momentous events taking place.

"The mines are clear," Elan said.

"What about the miners?" Kai asked.

"Some are already here, and the rest are on the way."

As Wade and three other workers unloaded the truck inside the fortress, they reported that Rosella came storming in and barked orders at the pukwudgies and guards. Jace sent a message when Rosella left the compound in her town car.

Unfortunately, many of the pukwudgies had popped out at her command, but Wade moved to step four and released those who remained by handing out pink tourmaline. He sent a message that he was successful, and next he was going inside the mansion to break all the mirrors.

It was hard to wait without fidgeting. Kai shifted his weight from foot to foot. We both wore three stretch bracelets on each arm. I ran my fingers over the polished stone.

"Together, your force is power," Wanda reminded us.

Muddy melted snow and mist flew behind the black sedan as it flew into the parking lot. The driver turned sharply by the viewing dock, sliding sideways until the car screeched to a stop. Guards popped out from every door, for a total of four. One helped Rosella out.

My chest tightened when I saw her sinister face and the black voids of her eyes. She lifted her head back and unleashed a threatening cackle.

"You just can't get away from me, can you?" She tapped her watch. "Isn't it about time for you to return to a slithering reptile, Mr. Handsome?"

"No, it is over. I will never be a reptile again," Kai said, his voice full of conviction.

Her eyes hardened in her pale face. Crow's feet made her look much older than before.

"Do you think you and your little lovebird can stop me?" She swirled her hand over her head. A few stone pukwudgies emerged from the trees, mingling with the crowds at the lake. The tourists didn't see them. Sky and Mia also moved unnoticed through the visitors, handing pink tourmaline to every creature in reach.

A notification sounded on our phones. Sakari confirmed that the mirrors in the employee entrances had been smashed. A second alert came from Wade, confirming the mirrors inside the fortress were destroyed.

I stood close to Kai, blocking the walkway to the viewing platform. Grandmother Kateri shuffled past one of the guards and pretended to trip. When he reached out to steady her, she slipped a large piece of pink tourmaline into his hand. Wanda pressed a stone into the palm of the other guard while he was distracted by the incident. Disgust replaced the initial surprise on both guards' faces.

Rosella was physically shaking now, and the color on her face turned dark red. She had to know her power was dwindling. But she waved her hands in the air again, chanting unfamiliar words.

Four more stone pukwudgies stepped out of the forest and moved toward us. The first stone hand brushed my wrist, hesitating as it touched one of my stretch bracelets. I quickly shifted the bracelet onto the creature's wrist. White smoke swirled around him.

One reached for Kai. When the pukwudgie raised its arm, Kai threw a stretch bracelet on it like a ring toss game. I lunged for the next one, slapping a bracelet on him. Kai caught the fourth one as she was reaching for my leg.

The white smoke swirled above all four creatures. Once they transformed, they disappeared with a pop. Sky and Mia continued searching for stone pukwudgies among the people.

Rosella's face twisted in torment. She chanted a few words, and our remaining stretch bracelets broke into pieces and scattered across the ground. She stomped a petulant foot and yelled in her strange language. She looked left and right, but no other pukwudgies came to her aid.

With laser focus, her black eyes stopped on me.

"It's you; it's all because of you. I think it is time you know what a real curse feels like."

Rosella pointed her skeletal finger in my direction, then waved her hand in a circular motion over her head. An overpoweringly acrid smell surrounded me, and I braced for disaster.

Kai pulled me into his chest, embracing me with arms of steel. The dark smoke swirled over me—but when I held up my hands and the object in them, the funnel of smoke changed direction and swirled over Rosella's head. Screams echoed across the lake, and the smoke dispersed.

I studied my hands for changes, but all I saw was the carved swan mirror gripped in them. Rosella was the one who was screaming.

"What did you do? You witch!" White feathers covered her head and hands as she spat and coughed. The curse had rebounded back onto her.

She yelled, "Guards, grab her!" The two remaining guards under her waning power stepped forward, one of them pulling a gun. I cringed back, and Kai stiffened.

An earsplitting crack accompanied the sudden appearance of the chief pukwudgie between us and the guards.

Rosella snarled, chanted, and flung black powder over his head, transforming him once again. Rosella's sneer turned into a satisfied grin as nausea swept over me.

With a shaky voice, I asked Kai, "Do you have any pink tourmaline?"

He shook his head no.

I swiftly took off my beloved necklace and tossed it to the chief. The creature cocked its head to the side. "A gift," I said with a shaky voice.

He scooped it into his stone hand, and once again, white smoke swirled over his head, returning him to his regal, bluish-gray form. The pukwudgie swirled his finger, and with an arc of orange sparks, the gun flew out of the guard's hand and landed in the lake.

Rosella's head snapped in my direction, and I held up the mirror threateningly. Her raven eyes narrowed when she yelled, "Guards, let's go! Now!"

She stormed to the car. As the guards made to follow, Wanda stumbled into one, handing him another large crystal. He froze and shook his head. Rosella barked again, "Now, you idiot!" Grandmother immediately handed the last guard a crystal of his own. He stared at it for a minute, turned, and threw the keys into the lake before stumbling away.

Rosella cursed and screamed, "Get back here." She was so focused on where the guard was going that she failed to notice the elder pukwudgie had moved to her side. White feathers shimmered on her head, and makeup was smeared under her eyes. "You will pay for this. You will both pay for this!" she spat.

The pukwudgie abruptly grabbed her hand, and the pair vanished with a bang.

Silence reigned. We were too stunned to speak.

Finally, tears streaming down my face, I turned to Kai and melted into his arms.

"I think we did it."

He had a look of awe on his fully human face.

"Look, I don't need pink tourmaline to block the curse anymore. We did it! When she lost her power over the pukwudgies, the curse lost its power as well," Kai said.

Grandmother Kateri hugged us from behind, and Wanda let out a cheerful cry. "We knew you could do it. Lily, we knew you were the one." She let out a raspy giggle. "I've always wanted to see a pukwudgie!"

Wade and his coworkers arrived, and they had brought the wealthy owner of the fortress with them. The businessman strode straight over to Kai and me. He did not even introduce himself; he just hugged us and cried.

He finally pulled back, wiping his tears with the back of his wrist, and extended his hand.

"I'm Andrew Hagstrom. Thank you for setting us free, saving my business, my home, and giving me back my life. I will find a way to repay you." He hugged us again.

I turned back to Kai as the enthusiastic Mr. Hagstrom joined the other celebrants. My hands traced Kai's face, and his moved across mine.

"Is this the beginning of normal?" I wondered aloud.

"Nothing about you will ever be normal. You are perfect."

CHAPTER 48

MANY OF US ended up at Grandmother Kateri's. My cheeks hurt from smiling. The setting sun cast a golden glow across the water, and cool night air crept in through the trees.

"Why don't we walk down to the lake and escape the crowds for a bit?" Kai suggested, filling a plate with appetizers.

"That sounds perfect."

We sat on the rock wall near the dock. I was nibbling on a carrot when I glanced up and spotted the chief pukwudgie drifting toward us from the forest. I touched Kai's knee, and he looked up.

The chief's expression was soft and kind. He stopped in front of me, placing an intricately carved wooden box on my knees. He motioned to open it. I picked it up and peeked inside, letting out a cry of joy.

"It's my swan necklace. Thank you." I hugged it to my chest, and Kai embraced me from the side. The regal pukwudgie bowed low, smiled, and returned to the forest.

"Thank you, my friend," I called out. He turned and nodded once more before he disappeared.

I held Kai's forearms while he fastened the necklace around my neck. Warmth spread through my body. "Where do you think he sent Rosella?" I asked.

"Someplace she fears."

"An active volcano, a lion's den, or something like that?"

"I don't really care, as long as it's far away and she never comes back."

I looked up to see another pukwudgie approaching. This one was a bit smaller, and his eyes sparkled. He placed a package between us.

We unwrapped the paper to find a wooden carving of two swans facing each other in the form of a heart. The details were breathtaking.

"Thank you for the gift," Kai said, smiling.

The pukwudgie bowed and returned to the forest.

A third one walked forward. This one looked like a female. She had delicate features and short, spiky hair. She placed a small box on my legs. The whole scenario began to feel ritualistic.

I bowed slightly and opened the box. It contained a small vial of liquid. She patted my hand, then patted her heart, touched her temples, and tapped her lips. She pointed to me and back to her temples. I wasn't sure what she was trying to tell me, but I nodded and said, "Thank you." She bowed and returned to the forest.

One by one, more appeared, each offering a small gift. A large clear-blue crystal, a wind chime, a dream catcher woven from vines and decorated with swan feathers, a carving of a raccoon, and more. The objects seemed like items the gods might once have given a mythical hero in preparation for a quest. Despite my happy ending with Kai, I got the sense that our story wasn't over yet.

Eventually, the procession ended. The wind swirled through the trees, whistling softly. The sun dropped low on the lake. Kai pulled me onto his lap and pressed his lips to my forehead.

"What did I do to deserve you?"

I buried my face in his silky hair. "It was meant to be. The spirits always had a plan."

Lily and Kai will return
in book two of the Salty Swan saga.

www.ingramcontent.com/pod-product-compliance
Lightning Source LLC
LaVergne TN
LVHW041751060526
838201LV00046B/970